DOWN CAME THE RAIN

ALSO BY JENNIFER MATHIEU

Bad Girls Never Say Die
The Liars of Mariposa Island
Moxie
Afterward
Devoted
The Truth About Alice

DOWN CAME THE RAIN

JENNIFER MATHIEU

Roaring Brook Press
New York

Published by Roaring Brook Press
Roaring Brook Press is a division of Holtzbrinck Publishing Holdings
Limited Partnership
120 Broadway, New York, NY 10271 • fiercereads.com

Our books may be purchased in bulk for promotional, educational, or business use. Please contact your local bookseller or the Macmillan Corporate and Premium Sales Department at (800) 221–7945 ext. 5442 or by email at MacmillanSpecialMarkets@macmillan.com.

Library of Congress Control Number: 2023013558

First edition, 2023
Book design by Ellen Duda
Printed in the United States of America

ISBN 978-1-250-23267-0
1 3 5 7 9 10 8 6 4 2

For Jill, for teaching me,
and for Houston, for loving me

HOUSTON

August 2017

We thought the rain would come in through the front door. Polite. Maybe it knocks first.

But it didn't, no matter how much we stared it down in the black of night. No matter how much we peered through our windows, wishing we could be lulled to sleep by the beating drums of fifty million raindrops into water that's been collecting for days instead of tortured awake night and day by the sound.

To be fair, water did come in the front door for some of us, leaking under wood and fiberglass and spilling everywhere like blood and guts. But for many of us, water came up like a ghost that can haunt you through any crack or crevice, through any space it wants.

Water came for us. It made us clamber up onto kitchen counters and climb up into attics and haul ourselves onto rooftops. It entered our homes and it entered our lives and it rose indiscriminately in every neighborhood across this city. And we had to run from it, or try to.

We were people on the news. Worldwide coverage. We were refugees in our own neighborhoods. We were pitiable and for good reason.

It rained and it rained and it rained and it rained. For four days and four nights it rained. We had built homes here and had done so much living. We had grown and thrived and endured and constructed a city of steel and freeways where once had stood swamps.

Like all human beings through all time and space, we believed there was something untouchable about us. Something powerful and resistant and strong.

But water does whatever it wants.

ELIZA

Clutching my junior year schedule in my hand, I scan my list of classes as bodies bump around me, waiting to be let into Southwest High School, a boxy behemoth of a building up ahead.

I can't believe this is my life.

I should be tired, actually. My baby cousin, Ethan, kept me up all night, fussing in his crib. It's hard to believe that six weeks ago I had my own room with a queen bed and an attached bathroom (two sinks!) and now I'm sharing a bedroom with a six-month-old. My aunt Heather came in around two in the morning to feed him, tiptoeing so as not to make the wooden floorboards creak.

They creaked.

I'd lain still, eyes closed, even though I'd wanted to sit up and scream that it was my first day of school the next day, and it was *junior year*, for crying out loud. The *most important year* of high school, so says everyone. So says me. The year I'd been waiting for since it dawned on me in fifth grade that UT Austin only lets in the very best of the best and I liked being the best and therefore I would be going to UT Austin.

But since I'm as conscious of being polite as I am of being good, I'd squeezed my eyes shut and dug my fingernails into my palms to keep from exploding, trying to keep my breathing nice and even, listening as Heather cooed to baby Ethan and fed him and rocked him gently in the glider that sits inches from the twin bed I've been sleeping in since my entire universe was flipped on its head.

I'm not sure I ever went back to sleep, even after Heather tiptoed out and Ethan gurgled and shifted, the crinkly sound of his diaper setting my teeth on edge until he finally settled. But I didn't settle. I'd just lain there, trying to adjust my 5'10" frame in a tiny twin, missing my old big bed like I missed my old everything. I'd frowned at the glow-in-the-dark star stickers on the ceiling, examining the outlines of animals and trees painted onto the walls of Ethan's nature-themed nursery, wishing that the actual planet could be as pleasant and lovely as the artificial universe my aunt and uncle had made for their miracle baby, the one they thought they'd never be able to have. The baby who, while superadorable and innocent and sweet, wears plastic diapers that will exist in a landfill for longer than either he or I will be around.

Who thinks this way about some poor, innocent baby? Sometimes I think I might be a terrible person deep down inside.

But terrible or not, tired or not, here I am. The first day of school at last.

"Eliza, is that you?"

I turn and spy Olivia Chen and Olivia Patterson, OC and OP as they call themselves, heading toward me, their faces as wary as mine must be. We've been in every advanced and AP class together since ninth grade, and they've joined me here at Southwest High, along with every other Baldwin High kid whose parents either couldn't afford private school or were too married to their liberal agendas to admit they were nervous about sending their kids to a high school full of Black and brown kids.

"Hey," I answer. "I'm so glad to see familiar faces." I pull out my reusable water bottle with its Reduce Reuse Recycle sticker on it from the side pocket of my backpack to take a sip and wonder briefly if Southwest has working water fountains. I hold my paper up in the air. "Wanna compare schedules?"

"Let's just hope the counselors haven't totally messed them up," says OC, sliding a crisp piece of paper out of her backpack.

Instead of getting ready to compare notes, OP crosses her arms and scans the crowd building around us.

"If this were a movie," she says, her girly upspeak punctuating every phrase with a question mark, "it would be a rom-com and Southwest High and Baldwin High are having a meet-cute. Only this isn't a movie. And this is just weird."

My eyes take in the scene again, even though I've been silently making notes since I got here. The Southwest High kids, almost all kids of color, wearing their uniform-issued blue Southwest High T-shirts and dress code–ordered jeans, and the Baldwin High kids, a mix of white and Asian and Black and brown, dressed in whatever we want because that's one of the perks of going to Baldwin.

It doesn't seem fair to me that the Southwest High kids have to stay in dress code and we don't, but nothing about the past few months has felt particularly fair to me.

Even though it's late September, over a month since we should have started the school year, Houston's humidity still reigns, and I start praying for the opening bell so we can enter this strange place that's supposed to be my school home for the next year. I've heard rumors about Southwest High's less-than-stellar facilities, but it's got to be against the law for a Texas high school to not have air-conditioning, right? Then again, it's air-conditioning that's helping destroy the planet, and for the millionth time in the last few weeks my stomach knots up as a wave of anxiety slides over me. I take a deep breath and ride it out, then will the opening bell to ring. At last it does, and amid shouts and curses in Spanish and English, the future of America troops up the front steps.

A buzz goes off in my pocket, and I slide my phone out as I walk through the front doors with OC and OP, the three of us venturing into a strange new world. My eyes look down. It's a text from my best friend, Isabella.

Have you gotten stabbed yet or what?

This is followed by several laugh/cry emojis.

A prickle of irritation races up my spine as I take in Isabella's assumptions about the sort of kids I'm in school with. She's supposed to be my oldest friend, so it might be nice if she could be supportive for half a minute. I roll my eyes as I'm bumped by bodies. I only half-hear OC and OP asking each other where they think a certain classroom might be.

I'm tempted to type back something rude, but I restrain myself. Instead I offer this response:

Have you been asked to debut at the River Oaks Country Club yet?

This gets a quick laugh react and nothing more, and I'm not

sure if I've annoyed her or what. In fact, I'm not even sure we're still friends now that we're not at the same school. The idea of not being friends with Isabella seems impossible to me, and as much as her text dug under my skin, I don't like it when people are mad at me. Especially the girl who is supposed to be my closest friend. So I hang back, off to the side of the crowded hall, letting OC and OP pull forward into the crowd along with their promises that we'll find each other at lunch. I type back It's not so bad honestly. Not, of course, that I have anything to base this assertion on. Just a sea of kids and an industry-standard school building and lots of voices and noise.

But I want "not so bad" to be true. It has to be true. I mean, this is my junior year.

The three dots pop up immediately, quickly followed by Isabella's next message: Just don't join a gang or anything. Jkjk I love you.

I bury my continued irritation in the back of my mind as I slide my phone into my back pocket. Classic Isabella. And for the millionth time in our friendship, I'm not sure if I'm angry, jealous, or amused.

Suddenly, there's a push from behind, and I turn around to discover a boy in a blue T-shirt and jeans.

"Hey, sorry," he says. He's obviously a Southwest High kid based on his uniform.

"No, it's fine," I say, almost having to shout over the stream of kids moving past us. "I shouldn't have just, like, stopped in the middle of the hallway. I just don't know where I'm going."

And even as I say this, I realize that we're both still standing in the middle of the hallway, both of us being jostled slightly by the people around us. Yet we're not moving. Just looking at each other for a beat or two.

"You from Baldwin?" he asks at last.

His voice is low and soft. He has clear olive skin. Jet-black hair. Dark brown eyes. Hispanic. A little shorter than me. Kind of elfin, actually, if I had to pick a word.

Not that I should be picking words. Not that I have time for boys. Not this year. Junior year of all years.

"Yeah, I am," I manage, remembering the task at hand. School. I tug my schedule out. "Can you help me find out where the 130s are?"

He points me in the right direction before saying, "That's right. Y'all got the first floor and the T-buildings, and we have to take the stairs." He doesn't say this unkindly or like he's territorial or anything. Just a fact offered up with a crooked smile.

"That's what I heard," I say, immediately and silently cursing myself for not being able to come up with a cleverer response.

Not that it matters. Not that I should be letting boys distract me. Even nice, dark-eyed boys with soft voices and crooked smiles.

"Anyway, that way," he says.

"Thanks," I say, figuring I'll probably never get the chance to lay eyes on him again.

"No problem," he answers, and I realize he still hasn't moved. Then he nods at my T-shirt.

"You into The Smiths?"

The question takes me by surprise. In this brief moment with this cute boy I'd forgotten that on my shirt is a black-and-white picture of a soldier wearing a helmet that has *Meat Is Murder* scrawled on it. It also says *THE SMITHS* in big green capital letters along the side.

I don't want to look like an idiot, so I tell him that I don't really know the band very well, and that I found the shirt at Buffalo Exchange, a used clothing store. I stop short from delivering a speech about the environmental harms of fast fashion.

"Huh," he says, clearly confused and probably convinced I'm a weirdo. "Cool. Well, welcome to Southwest High, I guess. Or Baldwin Southwest. Or is it Southwest Baldwin? Anyway, welcome to whatever it is."

He disappears before I can respond, and I have to shake my head a little to try and regain focus. Forget The Smiths. Forget boys. Forget anything but getting to class on time and getting started on this year, this crucial *junior year.*

But as I make my way to my first class, cute boy's last words ring through my head.

Whatever it is.

As in whatever has happened to my life?

~

My junior year (junior year!) at Baldwin was going to be perfect. That had always been the plan. A perfect list of extracurricular activities, AP classes, leadership opportunities, volunteer opportunities, résumé-building opportunities, opportunity opportunities.

I'd make my mark in any way I could, and the next fall, UT Austin would have to appreciate it. Right?

But despite being all too aware of the connection between climate change and extreme weather, my type A, to-do, worst-case-scenario brain hadn't counted on Hurricane Harvey barreling through Houston and laughing in my overachiever face, literally drowning my perfect plans. One minute I was rereading *Wuthering Heights* and *The Return of the Native* and reviewing my annotations in preparation for my summer reading tests, and the next moment the two-story home I'd lived in since I was born had been flooded out, and my parents and I had to move in with my mom's younger sister, Heather, and her husband, Dave, and precious miracle baby Ethan, born after five rounds of IVF.

My older brother, Mark, had already left for his second year at MIT when Harvey hit. *He* didn't have to help muck out our stinky house in the blazing August sun and *he* didn't have to listen to our mother sob in the upstairs bathroom and *he* didn't have to watch our father's face blanch when he listened to the insurance adjustor talk about deductibles and policy limits. *He* didn't have to have his junior year of high school uprooted and turned on its head. Naturally. Nothing ever goes wrong for Mark Brady.

But my junior year fate was sealed the evening three weeks ago when my mom came back to Heather and Dave's house after a meeting at Southwest High, the high school four miles up the street from our zoned school, Baldwin High.

"It's official," she'd said to me. I was sitting on the living room couch eating a frozen pizza I'd heated up and re-rereading *Wuthering Heights* in an effort to calm myself. "Baldwin High kids are going to share a space with Southwest High this coming school year while Baldwin's flood damages are repaired," she continued. "We're not sure how long the arrangement will last, but for the fall semester at least."

I couldn't speak. Just swallowed my pizza and stared, but Heather walked into the adjoining kitchen to make a bottle for Ethan.

"Southwest?" she said. "How can that even work?"

My mother sighed and walked to the refrigerator to pull out a bottle of white wine. She bumped into Heather. Honestly, it's a kitchen meant for one family, not two.

"Southwest isn't filled to capacity," my mother explained, pouring herself a glass and joining me in the family room, plopping onto the couch but careful not to spill any pinot grigio.

"That's because all the white kids who are zoned to Southwest are on transfers and their parents rent one-bedroom apartments in the Baldwin zone so their kids can go to school at Baldwin," I said. I was surprised I was able to speak. You would think my brain would be too busy processing that life as I knew it was over.

My mother tipped her head back, stared at the ceiling. "I know," she said. "When your dad and I bought our home, we bought it in the Baldwin zone for a reason."

"Isn't Southwest a little . . . rough?" asked Heather, shaking Ethan's bottle back and forth. As I watched her shake, I thought, *Nice metaphor for my life, Aunt Heather.*

"Well, some Baldwin parents aren't happy about it," my

mother told us. "They're threatening to move their kids to private school even though Baldwin will have its own space on the campus, and Baldwin kids will have Baldwin teachers."

"Well, I know you'll make the best of it," Heather reassured me before heading back toward Ethan's nursery.

I fake-smiled in her general direction, then pushed my pizza aside, my appetite suddenly gone. Maybe there was a part of me that thought my parents would spring for private school, but even though I knew my father made good money, enough that we were solidly upper middle class, I knew we didn't have *that* kind of money, especially after the flood and with the cost of my brother's college tuition. There was no way our skimpy insurance policy covered all the damage, and my parents hadn't bought additional coverage, convinced our house was in a part of the neighborhood that would never flood.

After Harvey, every Houstonian learned there's no such thing as "would never flood."

"What about clubs and sports and stuff?" I managed to ask. A text buzzed across my phone screen. Isabella. My parents are flipping. They're sending me to St. Augustine. My heart dropped.

"I'm not sure," my mother said, taking a sip of wine and sinking back into the couch before closing her eyes. "Principal Franklin assured us that the Baldwin experience would still be available to all Baldwin students and blah blah blah."

My phone kept buzzing. Texts from Isabella and other friends, no doubt. I turned the phone over on the coffee table, unable to look at it.

The Baldwin experience. It's what parents all over the city

fought to earn for their kids, faking addresses, sending kids to live with relatives, and buying or renting the cheapest possible address in the Baldwin zone, a strange little sliver shaped like a wriggly snake sliding through Houston's southwest side through older suburbs full of cute '50s ranch homes and the McMansions that had been built when the cute ranch homes were gone. (My family was a McMansion type, which is why I'd had my own bathroom, even in elementary school.) Back in the '90s, when my own mother and Heather had attended Baldwin High, it was ranked as one of the best public schools in the country. Baldwin was no longer as white as it had been when my own mother went there. There were plenty of middle-class kids of color whose parents did anything to win their kid a coveted spot there. But it was still pretty white for a Houston public school.

"Does Dad know?" I asked. My phone was still buzzing.

"I called him," my mother said, opening her eyes and sitting up. "He was distracted because he was heading over to the house after work to check on what the contractors managed to not finish today. Oh, Eliza, I was hoping we'd be back in our place by Christmas, but I don't know now."

My mom teaches at a preschool at the local Methodist church, and my father is in risk management for a Big Oil company downtown. The situational irony of a man in oil and gas being head of risk management when climate change caused in part by fossil fuels no doubt helped cause our home to flood isn't lost on me.

"I don't want to talk about Christmas," I said, standing up to dump my pizza crust in the trash can. When I opened it, I found a plastic water bottle.

"Am I the only person who recycles in this house or what?" I asked, fishing it out and putting it on the counter.

"Eliza, it's hard with the baby for Heather and Dave to manage to think about those things."

"Lots of things are hard," I answered. She didn't respond. I felt on the verge of exploding somehow, but what would that even look like? I couldn't burst into sobs in Heather and Dave's kitchen. That would disturb the baby. I couldn't run down the middle of the street screaming at the top of my lungs. The neighbors would call the police. I couldn't throw a glass and shatter it against a wall no matter how much the idea tempted me. That would make me seem unhinged. So I took my phone and, since Heather was in Ethan's bedroom with Ethan, I went out on the back deck. My mom didn't follow.

In addition to Isabella's texts, there was a flurry of messages from my overachieving, head-of-the-class friends waiting to be read.

Ummmm . . . are we srsly going to be at SW next year?

My parents are thinking about sending me to Austin to live with my sister because she's zoned to a good school.

Will we have access to our FULL SLATE of AP classes?!? Does SW even have science labs with the right equipment?! I emailed Ms. Franklin and demanded answers.

How am I supposed to put out a Baldwin yearbook when we are literally not going to be at Baldwin High?

I ignored all the messages, even Isabella's, and pulled up Southwest High on my phone. It had a three out of ten on whatever site anxious parents use to discuss schools. The website was clunky and out of date, with some sad club pictures from 2014 the only ones I could find.

Even though Southwest High is in a mixed-race neighborhood not that much different from the neighborhoods around Baldwin High, there were barely any white faces in the pictures. It had been decades since white kids zoned to Southwest attended there. Weirdly, until not that long ago, Southwest had actually been called Robert E. Lee High until the powers that be realized that was gross and problematic. Baldwin was named after the old white guy who founded the surrounding subdevelopments. Given that he was an old white guy way back when, he was probably problematic, too, but he got a pass, I guess.

Maybe I'll get a college essay out of this, I thought before getting grossed out by my own thinking. The UT-Austin thing is so embedded in my brain it's like my subconscious is constantly finding ways to increase my admission odds. I stared out at Heather and Dave's well-kept lawn and smacked a mosquito feasting on my calf. They'd been having a field day since the flood.

"Eliza?" I turned to find my dad, standing at the French doors that open to Heather and Dave's back deck. Dad went to A&M, and he probably wouldn't mind if his only daughter became an Aggie, too. But I'm not even going to apply. "Hey," I said, looking away and staring out at the backyard.

"Heard about school."

"Yeah, it sucks."

Pause. Nothing to say. Nothing to say. Nothing to say.

"I'm sorry," he said, and I could feel him tiptoeing around

the edges of this conversation, looking for an opening. I fought the tiny urge inside to give him one.

He didn't deserve it.

"Well, there's nothing you can do about it," I said, my voice withering. I didn't have to say it for him to know what I was implying. *There's nothing you can do about it except maybe quit working for the Big Oil company that's helping to destroy our planet.* I'd spent years trying to get my dad to understand this and gotten nowhere. We'd been outgrowing each other for a while, it seemed, but ever since Harvey, with the reality of climate change upending my entire life, I could barely stand to be around him.

My dad sighed deeply. Pointedly. And I kept my gaze trained on the backyard until he finally gave up and left. Burying my rage, I reminded myself of what I can control. Of who I am.

Eliza Brady, straight-A student, UT Austin–bound. A girl who's going to make her junior year a successful one. No matter what.

JAVIER

I haul myself out of bed and stare at the poster of Morrissey next to my closet. I once read a quote of his in some old interview.

What's the first thing you think when you wake up in the morning?

Wish I hadn't.

Hah.

Morrissey was the lead singer of my dad's favorite band of all time, The Smiths, and that band is now my favorite band. The Smiths have got, like, this pretty big cult following among Mexican people even though Morrissey is a straight-up racist now, saying all sorts of weird, hateful stuff. But my dad just puts on his CD of *The Queen Is Dead* (even though I tell him that CDs are what's dead), and he says it's all about the music to him.

I don't particularly wish I *hadn't* woken up in this morning, but I sure wish I didn't have to get to school for the first day of junior year. It's been a long summer since Harvey delayed the start of everything, and my brain and my body have gotten used to sleeping in until 10 A.M.

Speaking of my body, I stretch and pop my neck and my back and flex a little and assess myself in the mirror on the back of the bedroom door. Unfortunately, I haven't gotten any taller overnight. I'm pretty sure at sixteen I'm maxed out, but Mom says boys sometimes keep growing right on through their twenties.

My brother, Miguel, did, and now he's a real dude working on the refineries in Pasadena, all muscley and stuff.

Still gazing into the mirror, I flex a single bicep. Not all that impressive. If I'm being brutally honest, it's like watching a single lima bean shoot up through my skin.

I venture out to find the rest of the house apparently empty except for Diablo napping on our big living room couch. He startles when I waltz in, then yawns and curls back into a ball.

"Nice to see you, too," I offer.

There's a note from Mom on the kitchen counter, and probably a million texts on my phone, too.

Have a great first day!! Take a picture of yourself and send it to me! Please!

She'd want nothing more than to capture a "first day" shot to share on social media with her girlfriends, but she had to leave early for her job as a clerk at Monroe Elementary, the school around the corner where my sister and brother and I went as kids. Dad's gone, too. Sometimes he has the night shift at the print shop where he manages the warehouse, but this week, it's early bird for him.

"Daniela?" I call out, wondering if it's possible that my older sister is gone, too, leaving me alone in my house, a pretty rare occasion.

"I'm in my room!"

No such luck.

"Okay, just checking."

"Are you getting ready for school?" she calls.

"Yeah. You want coffee?"

"Do you have to ask?"

Soon it's Daniela and me drinking coffee and eating Life cereal, her on her phone and me trying to ignore my rumbling stomach. Not hunger but nerves.

"You okay?" Daniela asks from across the kitchen table. She has her black hair pulled back tight in a ponytail. I think she tweezes her eyebrows too thin and so does Mom, but she keeps doing it.

I shrug. "Just school. I'm not feeling it."

Daniela raises a too-thin eyebrow. "Well, feel it. Two more years and you're done at Southwest and then on to bigger and better things, like yours truly." She shoves the last scoop of Life into her mouth before rinsing her bowl and spoon and placing them in the dishwasher. Daniela is taking classes at HCC to become a nurse, and she takes that stuff seriously. She's up all hours studying, and after Harvey she went out with some other nursing students to help provide first aid and do intake at the shelters. Mom and Dad act like she's already a doctor, like, "Check with Daniela before you take that Advil." I mean, I can read the directions on the Advil.

Before Daniela disappears into her room to get ready, she asks if I want a ride.

"I'll walk," I say. "Meet up with Dominic." There are perks to living practically across the street from Southwest High. "But will you do me a favor?"

"What?"

"Take a picture of me for Mom?"

I stand up in the middle of the kitchen, still in my boxers and ratty T-shirt, and strike an overeager, kindergarten-style smile along with two absurd thumbs-ups.

"Perfect," says Daniela, capturing the moment with her phone. "I'm sending to the entire family."

I think for a moment what Miguel will think of my corny pose and redden briefly at the thought. I don't think my brother has smiled for a picture since he was in the fifth grade, even ironically. He'll probably think once again that he deserved a little brother who liked to play soccer and video games and listen to hip-hop, not some skinny younger sibling like me who prefers our father's music to anything kids listen to today.

Not to mention the other stuff that probably qualifies me as odd in his eyes.

I push the thought out of my head and take a hot shower, get dressed, grab my backpack, and head out the front door. I see Mrs. Green across the street, dressed in one of her big, billowy flowered housedresses and walking her little mutt, Frankie.

"Javier, are you heading on up to the school?" she shouts. "Is it finally starting today?"

She pronounces my name *Hah-vee-air*, but she's a pretty cool old lady. Some of the older white people in this neighborhood still seem bitter about the fact that their neighborhood isn't as white as it once was, but Mrs. Green never seems to care. She's a widow now, but her family has lived on this street since forever, and her own kids went to Southwest back when it was called Robert E. Lee.

"Yes, ma'am, this is the first day," I holler back, raising my voice over Frankie's barks. He always acts like we've never met before.

"At last!" she shouts, waving her hand at Frankie to try and shush him. It doesn't work. "Dang that storm. I bet you've missed all your friends."

"Haven't missed the homework, though!" I yell back.

She laughs, and we wave one more time, and then I head up the street, pausing to text Dominic that I'm on my way. That's another way I'm different from Miguel. Talking to older people, being friendly. Maybe I get it from my mom and a little bit from my dad. They're talkers. Daniela, too. Miguel is sort of a grunter. A grunter with muscles and tats and a pregnant girlfriend named Rosario who Mom wants him to marry ASAP.

And me? I'm Javier. Javi. I like The Smiths. I'm not good at sports. I make origami birds and do yoga videos with this chick from Austin who I found on YouTube.

And since Hurricane Harvey hit over a month ago, if it rains or there's even a chance of rain?

I feel like I might break down in tears and throw up.

~

Dominic rolls up to the outskirts of Southwest on his skateboard, his dreads shaking a little each time he picks up speed. When he spots me leaning against one of the benches that dot the perimeter of the campus, he pauses and kicks up the board in this supercool way I could never manage even if I tried, which is why I don't.

"Hola, primo," he says. Dominic loves to call me cousin in Spanish, and he jokes that we could maybe be related even though he's Dominican. The other thing he loves to do is mess with the minds of people who think Black people can't be Hispanic. His Spanish is better than mine, to be honest.

"What's up, cuz," I answer.

He sits down on the bench and peers around. We're quiet as we watch kids start to file up, gathering in little clumps, gossiping and shouting and play fighting. The Southwest kids like us are easy to spot, all of us decked out in our blue T-shirts and jeans and Southwest High student IDs on blue lanyards around our necks.

The Baldwin kids are easy to spot, too. They're the ones who don't have to wear dress code shirts. Plus, a lot of them are white. I think I've seen five white kids at Southwest High before today. The Baldwin kids look curious but also a little wary, and they keep checking out us Southwest kids and tapping on their phones.

"So, these are our friends from down the road, huh?" asks Dominic, reading my mind. "The Baldwin elite. We'd better get ready to bow or curtsey or whatever."

He's joking but not really. Ever since the school district announced that Baldwin and Southwest would be sharing a building this year, it's been on my mind about how this will actually *work*. Sure, they'll have one part of the campus and we'll have the rest, but we're going to share the cafeteria and our sports teams are going to have to share facility space. There's already been some grumbling online about the Baldwin football team getting the better practice times.

"Did you see some of the stuff on Twitter that the school district was posting?" Dominic asks. "Eagles and Tigers United! They even made a hashtag. Then some kids started tweeting out pictures of kids acting dumb with that hashtag, so the school district quit it." He laughs, and I do, too. Eagles and Tigers United? How? Baldwin is just a few miles away, but it might as well be a few hundred miles. Over near Baldwin, homes like the one I live in have been torn down to make room for big mansions, where guys who look like me get hired to mow the lawn every Friday.

I mean, there *are* kids who look like me at Baldwin. And kids who look like Dominic. But it's not just kids like that. And that's not the only way Baldwin seems different. They're always making headlines for their test scores and their twenty valedictorians and their National Merit Semifinalists. Truth is, there are smart kids at Southwest, too. And good teachers. I've seen it. But that doesn't make the papers for some reason.

"You think Principal Lopez is going to confiscate my skateboard?" Dominic asks as the crowd of kids starts to swell. It's got to almost be time for the bell. At least I hope so. It's hot as Hades out here.

"Why are you asking a question you already know the answer to?"

Dominic rolls his eyes and takes a moment to get in a last few tricks and flips on his board. I scan the crowd for anyone else I might know. Dom and I hang out with a small group of guys who aren't into sports. They aren't into yoga and origami swans, either, to be honest, but they each have their own thing. Dom is into skateboarding. Felipe is into anime. JoJo is into fat science fiction novels.

I don't spy any of my other misfit friends, but my eyes lock up on this girl not far from me. Baldwin girl. White girl. Tall, of course. What is it with me and height? I want it for myself, and I dig it in a chick. Jeans. Blond hair pulled back in a ponytail. No makeup.

She's cute. Really cute.

Plus she's wearing a Smiths T-shirt. The cover of *Meat Is Murder*.

Is it possible that a tall, cute (okay, *really* cute) girl around my age likes The Smiths? And she's here at my school? It doesn't feel possible, but it seems like it is.

Dom is flipping his board and doesn't catch me eyeing this girl, who is talking to two other girls not in Southwest High gear. The three of them are looking around, checking out the scene. I'll bet this feels a lot different from their first day at Baldwin. Like, I'll bet the principal and teachers applaud them or something when they enter the building.

There's no applause, just the ring of the morning bell. I manage to pull my gaze away from Smiths girl to see Principal Lopez standing at the front door, a big welcoming smile on his face. Standing next to him is a white lady in one of those suits they make for ladies. Maybe that's Baldwin's principal. Anyway, the two of them are smiling and waving like they're in a parade or something.

Dom yells something at me about finding the other guys during lunch, and I nod in agreement before losing him and Smiths girl in the crowd. And it is a crowd. This the fullest Southwest High has ever seemed on the first day of school. I know we have a lot of kids zoned to us who manage to get into Baldwin or whose parents scrape the pennies together to send them to private school, but right now it seems like we're at full capacity.

Not that I'm really going to school with these Baldwin kids. I have to remember that. They're here as visitors, and they probably can't wait to check out of the Southwest High Hotel.

Just as I'm about to reach in my pocket for my class schedule, I lose my footing and stumble into the person in front of me.

"Hey, sorry," I manage.

The person turns around.

It's her. It's actually cute Smiths girl in front of me, her blue eyes looking into mine from up above. Like, I mean, she doesn't have to peer down like I'm in kindergarten or something, but dang do I wish I were taller.

"No, it's fine," she says, but she doesn't move. Instead, she asks me about the 130s, and we manage some weird conversation about Southwest and Baldwin sharing space. The whole time I'm talking I'm not sure what I'm saying because all I can think about is how she has the lightest blue eyes I've ever seen. Cornflower, I think they call it. I'm not sure I know what cornflower even *is*, but anyway, her eyes are it. I can tell she has a sort of serious demeanor from the way she doesn't smile much. She's not rude or anything. Just very concerned about getting to class.

I help her out and then, just before I'm about to take off, I screw up the courage to ask her if she's into The Smiths. Like some part of my brain knows I just don't want to say goodbye to her yet.

Smiths girl gives me a confused look, then it's like she remembers what she's wearing.

"Oh, this," she says, peering down at the album cover pasted all over her white T-shirt. It's a black-and-white picture of a soldier looking stressed out, and on his helmet are scratched the words *Meat Is Murder.* She motions to it. "I don't really know the band that well, but I'm a vegetarian. I found it at Buffalo Exchange."

I nod, not sure how to respond. While I'm kind of bummed this cute girl doesn't know about my favorite band, the truth is her not knowing The Smiths doesn't make her any less cute. I don't know any vegetarians, but I've heard of Buffalo Exchange. It's like a resale shop for people with money who don't want to pick through stuff at Value Village.

There's nothing more to say, and I just mutter something about welcoming her to Southwest High and we part ways. But as I make my way to first-period English class, I can't stop thinking about those cornflower-blue eyes and that pretty, serious face.

~

I have Ms. Gomez again for English, and this pleases me. I had her freshman year, too. She's cool. She's always playing music for us and having us analyze lyrics, and she gets us up and moves around the room, too. Even though everyone acts like it's corny, deep down inside we all know it's better than sitting in a seat for fifty minutes filling out some dumb worksheet about parts of speech.

"It's nice to see some familiar faces," Ms. Gomez says, leaning back against the edge of her desk at the front of the room. She has her dark brown hair pulled back in a bun, like always, and she's wearing a light pink dress. The way she's standing, Ms. Gomez looks all business, too, just like Smiths girl.

Why do I keep thinking about Smiths girl?

"I see Annie and Jamarcus," says Ms. Gomez, her eyes scanning the room. "Oh, and I see Beatriz and Anthony, too." All of us are sitting in our clean, shining desks, last year's nasty graffiti wiped right off of them. The linoleum floors are gleaming something fierce. The pencils Ms. Gomez handed out when we walked into her class have perfectly clean pink eraser heads and sharp points that might break if you press down too hard. The entire school year stretches out ahead of us, new and open to possibilities. Anyway, that's how I'm thinking of it.

"And I see Javier," says Ms. Gomez. I blush a little from my third-row seat. I don't like being the center of attention much, but there was a part of me that was a little worried Ms. Gomez wouldn't remember me from ninth grade, and I'm glad to know she did. I give her a little awkward wave from my desk and feel like a dork.

"I understand it's been such a long and difficult summer for so many of us," says Ms. Gomez. "And it's *so* good to be here with all of you. I know it's going to be an unusual year for us, especially with our guests from Baldwin High using part of our building. I know we will make them feel welcome." She pauses, tips her head. A few kids shift in their seats. I feel like maybe some kids want to say something rude about the Baldwin High rich kids, but Ms. Gomez is too respected at Southwest for anyone to act a fool in her class.

"I also want to take a moment to say that no matter where anyone goes to school, all of us, all of us Houstonians, have been through such a trauma, haven't we? Hurricane Harvey was a trauma. A traumatic event. For our entire city. I think it's important to name that out loud."

Now I'm the one shifting a little in my seat. I take Ms. Gomez's supersharp pencil and press the tip gently into my skin over and over until it leaves a constellation of small gray dots. *Trauma*, I think. *Traumatic event.* Suddenly, I remember some phrase I heard on the television news. *Post-traumatic stress disorder.* I don't know what it means, exactly, but there's that word again. *Trauma*.

"If I can ask, and if you feel comfortable sharing, would you raise your hand for me if the place you were living in was flooded by Harvey?" she asks.

In our class of about twenty-five kids, six or seven raise their hands. I know one of them. Danny Rosa. We went to Monroe together and used to trade Pokémon cards at the park. He holds his hand up halfway until Ms. Gomez tells him and the others they can put their hands down. Then I realize Ms. Gomez is holding her hand up in a little half salute.

"I, too, am part of the flooded crew," she says, giving us a sad smile. "I just want y'all to know you're not alone. It's very difficult, isn't it?" One of the girls in the front row who had raised her hand nods at Ms. Gomez's question.

"Right now, my husband and our daughter and I are staying with his parents in Sharpstown, but we're hoping to get our house fixed up soon. I miss living so close to Southwest High and running into some of you at Kroger." She winks. It seems half the kids at Southwest are baggers or checkers or running after shopping carts at Kroger. Dad is always after me to get a job there myself.

"At any rate, to all of you who have had that extra struggle with Harvey, I want y'all to know I'm thinking of you, and I'm here for you if you ever need to talk or need more time on an assignment. Or anything." She smiles warmly at us, and it hits me that Ms. Gomez is one of those rare teachers that can be all serious and nice at the same time. It's like, some teachers are nice and get walked all over, and some teachers are tyrants who teach you but everybody can't stand them. Ms. Gomez manages to teach you and be nice to you, too, and I'm still not really sure how she does it.

When she says all that stuff about being there for people who have flooded, I feel a flash of guilt wash over me. We didn't flood in Harvey. So I shouldn't be so upset whenever anyone talks about it, should I?

I'm mulling this over when Ms. Gomez starts passing out papers to us. At the top is a little piece of writing and then some blank space at the bottom.

We put our names at the top just like Ms. Gomez tells us to, and then Annie Hernandez raises her hand when Ms. Gomez asks for volunteers to read the words at the top out loud.

"This is a poem by Henry Wadsworth Longfellow, just to get our brains stimulated for the day," Ms. Gomez says.

Annie reads in her clear, loud reading voice, and I follow along. Part of the poem talks about how rain is dark and dreary. That's certainly true. But in the last part, it says that rain "is the common fate of all," and that the sun will still be shining when it's gone. I guess that's true, too.

When Annie is done, Ms. Gomez thanks her, then asks us to write a brief response to the poem, and share with her anything we need her to know.

I run my thumb over the poem, like maybe I can absorb the meaning that way. Then I chew on my thumbnail. Kids around me are scribbling stuff down already. I tap my pencil on my desk, the *rat-a-tat* making the girl next to me turn and give me a dirty look.

I guess this poem makes me think about Harvey and everything we've all been through, I start. *I mean, I'm not sure, but I think that's what it's supposed to make me think about. The truth is we didn't flood and I'm really sorry you did, Ms. Gomez.* I almost write, "Harvey sucked," but I don't think that would be appropriate for school. So I just write, *Harvey was the worst thing to happen to this city in my memory.* That sounds sort of dumb. I mean, I'm only sixteen. My parents talk about Allison and Ike and when all those people had to flee New Orleans because of

Katrina, but I either wasn't born or was way too little to remember any of those events very clearly.

And honestly, even if I had, I still think maybe Harvey would be the worst.

I blink, and my mouth goes dry. This happens when I think about the storm for too long. That awful Saturday night. The band after band after band of rain sliding over our city and not moving. Just staying there, dumping what felt like oceanfuls of rain on top of us, hour after hour. Dad and Mom huddling with Daniela, and Diablo howling in his carrier in the hallway because of the tornado warnings. The thunder and lightning so loud and bright and terrifying I thought maybe our house would split in two, leaving us exposed under the horror of it all. Catching Mom giving Dad a certain look I wasn't meant to see. Lights flickering but still holding, somehow. Daniela texting her girlfriends, asking for updates. Mom texting Miguel and Rosario, checking to see that they were okay. Me, huddled up, pressing my spine into the wall, cracking my knuckles and trying to pray. Which is weird because even though we go to Mass sometimes, I haven't really prayed since I was a little kid, and I sort of feel like talking to God is like talking to Santa Claus at the Galleria.

"Javier?"

I look up. Ms. Gomez is standing there, smiling but clearly confused. All around me, kids are gathering their things, getting up from their desks.

"Did you not hear the bell?"

I flush, hard.

"Guess not."

"It's fine," she says. "But are you okay? You seemed a little lost in thought."

I stand up, eager to end this awkward moment.

"I guess I'm still getting into the groove of school or something," I say, handing her the paper. She takes it from me and nods.

"I get it. It's been a long summer. Although not because of anything fun."

"Yeah," I say. I make a move toward the door before I stop and tell her I'm sorry about her house.

"Thank you," she says. "I appreciate that. Your house made it through?"

I nod, heading into the crowded hallway. "Yeah," I tell her. "We were fine. Nothing happened to us."

As I head toward second period, I wonder why that feels like the truth and a lie at the same time.

ELIZA

For a first day, I guess things could be worse. I manage to find all my Baldwin classes on the Southwest High campus, and I quickly start to fill my to-do list with "musts" in my color-coded monthly planner. There's something so soothing about that planner. In the evenings, huddled on my bed with my headlight on low so as not to disturb a sleeping baby Ethan, I often relax with my colored highlighters and flair pens, making organized lists and plans and graphs and charts. My uncle Dave saw my planner once, left open on the kitchen counter.

"Whoa, Eliza, are you a Fortune 500 CEO or something?" he'd asked me.

"Maybe one day I will be," I'd answered back, oddly satisfied by his impressed remark. But the truth is, I'm not sure what I want to *do* or *be*. I'm not like my brother, Mark, who always knew he wanted to go into engineering. When I think about the future, all I can think about is getting into UT and the fact that the planet is on fire. It sounds absurd when I put it that way, but it's the truth. Those are the only two things I can really crystallize in my mind. The rest is sort of a blank, a mystery I'll deal with later. I mean, if the planet survives, I guess.

I used to save my planners in a storage closet in the kitchen and flip through them sometimes, just for the sense of accomplishment it gave me. Harvey took those, and if I let myself think about that, it leaves an ache in my throat and a prickly feeling. Maybe I'll deal with that later, too.

Or not.

Today there's too much to deal with just in the form of classes. I scan each teacher's syllabus and work through their predictable "get-to-know-you" first day rituals, all of them just corny stuff delaying the real work we all know is coming. In AP Calculus, we have to find partners based on formulas and share "fun" facts about ourselves. (*"I'm Eliza Brady. I have an older brother named Mark. I want to go to UT. I don't have any pets but I wish I did. I drive a Nissan Leaf. My middle name is Jane."*) In AP U.S. History, we have to make a brief timeline of major events in our lives (birth, elected president of fifth-grade class, chosen as class speaker of eighth-grade class, selected for National Honor Society, etc.). And in English class, we have to write a letter to our teacher. (*"My name is Eliza Brady, and I'm excited to be in this class. I'm an editor on the lit mag, I swim for Willow Pool in the summers, and I'm a member of Students for the Environment, Girls Who Code, the National Honor Society, the Key Club, the Current Topics Club, the French National Honor Society, the Quill and Scroll Honor Society, and the summer before last I was a counselor at Camp Paseo. You asked us to let you know of any issues that might inhibit our learning. I do want to share that our home did flood but we are staying with relatives and I don't foresee this having an impact on my academics. Looking forward to a great year in your class! Sincerely, Eliza Brady"*)

Only in AP Environmental Science, my last class of the day, am I spared the absurdity of putting off the point of why we're all here: to learn, do our best, and earn grades that will end up on transcripts that will determine our futures. The teacher, Ms. Bates, is sort of iconic at Baldwin. She's a tall, slim Black woman with very short hair who always, always wears small gold studs in her ears, red nail polish, and one of a rainbow collection of pantsuits. She notoriously tough, but word is she prepares kids for the AP exam like nobody's business.

And the legend is she also doesn't smile until Winter Break. Sometimes not even until Spring Break.

As she passes out her syllabus, she's already barreling forward, letting us know about upcoming quizzes, reading assignments, labs, and major projects. I sense myself getting excited by the challenge, even if I'm also a little bit nervous, too.

"I am fair, but I am firm," Ms. Bates intones, her polished black slip-on flats click-clacking as she walks up and down the aisles. "I am happy to provide one-on-one tutorials both before and after school, but you must make an appointment. I should tell you now that I do not offer extra credit, ever, so do not ask for it. If I catch you cheating, plagiarizing, lying, or conducting yourself in a manner beneath that of an AP student at Baldwin High, you will earn a grade cut, a phone call home, and a referral to administration. You'll also lose the privilege of asking me for a letter of recommendation." At this she pauses pointedly from the front of the room. "I should add here that I am known for my truly exquisite letters of rec."

She doesn't smile, not even a little. But I get the sense that this is Ms. Bates's dry attempt at humor. I like it. Other kids are staring straight ahead, practically holding their breaths. I'm not exactly grinning with excitement or anything, but there's something about Ms. Bates that *does* make me a little giddy. Maybe it's the challenge of an allegedly impossible-to-please teacher in a subject that's legendarily tough. Or maybe it's a teacher who treats us like grown-ups whose job is to learn, not play games and write get-to-know-you letters.

I shoot my hand in the air.

Ms. Bates turns to me.

"Yes, please remind me of your name?"

"Yes, ma'am," I say. "Eliza Brady."

"What is your question?"

I lower my hand into my lap and speak loudly and slowly. I've never had a problem speaking up in class. In fact, I find it utterly bizarre that so many of my classmates are so shy when it comes to participating in discussions and answering and asking questions.

"In this course, will we be . . . I should first say, given what the city has endured recently . . . I'm talking about Hurricane Harvey, of course . . . can we expect to discuss the effects of climate change on our planet?"

I wince a little that I stumbled slightly during my first question to Ms. Bates. I know I enunciated my words and made eye contact, but I wanted to impress her right away.

And I'm also sincerely interested in her answer.

"Eliza, that's an excellent question," says Ms. Bates, and I sit up a little straighter, a shiver of pride running down my spine. I nod, hoping I seem modest. "I appreciate you already trying to make connections between our learning and our real lives.

That's something we will be doing a lot of in this class. And yes, climate change is something we'll be discussing."

"Does that mean we'll be taking into consideration *all* points of view on the subject?" comes a male voice from the back of the room. I turn my head over my right shoulder. Jayden Scott. Superprivileged prep and member of the Young Republicans. I'm surprised his parents didn't put him at St. Augustine. I'm not surprised he didn't bother to raise his hand.

"Can you elaborate?" asks Ms. Bates, her face calm and neutral, not a hint of annoyance on it.

"I mean," says Jayden, loud and sure of himself, leaning back in his desk, taking up space, "there *are* conflicting reports on climate change and how real it really is. I mean, we've always had big hurricanes. Take the 1900 storm that destroyed Galveston. Was that climate change?"

I wait a nanosecond for Ms. Bates to answer, but when she doesn't, I can't help it.

"The vast majority of scientists now overwhelmingly agree that climate change is happening, and it's caused by humans," I say, looking him right in the eye. "And the data overwhelmingly suggests that climate change is having an impact on weather patterns, making storms, droughts, freezes, and wildfires more intense than ever before."

Jayden is smirking a little, probably enjoying this. Honestly, he's kind of been a jerk since we were in elementary school together.

"Okay, so prove it," he says, shrugging.

"Right now?" I counter, leaning forward a little in my seat. "I could pull up studies on my phone in two seconds, but you're not going to believe something that you'll see as inconvenient."

There's a rustle of movement around us, students shuffling in their desks and eyeing one another. I turn back, and my cheeks flush a little. Did I just cross a line? Am I going to get into trouble?

"Students," says Ms. Bates, clapping her hands lightly to assert her authority again, "I appreciate this enthusiasm and a desire to debate and learn on the first day of school, and during last period, no less. But let's table this conversation for another time. I want to turn our attention back to the syllabus."

I lower my gaze, my eyes fixed on Ms. Bates's detailed syllabus. I can almost feel Jayden's gaze burning into my back. How can anyone in 2017 living through what we've just lived through deny what's happening to our planet? How can anyone not care about this issue? I've cared about it since the sixth grade, when a school assignment on recycling sent me into a YouTube wormhole that had me watching video after video of starving polar bears and decimated rainforests. That evening my parents found me digging through our city-issued trash can, searching for anything recyclable that my family members had missed. Ever since then, the fact that so many people are like Jayden when the science is so clear boggles my mind.

And the fact that so many people like my dad still choose to work jobs that contribute to the problem makes me rage.

I don't want to think about Jayden or my dad. Instead, I curl my hands into fists, furious. I don't like feeling out of control like this, not ever. I take a deep breath, reach for my planner, and open it, fishing in my backpack for my colored highlighters so I can start organizing Ms. Bates's deadlines into my calendar.

As we wrap up the class, an idea strikes me. I wait until most of the class has filed out, including and especially Jayden, and I approach Ms. Bates, who is seated at her desk flipping through a stack of papers.

"Ms. Bates?" I ask.

She looks up, her face open and accepting even without her elusive smile.

"Yes, Eliza?"

I love how teachers always learn my name so fast. It's something I strive for.

"I hope I wasn't out of line in class," I say, shifting the straps on my heavy backpack. "I mean, in my response to Jayden."

Ms. Bates nods thoughtfully. "Not out of line. However, I trust that moving forward you'll always be sure to follow the parameters I put in place for our lessons and class discussions."

"Oh, yes, ma'am, absolutely," I say, nodding hard so she knows I'm serious.

"Was that all you needed?" She waits patiently, and even though she's not the warmest teacher on the planet, she's certainly not making me feel like I'm bothering her. I decide it's a good time to broach an idea that's been on my mind.

"Well, actually, I'm thinking about starting some sort of environmental club here at Baldwin," I say. "Or . . . I mean, here at Southwest. Baldwin at Southwest." I stumble, and now my cheeks really do flare red. I'm not used to phrasing any of this.

"A club focused on environmental issues?" Ms. Bates asks.

"Yes, and on climate change. I'm a member of Students for the Environment, but the president graduated last year, and, not to be impolite, but . . ." I pause here, thinking back to the old environmental club at Baldwin. Jackie Morrison was nice enough, but she wasn't the most dynamic leader, and our meetings were usually only a handful of kids talking about plans that never seemed to go anywhere. It always frustrated me. "Anyway," I continue, "I think there's an opportunity to inject some new life into the club. We could work to educate ourselves and others." At this I think of Jayden and the likelihood that he would even be willing to be educated. "But primarily, we would work on action items like a recycling plan for the school, and perhaps meatless Monday alternatives in the cafeteria?" Suddenly, my brain is blowing up with a million possibilities for this club, and I'm already making a mental color-coded to-do list.

Ms. Bates listens patiently before responding. "And let me guess. You'd like me to be the sponsor?"

"If you wouldn't mind," I say, grateful she brought up the question herself. Clubs can't exist without official sponsors, but sometimes teachers are reluctant to put another responsibility on their plates.

"You can ask Ms. Naylor of the lit mag or any of the other sponsors of the clubs I'm involved in," I say. "I'm very organized and efficient as well as responsible. You wouldn't have to lift a finger. The only thing we'd really need is to use your room."

Ms. Bates peers around the classroom we're sitting in. "I

must say, I'm still not used to this as my room," she says. "I've spent fifteen years in Room 125 at Baldwin. Of course, that was before Hurricane Harvey turned it into a swimming pool." She snorts ruefully, and it's the most un–Ms. Bates thing I've seen her do.

"I'm so sorry," I say. "My house flooded, so I understand."

"I'm sorry to hear that, Eliza," Ms. Bates says, frowning. "My home was spared, but my classroom was a home away from home, if I'm being honest."

I stand there, nodding, unsure of whether Ms. Bates has agreed to be our sponsor. I'm about to open my mouth to find a way to press the question once more when Ms. Bates speaks up again.

"I do already sponsor the Black Student Alliance," she says, "but if you're as organized as you say you are, I suppose I can't turn you down." She peers at me, like she's inspecting a specimen under a microscope. "You *are* organized, correct?"

I get that this is Ms. Bates's dry sense of humor again, and I smile.

"I swear," I say. "You'll never meet a more organized teenager in your life."

At this Ms. Bates actually smiles, her fuchsia-painted lips spreading into a wide grin. And then she laughs. Lightly and softly, and just for a second. Maybe it's more of a chuckle. But she *does* laugh. I feel that sense of pride again.

"Then I have to say yes," Ms. Bates answers. "A yes to the most organized teenager to walk planet earth."

"Great, thank you so much," I say. "I'm going to work on plans tonight!" I smile broadly and start to head to the door, but Ms. Bates stops me.

"Eliza?"

"Ma'am?"

She swivels in her chair to look at me.

"I'm thinking," she says, "that perhaps it would be a good idea to have this be a combined club of sorts. A club that involves Baldwin students *and* Southwest High students."

I don't consider myself someone who struggles to make conversation with an adult, especially an authority figure, but I find myself unable to speak. In fact, I'm fairly sure I stand there with my mouth wide open.

I certainly don't want to say *no*, of course. I don't want to displease Ms. Bates. I just wasn't expecting this.

More importantly, I'm not sure I know how to make this happen.

Ms. Bates finally fills the awkward silence. "The issue of climate change is so important, and I think it's something that could really serve to unite students from both our school communities," she explains. "Hurricane Harvey touched every corner of this community. Rich and poor. All colors. All circumstances."

"Of course," I manage at last, my mind recalling the image of the former mayor of Houston wading through waist-deep water, evacuating his house in the swanky Memorial area.

"Plus," continues Ms. Bates, "I think if our two schools are going to be sharing a space all year long, it would be nice if we found common ground, don't you?"

"Of course," I repeat. "I think this all makes total sense, and I'll get started on plans tonight, like I said."

Ms. Bates nods, the earlier smile and laugh forgotten. She's all business again. But before I leave, she says, "Sounds great, Eliza. I trust you'll do a more than capable job."

I wave goodbye and head down the hall, now mostly empty of students after the final bell. *More than capable.* I want to be *more* than more than capable! I want Ms. Bates to think I'm outstanding.

But how am I supposed to make sure this club represents both Baldwin and Southwest Highs when I don't even know how I'm supposed to meet any Southwest kids? The only time we are really given a chance to interact is lunchtime, when everyone sits with the people they already know. Today in the cafeteria I couldn't help but notice how strange it was to see a clear line of demarcation between us Baldwin kids, dressed in anything we wanted, and the Southwest High kids in their sea of blue shirts.

I also noticed that only one side had white faces in it. Baldwin.

The only Southwest kid I met today was the cute boy who'd told me he liked my *Meat Is Murder* T-shirt this morning and then mumbled something about his favorite band. He was so adorable I could barely find a way to sound like a normal person in front of him, so that doesn't leave me much of an opening to ask him to join my club.

Never mind, I scold myself. I'll figure it out like I always do. And I'll start tonight. As I head toward my car in the student lot, my mind is buzzing with all the tasks I can file into my ever-growing to-do list of tasks that will make this club super-successful. As successful as my junior year has to be.

~

I want to make it very clear that I am so grateful for Aunt Heather and Uncle Dave. My dad's parents live in Austin, and my other grandparents passed away when I was little. Without Heather and Dave letting us live with them until our house is repaired, we'd probably have to rent or live in an extended-stay hotel or something that could add to what seems like the ever-increasing cost of putting our lives back in order.

So like I said. I'm grateful.

But there is literally not any space to get my work done. Okay, my tenth-grade English teacher would not be pleased with my misuse of the word *literally*. There are spaces. But they're not really conducive to true productivity. In our house, I not only had my own bathroom, I had a bedroom massive enough for a large desk and several bookshelves where I could organize my stuff.

Not so at Heather and Dave's modest midcentury ranch house where I'm being forced to share a bedroom with a baby who still isn't sleeping through the night. So I make do. The back deck (if it's not too hot), the front porch (if there aren't too many people walking their dogs to distract me), or the dining room table (that nobody actually eats at and which mostly serves as a repository for mail, car keys, and yet-to-be-emptied bags of random things from Walgreens).

That's where I am at nine o'clock tonight, my glowing laptop sitting in the middle of an ever-widening circle of papers and books and flair pens and highlighters. A blank Google document is staring at me, challenging me to fill it up with as detailed of a plan as I've got. I reach out my hands, try to ignore my chewed-up fingernails, and type the words: Eagles and Tigers United for the Planet (ETUP)

That certainly sounds more exciting than Students for the Environment. My fingers hover over the keyboard, and I bite my bottom lip and stare off into the distance, letting my mind calculate and recalculate the next steps I've been considering since I first shared my idea with Ms. Bates. My brain picks up sounds—the squeak of hardwood floorboards as Dave paces back and forth in Ethan's room down the hall, trying to settle the baby to sleep. (I'll never think of it as my room, no matter how long we stay.) The low hum of the television in the nearby den as Heather and my mom drink wine and watch some dumb true crime show. The *yip yip* of some neighbor's annoying mutt.

The only creature not home to add to the symphony is my father, but I'm sure the jangle of his keys in the doorknob is just moments away.

That's the other thing about my old room. It was very quiet, just the way I like it.

I start to type out a bulleted list of ideas for the club. Guest speakers. Committees. Potential projects. I want this club to be action-oriented. Not just sitting around talking about the problem of climate change like the old environmental club at Baldwin used to do, but really *doing* something about it.

Meatless Mondays in the cafeteria? Recycling initiative? Organize carpools to reduce emissions? I furrow my brow as I brainstorm. After a little while, I crack my neck, stretch my arms, and take out my phone to start a club Instagram. I'm already envisioning the page filling up with pictures of Baldwin and Southwest High kids doing bayou cleanups and planting trees on the Southwest High campus. When my uncle walks by after finally getting Ethan down and says hello and something about me burning the midnight oil, I only pause long enough to look up and murmur a pleasant, "Yeah, I guess," before I get back to it.

Suddenly, my phone buzzes as a text appears at the top of my screen.

Let me guess. Already studying?

It's Isabella. We've been texting on and off all day, of course. Even though her earlier texts annoyed me, I've missed having her with me, gossiping in the halls and eating lunch together in the cafeteria. I can't believe after all these years of going to school together, we're on different campuses. I wonder if her parents will go ahead and just keep her at St. Augustine for her senior year. The Baldwin campus will have to be repaired by then, right?

Not studying . . . doing stuff for this new club I want to start to combat climate change.

I watch as the three dots pop up, not sure if Isabella is going to cheer me on or make a snarky joke. With her it could really go either way.

I'm not surprised at all by this initiative, my Type A Queen.

Only Isabella could manage to text a snarky cheer in one sentence. It makes me feel prickly. I hate feeling prickly.

Shut up, it's going to be amazing.

I don't like how this conversation already feels like an argument I want to win. After a moment, Isabella texts back.

Of course it is. I just miss you.

The prickliness eases up a bit.

I miss you too . . . so weird to walk the halls of Southwest High.

So weird to walk the halls of St. Augustine. You would not even believe the cars in the student lot. They're nicer than the teachers' cars.

I'll bet.

Then Isabella sends me that dumb GIF of some guy making it rain, dollar bills shooting out of his hands. Her commentary on St. Augustine life, I guess. Not that Isabella is hurting for cash. Her father does something in finance that Isabella doesn't even understand, and Isabella's mother comes from money. At least that's what my mom says. In fact, when Isabella's parents decided to send her to St. Augustine, my mother said she was surprised Isabella's folks ever sent her to public school in the first place.

I don't know how to respond to Isabella's GIF except to give it a ha-ha react.

Gotta get back to work. Maybe hang out this weekend?

Although it feels like something I'm just saying, not something I'll really do. I already have too much school stuff to get started on.

K. Have fun saving the planet.

I shoot back an eye roll emoji and set my phone aside.

When I first started getting obsessed about environmental issues in sixth grade after that recycling assignment, I tried so hard to get Isabella to understand why the issue mattered to me so much. She wasn't some climate change denier like Jayden or anything, but she just didn't seem to grasp the urgency.

"Look, I recycle," she'd said to me once. "And my parents already did their job by only having one kid. That's gotta, like, what, completely offset my oxygen footprint?"

"Your *carbon* footprint," I'd shot back.

Isabella just laughed. Scientists would figure it out, she told me. They always did. Not even Hurricane Harvey flooding her house had made an impact in her thinking. (Of course, Isabella was staying in a swanky rented condo in the Museum District, not sharing a bedroom with an infant relative.)

But while we waited for other people to solve the climate crisis, Isabella thought in the meantime we needed to enjoy our lives. Something she was certain I didn't do enough of. Isabella didn't care about getting into UT. Her father said as long as she got in somewhere, that was good enough for him.

Isabella's father's remark is sliding through my brain when my own dad shows up, just as I get my ETUP Instagram page set up, along with a first post of a bright blue-and-green planet earth and hot-pink letters spelling out the words WANNA SAVE OUR MOTHER? FIRST MEETING SOON! WATCH THIS SPACE!

"Hey, Eliza," he says.

"Hey." My eyes check the time on my phone. It's almost ten o'clock. "You're home late." I wish my mom had witnessed that last comment so she couldn't accuse me of not at least trying with my father, a favorite complaint of hers.

"Work was nonstop," he says, pausing to scratch the back of his neck. "And then I dropped by the house to check on a few things. I made the mistake of lying down on my bed upstairs and accidentally fell asleep." He yawns, like I won't believe him even though I do. My mother says I get my work ethic from my father, even if I don't think we're alike in any other way except that we're both tall and willowy, and my dad once had blond hair, too, before he lost most of it.

"How was your first day of school?" he asks.

"Fine," I answer. I have so much to do, and I really don't want to get dragged into a conversation. Especially when every conversation with my father feels like a job.

Just then, my mom's voice rings out from the den, asking if that's my father and saving me from having to provide him with more details.

"Yeah, it's me," my dad shouts in my mother's direction, followed by the sounds of Aunt Heather gently shushing us, reminding us once again that we're living in a house with a six-month-old infant.

"How's the house looking?" I ask. Less because I want to talk to him and more because I genuinely want to know.

"Eh," he says, setting a stack of papers and his keys on a free spot by the table along with a half-empty disposable water bottle. "They've made some progress on the kitchen, I guess. Not as much as I'd like."

"No smell?" I ask, cringing at little at the sight of the bottle.

"No, the smell is gone, thank goodness," he says. The foul, horrific odor born out of dirty floodwater and Houston summer heat was impossible to forget once you'd breathed it in, which we did, day after day in the wake of Harvey, hauling our unsalvageable family possessions out onto the street to be gawked at by anyone passing by. I ball my hands into fists for a moment and squeeze, willing the memory away, then turn my focus to my laptop screen.

"What's eat up?" my dad asks, peering over my shoulder. Why is he lingering? Ever since Mark left for college, I've noticed him trying stuff like this. Like he's trying to repair our relationship. Like he can transport us back to when I was in elementary school and we'd spend hours watching *SpongeBob SquarePants* marathons together and tossing the Frisbee in our backyard. We used to sincerely have a good time together, my dad and me. But at some point in middle school my attention turned to the climate crisis and my father's attention started turning more toward Mark, toward their shared interests in college basketball and science and math talk. Even if Dad had hoped Mark would be an Aggie like him, I thought he would explode with pride the day Mark got into MIT.

I doubt my dad will want to explode with pride over me starting ETUP.

"What?" I ask, peering up at him over my right shoulder. "What's what?"

My dad points a finger at the screen, right under ETUP.

"This," he says. "Eat up?"

Ugh. I hadn't even considered the sound the acronym makes. In my mind, I had spelled it out like a cheerleader. E-T-U-P.

"It's . . . a club I'm starting at school. A sort of combined club between the two campuses to work on climate change issues and take real action, like fighting against the fossil fuel industry."

There's a pause, and I know my dad is thinking of how to react. Sitting in this awkward silence, there's a part of me that wants to keep going, start in on one of the impassioned speeches I used to deliver to him starting in middle school. Point out for the millionth time that his job is directly contributing to the current crisis. Articulate all the ways a career change would be beneficial for the planet. But I haven't done any of that since Harvey. I'm so mad I don't know if I could do any of that without exploding. So I just keep my eyes trained on my laptop, hoping he'll take the hint and leave.

"Well, that will look good on those college apps, right?" he says at last.

"Yes," I admit. "But that's not why I'm starting this," I continue, choosing to talk to my screen instead of him. (*Eat up? Why didn't I catch this earlier?*)

"I didn't say that's why you started it," my father presses, and I can sense his discomfort. He's probably wondering why he bothered to talk to me at all.

"Well," I say, shifting a little in my seat, trying to stay calm, "I guess it sort of felt like that's what you were implying. I *do* care about my college applications. You know that. But I also care about, like, being able to live to retirement age on a hospitable planet. Even as oil and gas companies are attempting to ensure my early demise." Uh-oh. Here I go.

I know without looking that my dad is tossing his head back, staring at the ceiling in frustration. The pops in his neck followed by a long exhalation remind me of fireworks going off. *Pop. Pop. Pop. Swoooosh.*

"Eliza, I guarantee you're going to be able to live to retirement age on a hospitable planet," he says.

His on-edge tone tells me he for *sure* regrets starting this conversation with me. Whatever blog post he read on his phone about "How to Bond with Your Estranged Teenage Daughter" has failed him epically. I would almost feel sorry for disappointing him if he wasn't irritating me so much.

"Okay, I believe you," I say, my voice matching his. Curt. Irritable. Just then my mom wanders into the doorway separating the kitchen and den from the dining room. I look up.

"Sweetie, you must be starved," she says, leaning against the doorframe. I wonder if she can tell something's starting between us and that's why she's decided to interrupt. "I saved some lasagna. Want me to heat it up?"

"Sure, that would be great," my father says, reaching for his water bottle, the thin, cheap plastic crackling slightly under his fingers.

The moment he does this, my mind begins to perform this incredibly annoying trick it started doing around the time I watched the video of the starving polar bears. Sometimes—and a lot of the time, lately—when I spy a plastic water bottle or one of Ethan's disposable diapers or one of those take-and-toss

Starbucks monstrosities with the matching green plastic straws that holds a frothy mochafrappafrofro delight, my brain multiplies how many bottles or diapers or monstrosities that *one* person will throw out in just *one* month. Think about it. One person gets one Starbucks drink *every* single day for thirty days in a row. Five people. Ten people. Those cups would fill up this dining room in no time, plastic on plastic on plastic. Laundry detergent bottles. Hand soap containers. The bubble wrap that comes with every Amazon package. I can so easily envision these items multiplying, breeding, spreading, and building into Mount Everest–sized piles of junk that won't decompose for hundreds of years.

I mean, every plastic lunch sack my mother used to wrap up my peanut butter sandwiches in elementary school is still in existence somewhere. And I'm just *one* person.

When these images rip through my brain, when my mind starts running through these visual calculations, it leaves me so overwhelmed and helpless I have trouble catching my breath sometimes.

My heart picks up speed, and the crinkle of the plastic sets my teeth on edge.

"Seriously, Dad!" I snap, turning to face him again. I can feel red splotches of frustration begin to bloom on my face. "I have begged you like five hundred freaking times to use a reusable water bottle. I am *happy* to wash it out and refill it for you every single night if you'd like!"

"Eliza!" my mother responds. "That tone is so unnecessary."

That bottle is so unnecessary, I want to shout back, but I just sit back in my chair, crossing my arms in front of me defensively.

I shouldn't have said anything. I hate losing control like this. And now I've lost valuable time getting work done. Why should I bother trying to convince my father of anything? He's never going to listen to me anyway.

My father is still standing there, the water bottle in his hand. I keep my eyes on the dining room table. I'm pouting like a little kid who just got sent to the naughty chair, and I'm sure Aunt Heather and Uncle Dave can hear this entire embarrassing display.

"Eliza?" It's my father's voice, somehow managing to sound drained and angry at the same time. "I'm sorry I disturbed your *important* work. I won't bother to express curiosity in your extracurricular activities or schoolwork again, I promise." And instead of heading into the kitchen, he heads down the hall to the guest bedroom that he and Mom are staying in.

"Eliza," my mother says, her voice tight. "I don't have the energy to get into how unfair you've been to your dad lately, especially since we flooded. Your attitude is worse than ever. But your father has been under an enormous amount of stress lately. At work. With the house. With everything. I wish you could be a little more conscious of that."

I cross my arms even tighter and don't lift my gaze from the faux wood finish of Aunt Heather and Uncle Dave's dining room table. My heart is still racing.

"Sorry," I mutter.

"When he's cooled off, he deserves an apology."

"I know." Anything to finish this conversation so I can get back to work. Work will make me feel better.

My mother stands there for a moment, but I don't look up. I swear I've memorized the swoops and loops of this terrible table by now. After a few tense beats, my mother heads down the hallway, and I can hear her follow my father's path into their bedroom. No doubt they're commiserating about me and my behavior right now, their conversation forced into hushed, angry whispers so as not to bother baby Ethan.

I realize hot tears are pooling in my eyes. No. I refuse to cry over this. I squeeze my eyes shut tight, scrunch my face up for a count of five, then fix my gaze back on my computer screen. It's well past ten o'clock, and I still have homework and ETUP plans to attack.

I won't go to bed until I'm convinced they're perfect.

JAVIER

For what feels like the millionth time, Dominic commands me to watch him try a trick on his skateboard.

"I feel like a mom at the playground," I joke, leaning back into the grass as Dominic attempts one more complicated flip. I lift my voice into a child's pitch. "Mom, watch! Mom, watch!"

Dom laughs good-naturedly as he rolls off the paved trail he'd been skating on and settles down next to me in the grass.

This first Saturday of the school year finds us at one of our usual hangouts, Willow Waterhole. The waterhole, a collection of big, deep manmade lakes, is really part of a stormwater detention system that's supposed to help prevent flooding in the city, and it's within walking distance of Southwest High and my house. The city built some trails and bridges so people can enjoy it as a kind of park, and it's a favorite place for people to take walks, ride bikes, or, if you're Dominic, skateboard. After the rains of Harvey subsided, I'd walked here with Daniela and gaped at how the water level was so high it was over the tops of the trees that dotted the perimeter of the lakes. Hard to believe where Dominic and I are sitting right now was totally submerged during the storm.

The thought makes my heart quicken just a bit, and I have to remind myself that there's not a storm cloud in the sky and no rain in the forecast.

"The signs say there are alligators in there," says Dominic, his eyes trained on the water in front of us, "but I've never seen one."

"Freaky to think of alligators swimming around a couple of hundred feet from where we sleep," I answer, imagining the possibility. "Kind of cool, too, when you think about it." And it is cool, at least to me. Houston is so weird like that. I mean, you drive downtown on one of our enormous, sweeping freeways, and you're suddenly surrounded by all these sleek, tall buildings and big performing arts venues and whatever, but really the entire city is right smack on top of swampland and twisty, snaking bayous full of mysterious creatures.

"Kind of cool?" asks Dominic, pulling me back out of my thoughts. "Thinking an animal that could kill you with one bite is 'kind of cool' is very on-brand for you, primo." But the way he says it, I know he's admiring me more than making fun.

We sit there in silence for a little bit. My eyes catch on a plastic bag with the word *Kroger* stamped on it, fluttering in the bushes before it takes off, carried by a gust of warm wind. That's the one thing about Willow Waterhole. It is pretty, full of bluebonnets and other wildflowers in the spring, but it's gross how some people just leave their trash behind.

Dom has pulled out his phone and is messing around on it. I notice the time and remember I'm supposed to get home for a family cookout.

"I gotta be getting back," I say, standing up. "Want to come over to eat?"

"Thanks but no thanks," says Dom. "I want to stay and

practice a few more tricks. Even if my mom isn't here to cheer me on."

"Very funny, son," I say, dragging out the joke before I take off. My stomach is starting to grumble, and I pick up the pace, my mouth already watering at the thought of my dad's burgers.

~

"Miguel, toss me the hamburger buns," says my father.

"Only if you stop playing this corny music," Miguel answers from the back deck in my father's general direction.

"Not corny, Miguelito," my dad says, flipping a burger and then wiping the sweat off his brow with his big, beefy forearm. "This is the perfect band, son. Listen and love."

I laugh at my father's description of Mexrrissey, this band out of Mexico that does covers of Smiths songs with a twist, and all in Spanish, too. Of course my dad is listening to them on a CD out of an ancient boom box (his term, not mine) perched on the edge of our deck near his grill spot.

"Here, Dad, catch," I say, and I toss the plastic bag of buns. I overshoot by way too much, which I guess is sort of less embarrassing than undershooting? Especially with Miguel here. "Hold up, I got it," I add, trotting over to where the bread has landed before handing it to Dad, who takes it with a grin.

"Javi knows what I'm talking about with this music," my father says to Miguel. "Man, he used to love me singing 'Cemetry Gates' to him when he was a baby."

Miguel takes a long pull of his Modelo and sets the bottle down on the deck. "Dad, you don't think there's anything slightly messed up about the fact that you were singing about cemeteries and dead bodies to a baby? Maybe that's why Javi's so . . ." He pauses and eyes me carefully, pondering his next words. ". . . so *different.*" And here's the thing. Miguel doesn't say this in a mean way or with a smirk or anything like that. He doesn't say it unkindly. He just says it like it's a fact. Like we all know I'm the youngest of the family and I'm the odd one out. It's normal for someone my dad's age to like The Smiths and it's normal for someone my mom's age to enjoy yoga, but for a sixteen-year-old boy to like these things? Anyway. *Different.*

I settle back into my seat next to Miguel on the deck. His girl, Rosario, slides open the back door and joins us, pulling up one of our battered lawn chairs that have seen better days.

"Rosario, you want your burger well done, yeah?" my father shouts.

"I actually like it bloody, but that's not good for this one," Rosario shouts back, patting her tummy. "So well done it is."

My father laughs and keeps grilling.

I like Rosario, and I'm glad she's here with us, chilling with the rest of the family. I mean, she's family, too, really. She's been Miguel's girlfriend since they both were at Southwest six years ago. Now she works in some doctor's office yelling at insurance companies to pay their bills. Or at least that's how she explained it to me once.

"How are you feeling, Rosie?" I ask her. She smiles at the

nickname, sliding one of her dark curls behind her ear, the same ear with a string of shining piercings all the way up the earlobe. At least four. Maybe five?

"I'm okay," she says. "I still have a ridiculous amount of heartburn. And I'm still tired even though the doctor told me that in the second trimester you get a bunch of energy. Well, that dude doesn't work where I work." As if to prove something, she stretches her arms up in the air and her legs straight out in front of her and offers a deep, loud sigh.

At this, Miguel leans over and kisses Rosario's belly, a little peach wave that's peeking out of her pink T-shirt.

"Be nice to your mother, entiendes?" Miguel hollers. Then he kisses Rosario right on the belly button, and she laughs that same tinkly girl laugh I used to hear coming from Miguel's bedroom back when they were teenagers and I was a little kid and Miguel made me the lookout. ("Just knock on the door when you see Mom's car pull in the driveway, okay, Javi?")

As Miguel sits back up, I think about the fact that my brother—the same brother who used to hold me upside down by my ankles until I said the ABCs backward and the same brother who came home from junior prom totally wasted and puked in the azalea bushes in the front yard—is going to be someone's father. Yeah, Miguel has a good job at the refinery in Pasadena making even more than dad, supposedly. But it's still weird.

"Sorry you're so tired," I say as Miguel opens another Modelo and Rosario shoots him a *slow down* look.

"Yeah, well, it's also because Miguel and me are helping out at my mom's house in the evenings. Helping her get her house back in order." Rosario's mom's house flooded in Harvey, and she hadn't had any flood insurance because her home had never flooded, not in the decades and decades she'd lived there, and she couldn't justify the expense. Of course now the costs were crazier than if she'd had it. I'd overheard Rosario explaining to Mom how overwhelming it was to try and navigate the grants and assistance programs and loans and how she couldn't even imagine what it was like for people who didn't have easy access to the internet.

"And think about the people who don't have papers," my mother had said. "Who's helping them?"

Rosario had sighed in response.

The back door opens again. It's Daniela. Really, it's just her head sticking out. She avoids the heat by any means necessary, which is a heck of a task considering where we live.

"Can someone run to the Kroger or somewhere and get ketchup? Mom thought we had some and we don't."

Miguel claps his hands together.

"Your wish is my command, sister dear!" Miguel shouts, popping up.

"You've just had two Modelos," Rosario chides. "I kind of want the father of my baby to live long enough to *be* the father of my baby?"

Miguel rolls his eyes, but he tugs the keys to his ancient Chevy truck from his pocket and tosses them to me. Naturally, I don't react fast enough, and they land on the deck and sort of skid to my feet. I cringe at my lack of quick reflexes. Just one more thing for Miguel to add to the list of what makes me so "different."

"Javier can drive," he announces. "Right, little brother?"

I grab the keys and stand up, wishing away whatever genetic flaw I have that makes me incapable of throwing hamburger buns or catching car keys.

"Yeah, I'll drive."

We head around the side of the house and slide into Miguel's truck and head to Kroger. He cues up some super old-school DJ Screw and stares out the window as the bass reverbs through the cab of the truck.

"So, little brother, how's it really going?" he asks. "First week of junior year done."

"It's going good," I say. "I got Ms. Gomez for English again. I had her freshman year, too. She's cool."

"Yeah, I remember her," Miguel says, drumming his knuckles on the passenger-side window in time with the music. "She was kinda hot for a teacher."

I wince, thinking of kindly Ms. Gomez and her first day poetry exercise. "Geez, Miguel, she's a teacher."

"So?" he answers, laughing. Probably at my discomfort more than anything else.

We roll down Bellfort in silence until we reach the Kroger. As I maneuver Miguel's gargantuan truck into a parking spot, holding my breath as I try not to hit any other cars, he turns to me and asks, "Okay, so not Ms. Gomez. But are there *any* girls on your radar?"

I wait until we slide out of the cab and slam the doors before I say, "Not really, I guess." Miguel is probably judging my total lack of game right about now. I think about mentioning supercute Smiths girl, just to have something to say, but I haven't seen her since that first day. For all I know, her parents flipped out when she came home talking about how many brown faces she was surrounded by and they enrolled her at some swanky private school.

"Not really you guess?" Miguel repeats as we open the door and head for condiments. Miguel grabs a plastic clamshell of chocolate cupcakes as we pass the bakery.

"Daniela just said ketchup," I remind him.

"I can't get cupcakes with my own money?" Miguel scolds, laughing again. "Come on, little brother. Loosen up. It's not like we're going to get in trouble."

I shrug. I wish I could be half as relaxed as Miguel always seems to be. Even with a baby on the way he looks so chill. So cool. He throws some nice compliment to one of the older women stocking shelves about her smile, but not in that creepy dude way. Just in, like, a cool dude way.

I will never be as cool as Miguel.

And here's the thing. Sometimes I wonder if Miguel wishes I were as cool as he is. Like somehow I've let him down by not being the sort of little brother who wants to watch the Texans play and lose hours to GTA.

One time last year he stopped by unexpectedly when I was home alone to pick up some skirt Mom had altered for Rosario, and he knocked lightly on my bedroom door.

"Uh, come in?" I'd said, craning my neck up to see who was walking in.

"Bro, what's up with this?" Miguel had asked, Rosario's

butter-yellow skirt in his hand, a confused look as visible on his face as his five o'clock shadow.

"Um, it's Yoga With Adriene," I'd said, collapsing into an embarrassed heap from my downward-facing dog.

Miguel had peered at the iPad screen and assessed it carefully as Adriene went on in her soft, honey-smooth voice, encouraging her viewers to bend themselves into comfortable pretzels.

"She *is* pretty cute," he'd said, then eyed me again as I stood up and tugged my Southwest High shirt and athletic shorts into place. "But this is . . . yoga?"

I'd shrugged, my cheeks hot. "It relaxes me. I don't know. She's from Austin. She's Mexican, too." I added this last sentence as if this made it more acceptable for me to do yoga.

"Cool," Miguel had said, only because he didn't know what else to say, I'm sure. "Well, I gotta go, but say hi to the folks for me."

After he'd left, I'd closed the iPad and tossed it onto my bed before flopping next to it and staring at the water marks on my ceiling. Honestly, I think Miguel would have been less weirded out if he'd caught me flipping through some of Dad's old *Sports Illustrated* swimsuit issues.

After we get the ketchup (and the cupcakes and another six-pack of Modelo *and* two pints of Rosario's favorite Ben & Jerry's ice cream) *and* after I have to stand awkwardly to the side while Miguel cheerily catches up in the freezer aisle with some dude he knows from back in the day, we get in line to pay. The checker is a girl I know from Southwest. Not Smiths girl (she probably doesn't have to have a weekend and after-school job), but this girl named Yesenia. I had geometry with her freshman year. She likes to wear her jet-black hair in two braids that arc over her ears and land over her shoulders, like two little dog tails waving hi, but she dyes her bangs different colors. Today they're hot pink.

"Hey, Javi, right?" Yesenia says, sliding the cupcakes over the scanner. "What's up?"

I'm standing behind Miguel, who side-eyes me and does this little half smile.

I shrug. "Not much, I guess."

The pints of ice cream go by. *Beep. Beep.*

Silence.

"Weird with all those Baldwin kids at school, huh?" she asks. Miguel is digging in his pocket for his wallet.

"Yeah," I say. I want to say something more. Something about how it's so easy to spot them in their rich-kid clothes. Or that it's not really fair that we still have to wear our dumb blue T-shirts when they get free dress. Or maybe I could ask her if she thinks this little experiment will last the entire year? But each time I want to open my mouth to speak, it's like I keep thinking of how stupid my words might come out, and figure I better not risk it. Especially with Miguel there to judge my game.

Only being so quiet probably makes me look weird. Or worse, rude.

Yesenia makes change for Miguel, who takes it and grabs the plastic bag of our stuff.

"Well, see you, Javi," Yesenia says, offering up a little wave.

"Later," I say, following Miguel out the sliding door. Ugh, I didn't even say her name. And I know it, too.

We head back to the truck in a silence that doesn't get broken until we're seated and I'm putting the key into the ignition.

"She was cute," says Miguel.

I nod, embarrassed.

We're cruising home and Miguel is rapping his knuckles on the window. I glance over and can see the tattoo of Rosario's name on his inner right wrist bouncing up and down as he raps. Damn how Mom hated it when Miguel started getting tats. But that never stopped Miguel.

"Listen, little brother, I wanna ask you something," Miguel says. He clears his throat and seems uncomfortable, which is weird for a guy who always seems comfortable.

"Yeah, what's up?" I ask.

"I want you to know that it's cool with me, no matter what your answer is, okay? I'm an enlightened dude."

Miguel doesn't normally use words like *enlightened*. It sounds funny coming out of his mouth.

"Okay?" I ask, uncertain. And also a little embarrassed. Like somehow I can sense that this conversation is going to go nowhere comfortable.

"And if it's none of my business, tell me to shut up, okay?"

What is he getting at?

"Okay?" I say again. "I mean, whatever. I'll answer your question." I can feel my cheeks pink up, and I say a silent prayer Miguel is too focused on the road to notice.

He takes a big breath, exhales slowly.

"Maybe it's not so much a question as it is a statement from me," he says. He stops rapping his knuckles and cracks them instead. *Pop, pop, pop.* We come to a stoplight, and I glance over at him. He keeps staring straight ahead.

"I just want you to know, if you like chicks, that's cool with me. And if you don't, that's cool with me, too. Whatever floats your boat, as Dad would say."

My mouth sort of falls open, and then I shut it. I grip the steering wheel and look forward again, willing the light to turn green so at least I have something to do besides sit here in what might be my most awkward moment with Miguel since the Yoga Incident.

The light *does* turn, and as we pull forward, I say, "Uh, I like girls. Just to be clear." I squirm a little in my seat, embarrassed that I have to make this clear to my brother.

Miguel nods, and I keep my eyes pinned on the road. I want to disappear. I get that Miguel was wondering if maybe I'm gay. And I get that it's pretty cool that my big brother doesn't care if I am or not. But why is he thinking I might not be into girls?

I guess because I can't talk to them? Like, ever?

And maybe because of the origami and not liking sports thing, too.

Great. This again. I see stuff on social media all the time that kids like to tag as "toxic masculinity," but it's almost become, like, a joke. Just one of those things kids parrot without knowing what it means. But I don't think it's a joke. In fact, I think it's a real thing, and I've been dealing with it since I was a kid.

Ever since I started having to wear deodorant and realized they all had names like "Swagger" and "Wolf" and "Savage." I mean, what's savage about antiperspirant?

There are kids who are out at Southwest and one or two trans kids. It's no big deal. I mean, it's 2017. And even if it's Texas, it's still Houston. When I was in elementary school, a lesbian was elected mayor. So it's not like I have a problem with the idea of being gay.

It's just that I am very, very into girls. I'm into the way they look and the way they sound and, when I've gotten close enough, like when I'm turning around to pass back a paper to the girl behind me in class, I've realized I like the way they smell, too. Sometimes like cake and cookies. Sometimes like something I can't quite place but dig.

I mean, what I'm trying to say is that just because Miguel caught me doing yoga doesn't mean that he *couldn't* have caught me doing, like, other things.

Of course we are talking solo acts. I've never done anything with an actual, real girl. Not even kissed one. I think back to Yesenia at Kroger and figure the way I'm heading, I might never. I sigh, and I guess loudly, too, because my older brother starts talking again. He's turned down in his volume and his movement.

"Hey," Miguel says as we turn onto our street. "Listen, Javi, I hope you don't mind that I asked that. I was trying to be . . . like, supportive? Just in case? I screwed up, didn't I?"

"No, man, it's no big deal," I say, sliding the keys out of the ignition and handing them to Miguel. (I don't want to take a chance at tossing them, not even in this tight space. I'd probably overshoot and break the passenger window.)

"Okay," says Miguel. "Cool."

"Cool," I answer. Even though my big brother is the cool one.

I'm just the weirdo.

~

It's nice enough that we eat outside on the back deck, much to Daniela's irritation. Rosario keeps asking Mom about what it was like to give birth and whether it hurt a lot or not.

"This one"—my mom pauses to point at Miguel—"gave me the most trouble. But they say the first is your hardest." At this Rosario grimaces, pausing to rub the belly holding *her* first.

"Mami, por favor, cut me some slack with that," Miguel says, laughing. "It couldn't have been that bad. You had two more." He wipes at the corner of his mouth with his thumb, then burps, but softly, so Mom doesn't swat at him.

"Javi was the easiest," my father remembers, swatting at a mosquito. "Pinche zancudos! They've been so bad after Harvey. We need to go in soon."

"Please," says Daniela. She gets up to gather the plates and cups.

"Speaking of Harvey, how is it over at Southwest, Javi?" asks Rosario. "All those kids from Baldwin are there now, right?"

"Rich jerks," mutters Miguel.

"That's not true," says Daniela, coming back out onto the

deck. "There are lots of kids in my program at HCC that went to Baldwin. It's not *all* rich white kids."

"Yeah, but the rich white kids around here whose parents deign to send them to public school go to Baldwin," says Miguel. This time he does burp loudly, and Mom does swat at him. I can't help but grin a little at Miguel's vocabulary. First "enlightened" and then "deign." Modelo loosens his tongue.

"Can I maybe talk, seeing as Rosario asked *me* the question?" I ask. There's a ripple of laughter on the deck, and I feel a flicker of pride. It's not usually me who amuses my family.

Of course, I don't have much to follow up on after that. "It's fine," I say, both to Rosario and everyone else. I sense maybe they're all a little curious about this weird experiment that's happening at my high school. "They stick to their part of the building and we stick to ours. But we do have lunch together." I pause and realize maybe they all want more. "The halls are a lot more crowded now," I say, "and it's weird to see white people. I mean, not just teachers."

"Well, *I* think it's a good thing," says my mother, scooting her chair closer to my father and leaning her head on his shoulder. He leans over with his left hand and rubs her jeans-covered knee. They're always doing this sort of thing, acting all in love even though they've been married for a hundred years and have three kids. Dom's parents split up when he was a baby, and he tells me I should be grateful, and I guess I am. But it still makes me cringe sometimes. "The world is full of white people," my mother continues. "And Black people and brown people and Oriental people and whatever."

"It's Asian, Mom," Daniela says.

"Thank you, Asian," she says. "Anyway, this city and this world are full of all kinds of people so you might as well go to school with all kinds of people."

Smiths girl pops into my head again, a welcome surprise. Her light eyes. Her full lips. That *Meat Is Murder* shirt. The way she had her hair pulled back like she didn't care about it all that much, but somehow it still looked pretty. The way she disappeared down the hall into a Baldwin classroom with a bunch of other white kids.

"Hey, Javi, are you still with us?"

I jump a little in my seat at Rosario's question. She gives me a curious look and then a soft, knowing smile. "You look like you disappeared somewhere for a minute? Maybe to someplace nice?" Rosario has always been able to get a read on me, sometimes even faster than my actual big sister. It's one reason I like her so much even if there's no way I'm about to tell her or anyone else where my mind just drifted.

"It's nothing," I say, hoping any redness in my cheeks will be written off by the warm weather. "And, Mom, yeah, there are more people there, but it's not really like we're going to school together," I say. "It's just for this year. Just until they repair all the flood damage at Baldwin."

"Okay, just for the year and you're sort of going to school together," my mother allows. "Better than nothing. Maybe one silver lining from that damn Harvey."

I wince reflexively.

"You okay, Javier?" Now it's my father eyeing me carefully.

“Daddy, you know how Javi gets when we talk about Harvey,” Daniela says, standing up. “Now can we please all go inside and have ice cream in the kitchen so we stop getting eaten alive?” She leans over and smacks at her calf, hard. “Got one!”

“How does Javi get about Harvey?” Miguel asks as we file in through the open sliding glass door.

“It’s nothing,” I say. “Forget it.”

The last thing I want after this evening is any other reason for my brother to wonder what my deal is. I have to remember to get Daniela alone and tell her to cool it about that stuff. Sure, she found me pacing in the bathroom and fighting waves of nausea the last time it rained hard, but it’s one thing when it’s your sister who finds you like that.

It’s another thing entirely when it’s your cool big brother with the tattoos who already wonders how the two of you can be related.

ELIZA

The truth is, you can get used to anything if you don't dwell. If this moment in time is teaching me anything, it's teaching me that.

Strike that. Rephrase. Maybe not everyone can get used to anything. Maybe other people have to dwell.

I don't dwell. It's not my style.

I'm not saying that to brag. I'm just saying it to be realistic. When my house flooded and my school flooded and my parents and I had to squeeze into a three-bedroom house with my aunt and uncle and their sweet baby (with sleep issues) *and* I had to go to my old school in a different school, I just . . . did it.

How?

I'm not sure, but I don't think about it. I don't let myself. My whole life I've been like this. *Do* something instead of fixate on it. It makes me feel better. When I struggled in geometry, I found myself a tutor. When I started breaking out on my chin, I researched causes and developed a skin regimen that I still follow every night.

And when Hurricane Harvey decimated my world, I started ETUP.

"Eat . . . up?" Ms. Bates says, peering at the poster for our first meeting before glancing up at me from a seated position behind her desk. I created the poster on the computer, but I need her signature on it before I can make copies and post them all around the school. It's my last task of the day before I can head home.

"I didn't think about it at first," I say, "but I figure it if catches people's attention, maybe it's not such a bad thing?" I shift my weight from foot to foot, and Ms. Bates gazes over the poster again. At the top are the letters ETUP and then their meaning under that. And under that is a graphic of the earth splitting in two.

At the very bottom is the club's Instagram and the words WE CAN STOP CLIMATE CHANGE and information about when and where our first meeting will be held, in Ms. Bates's room after school this Thursday.

"I think the eat up part is fine," says Ms. Bates, taking a pen from a jar on her meticulously organized desk and initialing the lower right-hand corner, making it official. "I must say, Eliza, I'm impressed that you've put this all together in just a week's time. You're certainly ambitious."

I offer a quick, modest smile and a *thank you*. Ms. Bates's praise means a lot coming from one of the toughest teachers at Baldwin, but I confess that even though it's coming from her, it's not like this is a new experience for me. I'm used to teachers praising me. Probably not as much as they praised my genius, MIT-attending older brother, Mark, but still.

"I thought for our first meeting, we could introduce ourselves and talk about why we want to be a part of ETUP, and then we could start brainstorming action items for the club to complete," I say as Ms. Bates hands me back the poster. "I'm also wondering how you feel about officers? And maybe T-shirts if we can find an eco-friendly company. I'm not wild about doing that if we just end up adding a bunch of cheap shirts to a landfill in a year or two. Oh! And I forgot. Do you know how we can make sure to have ETUP's meeting included in the afternoon announcements? I know at Baldwin club officers filled out a slip of paper in the main office, but it had to be signed by the sponsor. Is there a similar protocol here at Southwest?"

At this, Ms. Bates pushes back in her desk chair and gazes at me, tipping her head ever so slightly like maybe she's seeing me for the first time.

"My goodness, Eliza, do you find time to sleep?" she asks. A gentle smile plays across her face. (So much for not smiling until the Winter Break. I've already amused Ms. Bates more than once. A flicker of pride works through me.)

I shrug. "Sometimes. I'm sorry, I can get . . . carried away."

The truth is, I don't find much time to sleep. My wired brain just won't let me, a lot of times. Neither will my to-do list. My mom is always after me to turn in before midnight, but given my class load and other responsibilities, I usually stay up way too late, and Ethan makes sure I get up *way* too early on some days.

"It wasn't a criticism," says Ms. Bates, holding up one hand. Maybe to make sure I don't start talking too much again. "I just . . . I think your energy and enthusiasm for this project is something to be commended. I do think you need to remember that it can take time for a new club to build momentum, but I hope that ETUP will inspire students from Baldwin *and* Southwest."

Southwest. Hmm. I know Ms. Bates wants a club with kids from both schools, and I nod when she brings it up again, but the truth is, I have no idea how to make sure we get representation from both groups. Last week, the first week of school, I mostly hung out with OC and OP and a few other Baldwin kids I know from the literary magazine and NHS. Because Baldwin kids are relegated to the T-buildings and the first floor, we don't see the Southwest kids all that much except for the beginning and the end of the day and at lunch. And lunch? Well, the cafeteria and the courtyard still look like a strange universe where half the population is legally mandated to wear blue shirts.

I just have to hope the posters and social media will generate some interest.

"I promise it's going to be a great club," I say.

"I'm sure it will be," Ms. Bates answers. "And I'll look into the afternoon announcements first thing tomorrow, all right?"

Suddenly, just as Ms. Bates says this, there's a splitting crack outside. It starts slow and then builds, like the world outside is breaking in two, just like the earth on my ETUP poster.

"Good grief," says Ms. Bates, frowning. She gets up from her desk and walks toward the big picture windows at the back of her classroom. I follow her, and our eyes gaze out on the dark carpet of clouds blanketing the sky. "It looks like it's about to pour."

"Rats," I say. "I don't want to get caught in it on the way out to my car."

"Well," offers Ms. Bates, "knowing Houston weather, you could put up those posters and by the time you're done, it could be one hundred degrees and sunny out there." She taps the window for emphasis.

"That's true," I say, my voice rueful. "In Houston it either rains for ten minutes or four days."

Ms. Bates shoots me a knowing look, then gives me the code to the first-floor copier so I can make copies of my poster. After that, I dig out the roll of painter's tape from my backpack so I can start spreading the word about ETUP. As I make my way through the Southwest High halls, I find them mostly empty except for the occasional group of students meeting with a teacher in a classroom, either for tutoring or a club, I guess.

My heavy backpack hanging off my shoulders and my painter's tape hanging around my wrist like a strange blue bracelet, I cover most of the first floor quickly, making sure I hit high-traffic areas like the bathroom doors and over water fountains. Once I cover Baldwin territory, I start hiking up and down stairwells into the land of the Southwest Tigers. I'm getting in some major exercise. Every so often I hear the crack and explosion of thunder. Peering through the windows reveals a classic Houston shower. Heavy and hard. Like Mother Nature's punch in the gut.

To live in this city is to have stories about rain. Even before I became invested in the environment as a middle schooler, I realized this. I was just a baby when Tropical Storm Allison wreaked her havoc, flooding the Medical Center and tens of thousands of homes. Mom and Dad were home safe and dry, their eyes following the multicolored blot of precipitation that looped back over the overflowing bayous and flooding roads like the villain in a horror movie. But my aunt and uncle were out at a club listening to Junior Brown when Allison unleashed hell. Aunt Heather had been standing by the stage, dancing to the music, and she'd assumed someone had spilled a beer on her feet.

"I looked down, and water was flooding in from the sides and the door and everywhere," she recalled. "And I looked at Dave and said, 'We need to get out of here!'" They'd spent the night in their Toyota on a freeway overpass, listening to the weather report on the car radio and praying their house was safe, which it was, fortunately.

It's nothing to have a heavy Houston rain send water spinning through the streets, forcing cars to drive up onto strangers' front yards, leaving deep, muddy ruts. My father is always reminding us that the streets here are designed to flood. That's part of how we cope with living so close to sea level. But it seems like in the last few years the rains have gotten out of control. The Memorial Day Flood. The Tax Day Flood. And of course, Harvey.

I shake my head, literally willing the thought out of my mind. I don't care what my dad and that jerk climate denier Jayden in Ms. Bates's class think. Climate change is causing all of this. It's not normal for it to rain for four days and send people up onto their roofs. Not in Houston. That's why we *need* clubs like ETUP. It's up to my generation to fix this, seeing as people like my dad are blissfully working away for Big Oil and seeing this as a total nonissue. I've known this is true for a while now, but since Harvey, it's like I've gone into overdrive. And I think that's a good thing. That means I'm going to make something happen.

But as I head up the stairs, a whispered fear grips me.

What if it's too late?

I shake my head again. No. Focus, Eliza. Focus.

And I do.

The sky is still crackling and the rain is still pouring when I finish up in what I'm pretty sure is the last stairwell in Southwest High. I pause at the second-floor landing and check my phone. Almost four thirty. I'm calculating how I should divide up the rest of the afternoon for maximum efficiency when I hear a strange sound at the top of the stairs, by the doors heading out to the third floor. Some sort of mix of snuffling and coughing. Crying, maybe?

"Hello?" I shout, my voice carrying up and echoing through the tiled walls and high ceilings like I'm alone at an indoor pool. "Is someone up there?"

The noise stops. I stand, my last ETUP poster clutched in my hand.

"Uh . . . hello?" I try again. "Do you need help?" I peer back down the stairwell, hoping this will be when some teacher or janitor decides to venture up this particular set of stairs.

"Um, sorry . . ." It's a guy's voice, but I can barely hear it. "I'm . . . uh . . ."

I wait a moment before deciding to charge up the last flight. Tucked into a corner off to the side is a boy in a Southwest blue shirt, sitting with his knees drawn up to his chest and his backpack in front of him.

Oh my. It's him. The very cute boy from the first day of school. The one who asked me about my *Meat Is Murder* shirt.

He peers up at me, a stricken look on his face. His dark eyes look glassy, but I don't spot any tears. He clearly would give anything to have me pretend I'd never seen him. But how is that possible when I'm the only other person in this stairwell and I'm staring him right in his face?

His very cute face. As cute as I remember it.

Stop it, Eliza. He needs your help, not your swooning.

"Hey," I say, acting like I don't recognize him from a week ago. I know from working as a counselor at Camp Paseo that you're supposed to always get on a child's eye level when they're upset, so even though this guy is my age, I crouch down, my big, bulky backpack almost sending me tipping backward. "How can I help?"

He runs a hand through his dark brown hair and takes a deep, shaky breath.

"Sorry, this is . . . embarrassing. I'm . . . fine." All of a sudden he scrambles up and then thinks to offer me a hand, hauling me up to standing position. His hand is warm. Sweaty. If it were anyone else maybe it would be gross, but for the few seconds my hand is in his it's like it's the only part of my body I'm aware of. Like my whole self is just my right hand, cozy and alive in his.

Then it hits us. We've gone from being awkward on the dusty, dirty tiled floor together to being awkward face-to-face at the top of an empty stairwell together. Our hands drop by our sides in one swift movement.

"You . . . don't look fine," I say, trying not to sound unkind. And he doesn't. I mean, he still looks adorable, but he doesn't look okay. I don't think it's safe to leave him alone. So I take charge like always and say, "I'm Eliza. I go to Baldwin. What's your name?"

"Javier," he says. "But honestly, I'm fine. I stayed late to print something on the library computers and now I'm going home." Beat. Pause. "Uh . . . has it . . . stopped raining?"

That last question comes out a little too fake-relaxed. I should know because I've gone through life being fake-relaxed many times, which is why so many people think I have it so together without trying even though I spend most of my waking hours writing up complex charts and lists in flair pens and maximizing my time in half-hour chunks. Not that it hasn't worked for me so far.

"I'm not sure," I say. "But we could find out?" He follows me down to the first floor and we peer out a glass window in one of the exit doors. The earlier pelting of water has tapered off to what appears to be a gentle spritzing.

Javier frowns (how does he even have a cute frown?), then

mutters, "I guess it's slowing down." He takes a breath. "Okay, it's cool. I'm taking off, I guess."

He has the nicest jawline. He has perfectly formed earlobes. And these very nice eyelashes, like miniature feathery fans.

And he seems very, very scared to go outside.

"Do you want a lift? I have a car. It would honestly be no trouble."

Like I said, I don't dwell. I *do*.

~

Javier slides into the passenger seat and glances over at me, his backpack clutched between his knees. There are some patches sewn onto the front. They look like maybe music patches or something, but nothing I recognize. Something tells me maybe Javier is cooler than I am.

"What kind of car is this?" he asks after he gives me his address. It's not far from the school at all, in one of the rougher parts of the area where people haven't started tearing down the old homes and building mansions. Not yet, anyway.

"Oh," I say, "it's a Nissan Leaf. It runs on electricity. I got it for my sixteenth birthday."

The minute it comes out of my mouth, I realize how stuck up I sound. But it's out there now. "I told my parents if they wanted to get me a car, it *had* to be a hybrid or fully electric. Even though my dad works for Big Oil." Great. Now I sound even brattier. Javier doesn't say anything, but I catch his eyebrows darting up ever so slightly.

I'm babbling because this boy makes me a little nervous, and I'm not used to that.

It's not that I haven't noticed boys, I guess. I have. I know when someone is objectively cute. But boys don't seem to pay much attention to me, and to be honest, high school boys are so immature and impulsive—even some of the smart ones—that they just don't seem like a good use of my high school time. My mom says I'm the sort of girl who will meet someone in college, but I wonder if maybe that's just the line moms use when they know their daughter is sweet sixteen and has never been kissed.

I grip the steering wheel a little tighter, definitely trying not to think about kissing too much with this cute boy just inches away from me.

The rain has almost stopped, and even on the lowest setting, my wipers start to drag a bit, so I turn them off. Just another brief yet apocalyptic Houston weather event.

"I really appreciate this," Javier says. Then, after a pause, he says, "I think we ran into each other on the first day of school? You had that shirt on? The Smiths?"

I turn onto his street. "Oh, that's right!" I say, like I'm just figuring it out. "Now I remember. Yeah. Only . . . I didn't know what the band sounds like. I didn't even know it was a band."

"Most people our age don't," says Javier. "My dad played them for me when I was a kid, and I just got into them. But they're not a band anymore. They're actually really good. Oh . . . that one's mine. With the sago palms right by the driveway."

He motions to a small, one-story ranch house with green

shutters and a lawn that needs to be mowed, but only just. An S-shaped crack runs the length of the driveway leading up to the attached garage.

I slide my Nissan over to the curb.

"Oh, I love sago palms even though they're poisonous," I say, staring at the proud green plants whose prehistoric slim green leaves fan up and out in the direction of the cloudy, post-storm Houston sky. "Did you know they're actually not palms? They're more closely related to conifers."

As my words hang in the air, I want to melt into the floor of my Nissan. With small talk like this, I don't think my mom's "you'll meet a boy in college" prediction seems very apt.

Only Javier just looks at me and nods. "I didn't know that. I mean, about the conifers. I knew they were poisonous, though. I dig them, too. They remind me of the dinosaurs."

This strikes me as a smart thing to say. We smile shyly at each other. I wonder if I should say something else about sago palms or just wait for Javier to get out. Only he doesn't. He just rests his hand on the door handle and turns to me.

"Eliza, this is weird, but . . . you really came along at the right time. I mean, I . . . appreciate that you were there in that stairwell." He pauses, and his olive cheeks pink up a bit. It only makes him more good-looking.

Suddenly, a thought occurs to me. I reach into the back seat for the ETUP flyer that I'd been about to tape up into that same stairwell where I found Javier. It's a little tattered now from my lugging it around, and one of the corners has been ripped clean off, but all the pertinent information is on there.

"Listen," I say, thrusting it in his direction. "I have an idea about how you could pay me back for this ride." *And how I might be able to see you again*, I think. Javier's brow furrows in confusion at my words. Rats. Now I sound like a jerk who is only into transactional favors or something. "I mean, not that I wasn't totally happy to do it!" I add in a rush. "I'm just saying . . . not that you *need* to pay me back, but . . . anyway, the reason I was in that stairwell was because I was putting up these flyers. We're having our first meeting on Thursday in Ms. Bates's room. She's a Baldwin teacher, but the club is open to kids from Southwest and Baldwin."

"E-T-U-P," Javi spells out carefully, and I want to kiss him for not saying "eat up." And also because his full lips seem quite kissable. Or what I think would be quite kissable. "This is, like, an environmental club?"

"Yes," I say. "And we're going to be very action-oriented. I mean, discussions and guest speakers maybe, but our main focus is going to be how can we work to make a tangible, positive impact on the planet." As soon as the words come out of my mouth, I realize I like the way they sound. I should use that phrase during our first meeting.

Javi's finger traces the splitting earth on the flyer. His nails are supershort and very clean. Another check mark in his favor.

"What made you want to do this?" he asks. "I mean, if you don't mind me asking."

"No, not at all," I answer. "The environment and climate change are something I've cared about a lot, for a long time." I choose not to mention my parents finding me digging for recyclables in the trash in the sixth grade and the YouTube and Reddit rabbit holes I like to throw myself down on a regular basis, holes that make me prickly with frustration, rage, and a looming anxiety that I try to bury when it bubbles to the surface. If I start telling him all that, I might never stop. Instead, I tell him that my house flooded in Harvey and between that and what happened to Baldwin High, I want to do something to get involved. "Plus, like I said, my dad works for Big Oil," I add, rolling my eyes, "so I figure someone in my family needs to offset the harm he's causing." I still haven't apologized to him for the dining room table episode, although this morning when he asked me for the half-and-half for his coffee and I handed it to him, he said thank you instead of grunting.

"My older brother works for Big Oil," Javier says, folding up the ETUP flyer and sliding it in his front jeans pocket. "But probably not in the same way your dad does."

"Oh?" I say, raising an eyebrow. "What makes you say that?" I still sort of can't believe I'm here in my car with a strange, cute boy I picked up in the stairwell. I'm still a little nervous because his face is so dreamy, but the more I sit here, the less nervous I feel.

"Uh . . ." he says, scratching at the back of his neck and looking into his lap. "Well, for starters, you live in the Baldwin zone . . ."

"All sorts of kids live in the Baldwin zone," I counter, but I smile when I say it so he doesn't think I'm offended.

"You didn't let me finish," Javier continues. He motions around him. "You got a car on your sixteenth birthday? Like a fancy car you plug into an outlet like a microwave or whatever?" He grins. I like that he's funny, too.

"Yeah, exactly like that," I say, still grinning. "Okay, so my dad's an oil executive. You got me. But hey, it's not like my parents sent me to St. Augustine the second they found out I was going to have to go to Southwest."

The minute the words come out of my mouth, I regret it. It's the *have to.* I mean, Javier goes to Southwest all the time, not just when a natural disaster requires it.

"I'm sorry," I say, flustered. Embarrassed. "That came out . . . weird. I . . . I'm . . . I'm glad I'm at your school."

Now it's Javier's turn to raise an eyebrow, a move he pulls off much more smoothly than I would. But I don't think I've hurt his feelings. At least I hope not.

"Okay, my brother, Miguel, is an operator at one of the refineries in Pasadena," he says. "So I was right from the start."

"Fine, guilty as charged," I say, holding up both hands in mock surrender. "Clueless Baldwin white girl over here."

"Southwest brown dude who acts weird in stairwells over here," Javier answers, matching my hand movements.

I smile again, and then it's still for a moment. The only real noise is some dog barking in a backyard a house or two over. His dark eyes meet mine. A lock of his hair falls just so over his gaze. I would never do it, of course, but I feel the urge to reach over and gently brush the hair out of his face. The idea makes me a little dizzy.

"Well, I'd better get in, get started on homework," Javier

says, probably sensing my weird thoughts. "But . . . thanks for the ride. And for this club flyer."

"Do you think you can come to our first meeting?" I ask, sort of hoping I don't sound like I'm pressuring him but kind of hoping I am. "Please? I'm scared no Southwest kids will come, and I really want both schools to be represented at the meeting."

And also I think you're pretty cute? Of course I don't say that part. I may do and not dwell, but I have limits.

Javier nods and pats the pocket holding the flyer. "Yeah, I think I can make it," he says. "I'll be there."

"Cool!" I say. "And bring friends. Or whatever." I don't want to be too pushy. It's enough right now to know he's going to be there.

"Okay." Javier nods, and then he gets out of the car. But before he starts to make his way up to the front door of his house, he leans his head in and thanks me one more time for the lift.

"No problem," I say.

I drive off, thinking about Javier's face and voice, which is deep and warm and one I wouldn't mind hearing again.

I'm not sure why I can't stop thinking about him. My history with boys is essentially nonexistent. I've come to terms with this, choosing (or is it hoping?) to believe my mom is right when it comes to what awaits me in college. But Javi isn't a college boy. He's not even a Baldwin boy. He's a very sweet-faced, deep-voiced Southwest boy who appeared to be having some sort of meltdown in a stairwell today and who may or may not come to the first ETUP meeting.

I really hope he comes to the first meeting.

I am hoping and thinking and wondering so much that I don't realize until I pull into the driveway that instead of heading to Aunt Heather and Uncle Dave's, I've driven all the way to our old house on Ferris, its windows dark and the garage blocked by a large blue dumpster full of pieces of what was once our house.

The contractors aren't here. No one is. It's a hulking, sad shell, and I don't get to live here anymore. My throat tightens and my mouth goes dry, so I put my car into reverse and get out of there before I fall down a rabbit hole of feelings far deeper and scarier than anything I could ever find online.

JAVIER

"Come on, Dom, it won't be that bad," I say, shoving the last part of my sandwich in my mouth and talking between bites. I lean back on the bench my group always claims during lunch. "It's just a meeting."

Dom scowls between flips on his board, every so often scanning the courtyard in advance of a teacher on lunch duty who will tell him to put it up in his locker. "I don't do meetings," he says. "Like, clubs. Unless there's a skateboarding club around here. And even if there was, I don't think I'd go to meetings unless all we did in them was skate." At this he pauses and reconsiders. "Nah, not even then."

"What about you, Felipe? JoJo?" I ask, trying to rope at least one of my friends to come with me to the ETUP meeting after school.

Next to me on the bench, Felipe stares into his phone and shrugs. "Can't. I'm helping my dad. I have to get out of here the second the last bell rings." Felipe's dad roofs houses, and Felipe sometimes helps him when a job is going longer than planned.

"I just don't want to," JoJo tells me without looking up from his book. Speaking frankly has always been JoJo's strong suit.

I sigh. All week I've been thinking about this ETUP meeting.

Ever since Eliza took me home that day I flipped out in the stairwell because of the rain.

Ever since something strange gripped me and I was able to . . . talk to a girl.

Monday after Eliza had dropped me off in her fancy electric car, I'd headed straight to my bedroom and stared at myself in the mirror, at my dark brown eyes and eyebrows that are maybe too bushy and my nose that I sometimes think is too big for my face. I'd stared and stared as Diablo meowed for an afternoon snack.

"Who are you, Javier?" I'd asked my reflection, curious as to who this person was staring back at me. Like I'd transformed into some new creature who could suddenly and inexplicably talk to girls.

Or maybe just to Eliza.

I'd been embarrassed when she'd found me in that stairwell. Had I known a storm would hit so hard and so fast, I would have figured out another time to print my paper for Ms. Gomez's class. I could have come early the next morning or asked Ms. Jimenez next door to let me use her printer like she sometimes does. But I wanted to get it done, and so I went to the library and then I couldn't get it to print and Mr. Casteel the librarian had to help me, and then when I was ready to go, I caught a glimpse through the library's picture windows of the thick, rolling black-and-purple cloud rolling in, and my body was gripped with panic.

I think it was the way Eliza squatted down to look me in

the eye. Or maybe it was the way she just demanded I let her take me home. Or was it the fact that she didn't know anything about The Smiths and I got to tell her about them? Or the way she got all dreamy-eyed about something like sago palms? I don't know what it was, but for some reason sitting in that car with a white girl from Baldwin, it was like a magic spell had been cast on me. Forget clamming up in front of Yesenia with the pink bangs at Kroger. With Eliza I was chill. I was even funny.

And now I was on her radar for this ETUP meeting.

"Why do you want to go anyway?" Dom asks, pulling me out of my head. "You don't do clubs, either."

I kick my feet out in front of me and study my Converse like they'll have some reason on them that I can give Dom. I end up mumbling something about Harvey and wanting to do something to prevent it from happening again. At this Dom and Felipe and JoJo exchange looks. They don't know about how the rain makes me want to puke, but they do know I hate talking about that hurricane.

"You didn't even flood, man," says Felipe, sliding his phone into his back pocket as the bell for fifth period rings. "So what's up?"

I get up and stretch out my arms all fake-casual. I'm not about to mention Eliza to the guys, or the fact that I have Eliza's tattered ETUP flyer taped to my wall next to my Morrissey poster. They're cool guys and not jerks about most things, but a Baldwin girl whose rich dad bought her her own car? I'd rather not open myself up for that sort of humiliation.

We head back into the building, and I use the noise of the bustling crowd as an excuse not to answer Felipe's question. And, as I've done for the past few days, I scan the crowd, looking for Eliza. Before and after school and lunchtime is usually the only opportunity for Baldwin and Southwest kids to mix even though the two groups tend to stay separated even then. So much for Mom's fantasy of all of us learning together as one.

I don't spot Eliza. That means the only way to see her again, probably, is to go to this meeting. Alone. Maybe I can get there a few minutes after it starts. Hide at the back or something.

I remember her light eyes and that take-charge way of hers. I remember her broad smile as we sat in front of my house, joking around. I remember how she made me feel as I stared at my reflection, like I was suddenly transformed into someone else. Someone funny and cool. I wonder if that feeling will ever happen again.

I guess going to the ETUP meeting is the only way I'll ever find out.

As I turn the corner toward Room 155, my heart starts picking up speed. Sort of like when it rained the other day, only this feels different. Better. I remember as a little kid when I'd tell Mom I was nervous, she'd always say, "Nervous or excited, mijo?" I get now that it was her way of trying to get me to see my anxiety in a different light or whatever, but it used to annoy the heck out of me.

Except now it makes sense. I'm heading toward the ETUP meeting, and I'm going to see Eliza. And yeah, I'm nervous.

But mostly I'm excited.

"Welcome, welcome," says a Black woman standing by the classroom door, obviously a teacher. "Welcome to ETUP. I'm Ms. Bates." The way she says it, like "eat up," surprises me. I guess I'd never considered it could be pronounced that way. Makes it sound more like a food club than something about the environment.

A handful of kids are streaming in, mostly Baldwin kids dressed in their own clothes and not the same tired blue shirts Southwest kids get stuck with. You'd think Principal Lopez would have considered suspending the dress code for, like, one stupid year.

And suddenly, there she is. I spot her as I head into the room. She's standing at the whiteboard, her back to the growing group of students. She has a blue Expo marker in her hand, and she's writing stuff on the board. Her hair is pulled back in a ponytail and she has on jeans and a green T-shirt. My eyes coast over her figure before I start to feel like a creep, so I just dip toward the back of the classroom and pull out my phone to give myself something to do.

"Javi?"

I look up and spy Yesenia and another Southwest student, a boy I think is named Rodrigo. They slide into the desks next to me.

"Hey, what's up?" I ask. "You interested in this club?"

"I told Rodrigo I wanted to check it out," Yesenia says, confirming my guess about this dude's name. Then, the way she loops her pinkie through his confirms that she wasn't flirting with me at Kroger. Just being nice. Rodrigo is clearly her guy. He doesn't say much to me, just offers me a *what's up* nod. I offer one back, grateful that I'm no longer sitting alone.

Eliza has finished writing on the board and her eyes are gazing out at the filling classroom. Suddenly, her eyes lock on mine, and she smiles broadly and waves. At me.

I lift my hand, suddenly shy. "Hey," I say. Like she can hear me from this row of desks. I feel like a dork.

"You know her?" Yesenia asks.

"Yeah, just talked to her once," I say. "She started this club."

"Cool," says Yesenia. "I think this is a superimportant topic. Rodrigo agrees with me. Right, Rodrigo?" She says it in this way that doesn't leave Rodrigo much room to disagree. He just bobs his head again and stretches out his hand until they're not just grasping pinkies but all five fingers and palms, too. I imagine for a minute what it must be like to have a girlfriend. Of course this brings my focus back to Eliza, who is now moving toward the front of the room and clearing her throat, like she's trying to get our attention.

When this doesn't work—the room *is* pretty crowded, which seems cool, honestly, but it's also noisy—Eliza claps her hands three times, loudly, like a teacher.

"Hey, y'all, could I get your focus? Thanks." She tosses her ponytail back and stands up a little straighter. She's got at least three inches on me for sure. She squares her shoulders and waits, a calm smile spreading over her face. She's got that same I've-got-this vibe that she had when she found me in the stairwell.

Not gonna lie. It's really attractive.

"So, hello, everyone. My name, for those of you that don't know me, is Eliza Brady. I'm a junior at Baldwin, and I approached Ms. Bates last week." At this, Eliza motions to the teacher at the door, who is standing and nodding at Eliza, a gentle smile on her face. "I asked if she wouldn't mind sponsoring a club that focuses on environmental concerns, and she made the terrific suggestion that it be a club that unites both of our schools. After all, we may normally be on different campuses, but we still share one planet, right?"

The casual, sure-of-herself way that she tosses off this rhetorical question makes me think she just came up with it. If it were me up there leading a meeting of dozens of kids my own age, I would have probably written out some dumb script to read word for word while never letting my eyes leave the paper.

"Eliza, I have a question," a tall, slender Black girl in the front row says, raising her hand. She's got on a cherry-red blouse, so she's Baldwin, and the way Eliza calls on her by name, it's clear they know each other.

"Yes, Yvonne?" says Eliza. "By the way, I love that you have a question already."

"Well, this may be silly, but is this club pronounced E-T-U-P or . . . like, eat up?"

Eliza's eyebrows pop, and she actually seems a little caught off guard. "So . . ." she starts, choosing her words. "I, uh, didn't really think about the sound of the word when I came up with the club name. In my mind I just spelled out the letters?"

The way it should be pronounced, I think.

"I like eat up," says a white boy off to one side. "It's catchy. Eat up carbon emissions or whatever. You know?"

Eliza grins widely, showing off a gleaming smile.

"Oh, that's . . . clever, Matthew." She turns and looks at us. "I don't care one way or the other," she says, and I wonder if this is true. Eliza Brady strikes me as someone who cares very, very much about everything, even small things like club name pronunciations.

"I say go with eat up," says a Southwest girl. "Like that boy said, it's catchy."

"Okay, perfect," says Eliza, glancing over toward Ms. Bates, who nods again. "That takes care of that." She takes a deep breath, peers around at all of us. "Before we go on, I just want to say that I'm glad we're all here. I know all of us as a city suffered through Harvey, and I'm willing to bet that's a big reason why some of us are here." There's a ripple of nods, but I notice that Eliza doesn't bring up the fact that her house flooded or anything personal. I wonder why she shared that with me in her car but not here, in the club meeting when it would be really relevant.

"So my hope with this club and with all of us"—at this she spreads her hands out, indicating that we're all in here with her—"is that we'll be an action-oriented club. That we'll take real steps to work against climate change here in our community and even beyond."

After that, she grabs her Expo marker again and starts asking for people to brainstorm ideas. Kids begin tossing out thoughts like starting a recycling program and encouraging people to talk about reducing plastic use in their homes. Yesenia raises her hand and says she wants to do something about encouraging reusable bags at Kroger where she works. Eliza jots everything down on Ms. Bates's board. Her handwriting is perfect, and she can even make her words straight without lines on the board to guide her.

Suddenly, I feel my hand shoot up.

"Yes, Javier?" Eliza asks, locking eyes with me and smiling.

"Uh," I say, initially caught off guard that she calls on me by name. "What about doing some cleanups at the Willow Waterhole near the school? My friend Dominic skates around there, and the last time we were hanging out there, I noticed how there's a lot of garbage people just leave."

"That's a great idea, yes," says Eliza, jotting it down in her perfect lettering. Then she turns back to me and asks, "I haven't been to the waterhole much. Can we talk more about it after the meeting?"

I nod yes reflexively, then mutter, "Sure," for good measure. But my heart is starting to pick up speed at the idea of having a reason to hang back and speak to Eliza after the meeting ends. *Are you nervous or excited?* I ask myself. Damn, this time it really does feel like fifty-fifty.

Once a few more brainstorming ideas are on the board and

Eliza has taken a picture of them to save for later, she reminds everybody to follow the club on Instagram and takes a few more photos to post, plus she sets everybody up to get text alerts about club activities.

"Let's make our next meeting two weeks from today, okay?" she says as kids start filing out. I linger awkwardly.

"Great work," says Ms. Bates to Eliza before offering me a handshake. "And nice to meet you, too. Javier, I think Eliza said it was?"

"Yes, ma'am."

Ms. Bates heads back to her desk, leaving Eliza and me to move toward the side of the room, Eliza dragging her backpack, which looks like it must weigh five hundred pounds for all the stuff she's carrying.

"Hey," she says, smiling at me, her bright blue eyes shining. I wish it didn't feel like I was gazing up at her. I try to stand tall, wishing not for the first time that I had a few extra inches on me. This felt easier when we were both sitting in her Nissan.

"Hey," I say, cool Javi from the car suddenly absent.

"So Willow Waterhole was a great idea," she says. "And it made me think about something." She pauses, fiddles with a strap on her backpack. Is it possible Eliza is nervous, too? After the way she acted in the stairwell the day that it rained and after watching her lead that meeting, it doesn't seem like she could ever be nervous about anything.

"Yeah, what did it make you think of?" I ask. At least my response is more than one word this time.

"Not to put you on the spot," she says, "but would you be interested in serving as copresident with me? Like, of the club? That way we could make sure both schools are equally represented."

Me? A club president? It's like she's asking me to become a trapeze artist.

Eliza senses my hesitation, I guess, because she fiddles with her backpack even more, then glances toward Ms. Bates, who is grading papers at her desk but can obviously hear the conversation.

"Ms. Bates, don't you think that would be a good idea? For a copresident of the club to be from Southwest? For it to be Javier?"

I notice her voice is a lot less sure of itself now when it's just us. How can Eliza be so confident in a big group and suddenly so much less confident now? I consider this. The possibility that *I'm* the one making her nervous is so dumb I put it out of my mind almost the instant it occurs to me.

But what else could it be?

"I think that would be a great idea," says Ms. Bates, pausing her work to focus her attention on us. "Javier, do you think you have the time?"

How can I possibly say no when Ms. Bates and Eliza so clearly want me to say yes? And anyway, how can I say no if I know this is a way for me to see Eliza again, and maybe not just every other week when the club meets in Ms. Bates's room?

"Okay," I say. "Yeah, I'll do it."

"Great," says Eliza, her smile widening. Man, she has the best smile.

Trying to act cool, I exchange numbers with her. At this, she seems to lose a little of her nervousness. In rapid-fire sentences punctuated with smiles and nods, she says we'll be in touch soon and asks me to text her about when would be a good time to meet. She even gets Ms. Bates to take a picture of the two of us for the club Instagram. I stand there awkwardly, offering up a half smile. I'm sure it's a terrible shot. Afterward, I end up leaving the two of them alone as I head for home.

It's too late to meet up with Dom or any of the other guys who abandoned me when I wanted to attend this club meeting. A club for which I'm somehow currently copresident.

Daniela would think this was cool. She was real active at Southwest when she went here, always staying after school doing a million things with yearbook and the Spirit Club and a bunch of other stuff. Miguel, though? He barely graduated. I wonder what he would think of me being president, excuse me, *copresident*, of an environmental club. Probably add it to the list of Weird Things About My Little Brother, right after "afraid of rain."

As I'm heading out of the building, my eyes get pulled to a sign next to a door on the first floor. Printed in red letters on white posterboard complete with a smiley face is a sign that reads:

SOMETHING ON YOUR MIND?
THIS IS A SAFE SPACE TO ASK FOR HELP!

School is over and the door is closed with the lights clearly off behind it, but I know this is Ms. Holiday's office. She's the school social worker for Southwest, and even though this is technically Baldwin High territory now, her space is still there. In fact, there's another, smaller sign under it that says TIGERS *AND* EAGLES—BOTH ARE WELCOME!

You'd think from looking at her that Ms. Holiday is just one of those smiley white ladies who could act all nosy about your personal life and get on your nerves, but kids at Southwest love her. After Juan Castro died in a car wreck during my freshman year, she'd stayed for hours and hours in the library counseling kids who couldn't stop crying. I didn't know Juan, but he'd been really popular, and from the way kids were clamoring to get in to talk to Ms. Holiday, I knew she must have a way of making people feel better. She always seemed to be in ten places at once, though, because I would always spy her consoling some upset kid in the hall or guiding them to her office. It's kind of wild to me that we have, like, five cops on campus and just one Ms. Holiday.

Something on your mind? The words on Ms. Holiday's sign run through my head as I bust through a set of side doors and head for home, the mid-October Houston heat still enough to irritate. I'll be honest, Eliza Brady is on my mind. Her cute face and the way she takes charge are pretty tough to forget.

But if I'm being real honest with myself, not even Eliza can push out the background buzz of worry about the rain. That's always "something on my mind." It's an ever-present buzz that hasn't lessened any since Harvey. Instead, it thrums constantly in the atmosphere, as threatening as the dark clouds that could roll in at what feels like any moment.

Oil built this city. It constructed its skeleton and strengthened its muscles and made its heart pump like a pumpjack, steady and strong.

The pumpjack has many nicknames. One is Big Texan.

We called the old football team the Oilers. Their logo was an oil derrick the color of the big Texas sky. Those of us who are old-timers can remember the oil booms of the past, with people flocking here almost overnight to make their fortunes, and quick, too. Fortunes built on Texas tea. On this magic buried deep in the earth.

We remember the bumper sticker—Drive Fast, Freeze a Yankee. We remember the good times. The boom years. The oil money that built this city. Funded the arts. Donated to schools. Bought politicians. Emblazoned its name on every stone surface available.

Yes, we remember the good times. And the inevitable busts.

Of course, we've changed. We want you to know this. We've diversified, to use a favorite term. Biomedical. Aeronautics. Academia. Health care. We bristle at the suggestion that we are still just an oil town. When the football team came back, we didn't name them after oil. We talk about renewables now, too.

But out on the east side of town and near the port—where the houses are smaller and older and the people are poorer—busy oil refineries still stand like supernatural cities from another planet. Mile after mile of enormous white tanks squat solidly next to tall silver towers. Bright orange flares still spark up the sky.

We hear about the science that says the closer you live to these places, the higher your risk of cancer and other health issues. We read about the connection between fossil fuels and climate change, including our notorious Houston floods.

Sometimes we get angry and upset. Worried and sad.

And sometimes we try not to think about it.

ELIZA

My backpack weighs a ton as usual, and when it lands on the floor by the front door and Aunt Heather gently but firmly reminds me about the noise and baby Ethan, I already get a sinking feeling that it's going to be a lousy Friday night.

"Sorry," I say, wandering into the kitchen, where Heather is marinating some big hunk of red meat for dinner. Yuck. Raw meat makes me want to vomit, not just because of the blood and how gross it looks, but because it reminds me of the acres of rainforests that were sacrificed just to get it to the table. I gave up meat in eighth grade, not long after learning about its connection to the planet, and it wasn't even that difficult given all the other stuff there is to eat. Heather is always going on and on about how she shops organic at Whole Foods, but meat is meat. It just seems so lazy to not do this one easy little thing that makes such a big impact on the planet. But I keep my mouth shut.

"Don't worry," says Heather, brushing off my doorway noise. But I can't help but think that she and Dave have to be ready for my parents and me to move out. After all, they went through, like, five million rounds of infertility treatments to have Ethan, and just as they're supposed to be enjoying their new baby, we invade their house.

"Are you the only one home?" I ask.

"Just me and Ethan," Heather says, smiling at the sound of his name. "He's taking a late nap. Probably going to keep us up all night tonight."

Great news considering I share his bedroom, I think. But again, I keep my mouth shut.

"Your folks are at your house," she says, "and Dave is stuck at work, but he should be home soon." Dave is a lawyer like Aunt Heather was before she quit to stay home with Ethan. "How was school?" she asks.

"Fine," I say, grabbing a glass of ice water and moving to the couch in the adjoining den. "I had lit mag after school today plus some tutoring for AP Lang."

"What's the trouble in Lang? Anything I can help with?" Heather asks. "I loved English class."

"Thanks," I say. "I got a 90 on my last rhetorical analysis essay and wanted to know how I could improve. The teacher gave me some pointers."

Heather grabs some jars of spices from a cabinet. "Eliza, a 90 is a great score," she says.

"I guess," I say. "But it doesn't mean there's not room for improvement."

I set my water down and go back and get my planner from my backpack, then bring it back to the couch. I carefully cross off today and look at the week ahead, mentally prioritizing certain commitments and sectioning off the weekend into the most efficient chunks I can come up with. It's been a week since the first ETUP meeting, and I need to start strategizing for the next one.

The thought that I need to text Javier has been humming quietly in the back of my mind, basically at all times, but I keep overthinking what I should say. And maybe there's a tiny part of me that's been hoping he'll text me first? My mind wanders off to those deep brown eyes and thick eyelashes. Is it weird to be attracted to eyelashes?

I shake my head in an attempt to regain focus when I hear the front door open. It must be my parents because I can hear my dad speaking to someone in a loud, booming voice.

"That's great, Mark, wow. Terrific!"

My mom enters the kitchen and den area, leaving my dad yammering away.

"Your father is FaceTiming with your brother," she informs my aunt and me. "Mark got some internship for the spring semester that he's very excited about, so he called when we were in the car on the way home."

I cringe. "Can someone tell Dad that he doesn't have to, like, speak more loudly just because he's on FaceTime?" I say. "The sound works just as well whether you see Mark's face or not. Plus, the baby is asleep." I admit I say that last part to get Heather on my side, but she doesn't react.

"And good evening to you, too, my dear," my mother says, her tone withering. "Let your dad be loud. He needs good news."

I shut my planner and watch as my mom and Heather murmur to each other and my mother seamlessly integrates herself into Heather's dinner preparations. The two of them are really close and always have been. Their parents died two years apart from cancer when the two of them were only in their early twenties, and my mom always says she and Heather are the only real family either one has. Even when we weren't living here, it wasn't unusual to find my mom and Heather prattling away on the phone or meeting up at Brays Bayou for a jog or a power walk.

Mark and I are not close like that. Not by a long shot. We never disliked each other or even fought like siblings on television. We just had our own circles of friends and our own lives that didn't seem to intersect all that much. Mark was a huge engineering savant right from the start, making his own Rube Goldberg machines in his bedroom out of string and LEGOs and anything else he could find, and he and Dad bonded more and more over that as time went on, leaving me to be mostly good at everything and not great at any *one* thing. Not great enough for my dad to notice, I guess.

"Sounds good, son," my dad is booming, holding his phone out in front of his smiling face as he walks into the kitchen. "Here, say hi to everyone before you go." Dad flips the camera and I dutifully wave hello from my position on the couch as I fake-smile at Mark's faraway voice calling out goodbye.

My mom hands my father a glass of wine as he sits down on the couch catty-corner from me, his smile still broad.

"This is so great," he says, that smile still cracking his face in two. "An internship at Boston Scientific is truly a coveted one."

I pick at a thumbnail and don't respond. After all, he wasn't speaking to me. Mom pipes up that it sure is great. I want to ask Dad if he's already making a plan for Mark to come work with him, imagining some snarky question I could come up with. But it doesn't feel worth it.

"You're quiet over there," Dad says, noticing me at last.

"Yeah," I respond. "Sorry no big internship news from me."

There's an awkward beat. It's not as passive-aggressive as I could be, but there's subtext anyway. I feel prickly and irritated with myself. My father sips his wine and ignores my reply. Aunt Heather starts filling the space with questions about dinner and what everyone wants for a side dish and blah blah blah.

Suddenly, Ethan starts crying.

"I'll get him," I say, jumping up, anxious to get out of the den. Nobody says thank you or anything. Maybe they're glad I'm gone, too.

When he sees me coming into the nursey, Ethan smiles. He likes me, I know he does. He looks right into my eyes when he sees me, and sometimes if he's upset he does this little baby death grip around my neck when I pick him up. Aunt Heather likes to call him the Michelin Man because of his sweet baby rolls, rolling one right into the next, and when I shower him with raspberries on his neck and tummy, he giggles the greatest laugh that was ever laughed.

Surrounded by the fake-natural world Heather and Dave have created all around us, I rest Ethan on his changing table and change his diaper. I wish for the millionth time Heather and Dave would consider cloth; I've even texted Heather articles about the topic. But they never explored the possibility.

"One more diaper in the landfill, buddy," I whisper to him, snuggling his button nose with mine. "Not that that's *your* fault." I kiss him on the forehead, and he reaches out, grabs a few strands of my hair and tugs like he understands me. I wonder if he understands that the plastic glow-in-the-dark stars on the ceiling and the rosy red apples painted on the trees on his walls are the nicest version of nature that he might ever get to experience if people don't stop and do something about what we're living through.

After snapping him into his Curious George onesie, I scoop him into my arms and stand there in the middle of our, really *his* bedroom. I can hear my parents and my aunt prattling on about something. The thought of spending Friday night at home with them or trapped in this room with a baby, however cute he may be, suddenly makes me claustrophobic.

Just then, my phone buzzes in my pocket. For not the millionth time I find myself hoping it's Javier getting up the courage to text me. After all, I told him to reach out and let me know when would be a good time to meet up and discuss club business.

Hey. Parents are out of town. Come over and spend the night and save me from total boredom.

It's Isabella, not Javier. Just then, Ethan's rear end emits an explosion so loud I just know the result is going to be another diaper in the landfill. I sigh.

I'll be there as soon as I can.

Isabella's house flooded in Harvey, too, but her parents are so loaded they can afford to rent a swanky two-bedroom apartment overlooking Hermann Park and Miller Outdoor Theatre. I have to announce myself to a doorman before getting buzzed in, and as I coast up quietly in an elevator to the seventeenth floor, I think about the fact that I haven't seen Isabella since before school started, even if she is supposed to be my best friend.

"Finally, we meet again," Isabella says, tossing open the door and reaching out to hug me. When she pulls back I see she's wearing a St. Augustine T-shirt and yoga pants that I know she never does yoga in. Her honey-blond hair is piled up on the top of her head in a way that looks messy but may or may not have taken an hour to get just right. With Isabella you never know.

"Hey," I say, dropping my backpack by the door. "Wow, this place is nice."

Isabella looks around like she's noticing the sleek surfaces and subdued, modern furniture for the very first time. "Yeah, Mom got one of her decorator friends to do it cheap or something. Or her friend's decorator? I don't know. My room looks like a nice hotel in a family friendly resort, though, which sort of sucks."

I wonder if she knows how much it can suck to share a room with an infant, I think. But I don't say that out loud.

I follow her into the kitchen, the stainless steel appliances so shiny they practically blind me. Isabella slides a tub of expensive-looking gelato out of the freezer, then grabs two spoons.

"I asked Andrew to get chocolate, but we're going to have to make do with strawberry," she says with a dramatic sigh. Isabella loves to refer to her father by his first name for some reason. He just laughs when she does it.

"So . . . who are you talking to at Southwest?" Isabella asks as I follow her into her bedroom, which does indeed look like a nice hotel room, complete with framed paintings of abstract images in soft, golden hues. Nothing like Isabella's messy room at her old house, the walls littered with images of gorgeous models torn from *Vogue* and photographs from her family vacations to Maui and Greece. Isabella and I sit on the floor, covered in a lush, thick cream carpet.

"Don't spill," she warns me, handing me the gelato before she slides a spoonful into her own mouth.

"I'm not really *at* Southwest, you know. I'm at Baldwin still, technically." I take a small scoop with my spoon. For some reason, I'm not hungry.

Isabella rolls her eyes at me. "You *know* what I mean," she says. "You're on the Southwest campus. What's it like? Are there, like, fights every day?"

Now it's my turn to roll my eyes. "There were fights at Baldwin," I say, suddenly defensive. "Remember that one in the courtyard with the two baseball players fighting over Melanie Jacobs?"

"Ew, yes, like who would ever fight over her? She's not even that pretty," Isabella responds, setting the gelato aside and sliding onto her stomach before pulling out her phone. Her gaze gets lost in the glow of her screen.

When Isabella and I were in Ms. Coughlin's third-grade class at Condit, she once wet her pants just a little bit while we were waiting in line for the bathroom, and when Joshua Flanagan pointed out the wet, orange-sized circle at the back of her salmon-colored shorts, I'd pushed him so hard he'd fallen down and busted his chin, and I got in trouble.

When Isabella and I were in Mr. Olsen's sixth-grade English class and I was pretty sure I'd started my period and didn't have anything, it was Isabella who'd bravely approached Mr. Olsen's desk and discreetly whispered that she needed *feminine protection*, after which he, flustered and blushing, went through the school nurse–provided first aid kit in his desk and slipped Isabella a pad, which she quickly gave to me when the bell rang.

We've spent countless hours silently scanning social media together and dancing to stupid music together and blaming each other for our own farts together and eating raw cookie dough straight from the tube together.

When did I start to outgrow her? Was it when she started justifying cheating during AP World History class because Mr. Christiansen was notoriously difficult? Was it when she stopped reading books just for fun? Was it when she lost her virginity in June to a guy at camp that she didn't even like all that much, just because she wanted to "get it over with"?

Or was it right now, thirty minutes into this sleepover and already feeling like I'd maybe rather be at home in bed with Ethan in the crib near me, his baby snores mixing with the ambient music Heather and Dave like to play to get him to soothe himself to sleep?

I take another small bite of the gelato before deciding it's my last.

"Can I have a glass of water?" I ask.

"Yeah," says Isabella, glancing up from her phone. "Hang on." She darts off and by the time she comes back, I'm scrolling through my own phone, my eyes running over texts from kids like OC and OP asking about deadlines in AP Lang and other school stuff. It strikes me that I've always had Isabella and then, like, school friends. Lunch friends. Club and yearbook and National Honor Society–volunteering friends. The realization sinks me down into a mood that's even yuckier than the one I had earlier in the day when my dad lit up the den with his excitement over Mark's internship.

I consider trying to explain the afternoon to Isabella and start to open my mouth, but the idea of trying to describe all the particulars just feels exhausting. Besides, all she'd probably say is to get over myself.

"Look at this house," Isabella says, shoving her phone in my face. "This is a girl in my chem class at St. Augustine. I mean, she has an actual room for ballroom dancing. And an elevator. I was over there last week."

"Wow," I mutter, feigning interest at the architectural monstrosity in front of me, complete with a tanned white girl in a lime-green bikini posing by a pool, her perfect smile ready-made for an orthodontist's billboard.

"That's Kennedy Walter," she says. "Totally loaded. And her house didn't even flood. Life isn't fair."

It sure isn't, I think. But instead of saying that, I toss my phone off to the side and press the palms of my hands into my eyes until

I see exploding stars and sunbursts. "Ugh, don't mention flooding. It's going to be Winter Break before I get back home."

"I don't even ask anymore," says Isabella. "Mom is obsessed with the repairs and the decorating. Redoing the house is a full-time job or whatever."

Even though I don't want it to, my mind floats back to the images that wouldn't stop playing on the news in the wake of Harvey, images that rotated on Heather and Dave's television in the immediate aftermath. Families of six or seven wading out of apartment complexes on the north side or tugging moldy carpet out of modest homes on the east side.

"Sometimes I wonder what happened to the people who didn't have flood insurance or families to stay with. People without our, you know, resources," I say, pulling my hands off my face and opening my eyes. Isabella's room is suddenly uncomfortably bright.

"Yeah, that sucks," says Isabella, still buried in her phone. "They probably have a lot of government programs and stuff, though. To help. I mean, probably." Isabella says this like she doesn't really believe it, and I nod like I want to.

"Anyway, aren't you solving climate change with your new club?" she asks. "What are you on Insta?"

Once I tell her, she flips through ETUP's pictures, including the picture of Javier and me that Ms. Bates took.

"Who's this?" she says.

A charge of excitement moves through me, but I hide it well enough from Isabella. I should want to share my crush with my oldest friend, I guess, but it doesn't feel like the right time. Or maybe I just don't trust Isabella's reaction.

"That's Javier Garza," I answer. "He's a Southwest kid. Copresident of the club with me."

"Hmmm," Isabella determines. "He's cute. And, like, three inches shorter than you."

I shrug. "I guess." It doesn't really bug me that Javier is shorter than me even though it doesn't surprise me that this is one of the first things Isabella notices. I grab my phone, silently hoping once again for a text from Javier. Or from anyone who might pique my interest. But there's nothing.

The night plays out like it started. Nothing that exciting. The same conversation in circles. Isabella finishes the gelato. By the time we fall asleep in her double bed, Isabella's not-so-baby snores punctuating the darkness, I wonder if I wouldn't have had a better night staying home alone, feeling sorry for myself.

I lean over my side of the bed and grab my phone off the carpet. It's almost midnight but I'm wide awake. After all, my late nights finishing homework and doing club and school stuff haven't exactly set my body clock to a healthy sleep schedule.

I scroll mindlessly for a while and then find myself back on ETUP's Instagram. My eyes fix on the picture of Javier and me. The way he's standing sort of awkwardly like he doesn't know what to do with himself except to lean, sort of, in my general direction. Something about this awkwardness endears him to me even more.

I examine my own image, smiling brightly for Ms. Bates as she snaps the picture. Shoulders back. Eye contact exceptional.

Anyone who didn't know me would think I was the most confident, put-together girl on the planet. And that's what I want them to think.

That's what *I* want to think.

But in the dark, scary place that I don't talk about with anyone—that I *can't* talk about with anyone, because I've outgrown the person who used to be my someone—I know that deep down inside, I'm worried that I'm always two steps away from screwing it up.

These thoughts aren't thoughts I like to have. *Don't dwell, Eliza. Just do.*

Glancing back at Javier's face, I decide to forge ahead. Opening up a new text message, I type in a name. My thumbs hover, then dive in.

Hey, it's Eliza from ETUP. I was wondering if you wanted to get together sometime early next week to talk about club stuff? Preferably Monday? Since we have a meeting this coming Thursday and everything? Let me know.

My thumb twitches. My breath is held.

The text is sent.

I place the phone facedown on the carpet by the bed and count to one hundred. No buzz. I get up and go to the bathroom, then wander around Isabella's fancy apartment for another five hundred counts. I do thirty squats in a row in an effort to make myself tired. I check out the contents of the refrigerator. (Half of Whole Foods shoved in with too many takeout cartons to count, some of them Styrofoam, which makes me cringe.)

I creep back into Isabella's bedroom even though I'm fairly certain fireworks wouldn't wake her.

I pick up my phone.

I flip it over.

Sounds cool. What about Monday after school?

Alone in my former best friend's bedroom, I grin so broadly my cheeks hurt. It feels like the first real smile I've had all day.

JAVIER

There she is. Standing at the front door of Southwest, her eyes on her phone, her thumbs tapping away.

Waiting for me.

My breath quickens, and I find myself wanting to dart into the nearest boys' bathroom and hide, hoping maybe somehow she'll think I've given up on our plans. Plans that I made from the safety of my bedroom through my phone. Plans that involve *Eliza Brady coming over to my house.*

Dang, she's so good-looking.

As I dodge kids bolting in various directions down the first-floor halls, shouting and hollering so loudly the sounds echo off the tiled walls, I screw up the courage to keep going. Twenty feet away. Ten feet away. So close I could smell her shampoo if I were that kind of creep, which I'm not.

"Hey."

Blue eyes. Big smile.

"Hey, Javier. Or . . . Javi. Is there one you prefer?"

"Either is fine," I say, trying to seem relaxed while processing the fact that this girl is about to come over to my house and I'm supposed to be cool about it. I squeeze my hands around my backpack straps, wondering if I can get back to the relaxed, funny Javier I was the first time I met Eliza and she drove me home. How'd I do that? How'd I pull off being so chill? I can only guess it's because I didn't see it coming. It all happened so fast I had no time to overthink everything.

Not like this. Nope. I've been overthinking this scenario since she texted me on Friday night and I realized she really had wanted to meet up in between club meetings.

"Uh, I'm parked in the student lot, same as before," she says, and we begin the walk out to the back parking lot, passing the school buses lining up to take home kids who can't walk, bike, or drive. "Ew," Eliza says, the fumes crossing our path, making her wrinkle her nose in a way I can only describe as adorable. "Seriously, those diesel engine emissions are so bad, worse even than regular cars. And look." She pauses in mid-stride and scowls judgmentally, like the buses are villains in a story she has to analyze for English class. "These buses are empty. It's going to take forever before they're filled, and they're just idling for half an hour or whatever, spewing carbon all over the place." She waves her arms for emphasis and then keeps walking. "Maybe we should make this a club project along with organizing more carpools."

"Yeah, sure," I say, following her to her Nissan. Not for the first time I realize that most of the kids who are parked back here are Baldwin kids. They're more likely to have their own vehicles.

Slamming the car doors shut, we're sealed back up in our original hangout bubble. This car where I once acted like a normal human teenage boy who could joke and smile and talk. I slide my seatbelt across my lap, hoping my brain will subconsciously absorb the environment and transform me from nervous weirdo into Cool Javi.

"Thanks for letting me come over to your house," Eliza says. "I'm staying with relatives since Harvey and I don't have a lot of privacy."

"No problem," I say, my eyes focused on the sidewalks in my neighborhood. Suddenly I'm seeing them with Eliza's eyes. The houses around Southwest are sturdy, squat little brick homes from the '50s and '60s. Tidy gardens mixed in with yards overflowing with weeds. The occasional car on cement blocks. Abuelitas chatting on front porches and older white residents who never left, like Mrs. Green, sorting through mail in their mailboxes or walking their scruffy mutts. I wonder if Eliza is judging all of this. Surely before Harvey she lived in some swanky mansion near Baldwin. One of those fake Spanish villas or Italian castles or something, where everyone has their own bathroom and you can probably go years without seeing another member of your family if you want to.

We park and head in, my anxiety fading a little bit. But only a little. I wonder if she's judging my small living room with the low ceilings, the twenty-year-old couch with cat scratches. The adjoining kitchen with a refrigerator covered in corny magnets that my mom loves to collect. But Eliza doesn't say anything. She just follows me inside.

"My parents are at work," I say. "And my older sister is at class. So we have the place to ourselves."

"Okay," says Eliza, and immediately I cringe inside, wondering if she thinks I'm implying something.

"So we should have a lot of peace and quiet to get this recycling plan going," I add, to make myself clear.

"We're not totally alone. What a sweetie!" Eliza says, noticing Diablo curled up like a little orange donut on the couch, dozing blissfully.

"That's Diablo," I say, "and watch out because he can earn his name sometimes when he gets too frisky."

But Diablo is all sweetness as he wakes up, notices us, and proceeds to rub himself around Eliza's legs, leading her to giggle. "I want a cat or a dog so bad," she says. "Our dog, Grover, died the week before Harvey, and my parents say we can't get another pet until we move back into our house."

"That sucks, I'm sorry."

"Yeah," she says, in a voice that makes me think she's done talking about it.

I suddenly remember what my mom would say about being a good host. Motioning toward the kitchen, I ask her if she wants a soda or something. "I have my water," she says, sliding a reusable bottle from her backpack, one of those fancy flasks that probably cost more than one of my parents earns in a day.

I grab a can of apricot Jumex out of the fridge and ask Eliza where she'd like to work.

"Your room, I guess?" she asks. "Or wherever." She seems flustered when she answers, and this somehow boosts my confidence a little. I made my bed this morning and tidied up, just in case we ended up working in there.

"I have a desk in there," I say. "I'll bring another chair in so we can sit together."

"Cool," she says.

As we set up, Eliza scans my bedroom, and once again I find myself viewing it through her eyes. The Morrissey poster. The collection of origami swans and creatures dotting the top of my dresser. The dusty used acoustic guitar I begged for two Christmases ago and still haven't really learned how to play.

"Oh, that's the *Meat Is Murder* guy," Eliza says, motioning toward Morrissey.

"Yeah," I answer. "Like I said, he's a total jerk now, but . . ."

She nods knowingly. "Yeah. How do we manage that tension between the artist and the art, you know? Especially when the artist is problematic. Tricky stuff." Geez. She sounds like she could be in college already. The fact that she's so smart just makes her cuter somehow.

"I could play you some," I say. "I mean, later. After we get work done."

She tucks some loose strands of hair behind her ears and slides her MacBook out of her backpack, setting it up next to her fancy flask. "Sure," she says. "That will be our motivator to get all our planning done as efficiently as possible."

I nod like I think this way all the time, then sit down to her right. I take a deeper than normal breath, but I don't smell her shampoo or any perfume or anything. I just spy freckles on her forearms and a second earring on her right ear, a little silver hoop behind a tiny silver stud. And I notice this way she quietly clicks her tongue as she scans through a spreadsheet.

I guess she must sense me sort of glancing at her.

"I'm sorry, is that clicking thing annoying? It's, like, this habit I do when I'm thinking."

I shake my head no. Of course I don't mention that it's kind of appealing, actually.

Eliza pulls up a Google form she'd texted out to the club late last week, asking for availabilities for recycling shifts. Humming and clicking, she starts plugging names into shifts, both before and after school.

"What about bins?" I ask. "I mean to actually collect the recyclables to take to the city recycling dumpsters?"

"So the gross oil company my dad works for actually bookmarks funds for charity work," she says. "I guess for tax deductions or to feel less guilty about destroying our futures." I can't tell if she's serious or joking as she says this. "They're donating the money to buy the bins we'll use. Of course, plastic comes from oil, so I suppose it's actually a win for them." At this she rolls her eyes.

"Do you ever think about how screwed up it is that this city is so dependent on oil and gas and it's, like, that's what's also helping destroy us at the same time?" I ask, thinking of Miguel and his job on the east side.

Eliza turns and stares at me. "Literally *all* the time," she says. "Like, in my sleep."

I nod, but my brow furrows in concern. "The problem is, there are good jobs in that field. I mean, like my brother. He doesn't have a college degree. What's he supposed to do, you know? Get a job at Whataburger for minimum wage? Or work at the refineries and help feed his family?"

Eliza shifts in her seat, and she doesn't fire back an answer right away in that confident way of hers. I almost think I've made her uncomfortable. "That's true, yeah. I mean for *your* brother. But . . . my dad. He does have a degree. He could go do something else. *Anything* else."

From the way Eliza speaks about her father, she doesn't seem to like him much. I don't push her as to why, of course, but I can't help but think it might be hard for anyone to start a brand-new job if they've had an old one for a superlong time. A few years ago before he started working in the warehouse, my dad got laid off from his job as a fabricator, and it had taken him a lot of time to wrap his head around the fact that he wasn't what he used to be anymore. But I don't say any of this to Eliza. I think she would listen, probably. But I also sense that she'd be ready with an answer and then *I* wouldn't know what to say. I'm pretty sure she's smarter than me like that.

"Here, let me take over," I say. "I can help with these last few shifts."

"Perfect," she says, sliding her latest-model laptop over to me. It sure is nicer than the one the school district issued to me. "I can look up stuff about a movement for Meatless Mondays on my phone," she continues. "And maybe something about getting those school buses to stop idling."

Eliza and I work together mostly in silence, punctuated only by the clicking of her tongue and the occasional humming. She takes notes in a planner covered with a rainbow of highlighter marks and lists.

"Whoa," I say, when she opens it up.

She grins, like she's pleased she's impressed me. "This is my life bible," she says, patting it. "I find it, like . . . soothing."

"That's like me and yoga," I say, and as soon as I say it, my brain can't decide if it wants to implode from embarrassment or be proud that I've just said that out loud.

"Huh," says Eliza, sitting back in her desk, dropping her phone into her lap. "Interesting." She pauses, examines me carefully. My heart picks up speed when she does. "Like at a studio?"

I laugh. "No, like on YouTube."

She grins, her smile making it all the way up into her eyes. Geez, she's so cute. This cute girl in my bedroom.

I mean, we're making a recycling spreadsheet, yes. But still.

"I can't do stuff like that," Eliza says. "Relax in that obvious sort of way. I just like to . . . do. Be in motion." She stops, breaks eye contact, and looks down at her phone. "If we're going to work together, I should probably say now that I'm most likely going to annoy you."

"Doubtful," I say, and she smiles into her lap again. The word hangs there, and there's this quiet around us that feels like a different sort of quiet from before. Like it's laced with something else. A possibility. A hope. From me, definitely. From her? Who the heck knows.

"Let's take a break," she says after a little while, and she stands up, stretches her arms up over her head. "Play me some of that *Meat Is Murder* band." She bends and twists a little, her back setting off a rapid-fire set of snaps and pops. "Hey, can I, like, sit on your bed? That chair is killing my back."

"Sure," I say, and my voice wobbles a little when I say it and I basically want to die.

I pull up The Smiths, some of my favorite songs from my dad's favorite album, and mine, too, I guess.

"This record is called *The Queen Is Dead*," I say.

"Okay," says Eliza, sitting cross-legged on the middle of my twin bed and leaning back against the wall, half-closing her eyes. She listens, contemplating. I take a beat to consider her face, the intensity of her expression, even when her eyes are closed. Like you can tell she's really *listening*. Holding my breath, I crawl as casually as I can to the foot of my bed, noticeably far away from her. I lean up against the wall, too. When she senses the bed move, Eliza opens her eyes and peers at me.

"They're different," she says. "Pretty good. Weird. Do they actually have a song that's called 'Meat Is Murder'?"

"Yeah," I say, pulling it up. She listens thoughtfully as Morrissey wails about animals being sacrificed for human consumption. I think about the hot dogs they were serving in the cafeteria today. So much for my own Meatless Monday.

"Wow," says Eliza, keeping her eyes open now. "These lyrics are intense." She listens seriously as the song closes out. "I stopped eating meat more for the planet . . . because it murders the planet. I guess I wasn't thinking so much about the animals. But yeah . . . that song doesn't exactly make me question my choices."

I feel sort of embarrassed that I don't know, but I go ahead and ask Eliza what eating meat has to do with saving the environment.

"Oh!" she says, reaching over to my desk for her laptop. "That's such a good question. And something we'll want to explain to the club members. Let me show you something."

Her laptop in her lap, Eliza scoots a little closer to me. Her fingers fly over the keyboard as she opens up page after page and explains how not eating meat helps conserve water, limits pesticide pollution into our rivers and oceans, and stops deforestation, not to mention the positive impact it has on reducing carbon emissions.

"I mean, honestly, Javi, there is so much on here that's so devastating," she says. "And the thing is, we *know* what we have to do to stop carbon emissions and the greenhouse effect. We're just choosing not to do it."

Eliza opens up articles from the *New York Times* and the *Washington Post* and YouTube videos with climate scientists warning about melting polar ice caps, more widespread wildfires, food shortages, long-lasting droughts, killer heat waves, and bigger, more intense hurricanes. At this last mention, my mind flies to Harvey. To sitting in this very room, listening to the rain pound on our roof all day and all night, punctuated only by the sounds of my parents walking up and down the creaky hallway, debating how many inches more we could handle before the rain breached the only house I'd ever known.

My eyes are on one of Eliza's videos about storms, images of trees bending and breaking in some windswept hellscape, rain pounding hard on twisted metal and trash blowing down some nameless street. I can sense my breathing growing shallow, my face getting hot. I don't want to lose my cool in front of Eliza, and I glance away, cough hard in an effort to make the nausea creeping over me subside.

"Hey, Javi?" Eliza asks, her voice soft. She clicks out of the video and shuts her laptop. "I'm . . . Are you all right?"

I exhale, my breath shaky. I'm so embarrassed I can't look at her. I don't think Eliza is the sort of girl who thinks guys should be tough and never cry or whatever, but what kind of wimp can't even watch YouTube videos about this? My eyes fixate on the window over my desk. It's sunny out, not a rain cloud in the sky. I try to focus on that reality.

"Javi?" It's Eliza's gentle voice again, checking on me.

"I'm . . . fine."

"You don't look fine. Wait, let me get this." She reaches for the half-finished can of Jumex on my desk and hands it to me. I take a few sips, then reach over and put it back down. I take one more deep breath.

"Thanks, I'm . . . I'm better."

"Was it . . ." Eliza looks at me, then at the closed laptop on her lap. "I'm sorry. I . . . I go off sometimes. I know. It's just that I'm . . . This stuff is so important to me. I get that it's overwhelming." She puts a hand on my shoulder, and this makes my heart start to race again, but in a different way, I guess.

"It's . . . I mean, the climate stuff is scary, yeah. But . . . ever since Harvey . . . thinking about the weather, the rain . . . it . . . makes me sort of . . . I don't know."

Eliza tips her head, and I can sense her thinking, trying to understand something I don't even have the right words for.

She probably thinks I'm a total freak.

"Oh. *Oh.* Javi, is that why you were so upset when I found you that day in the stairwell?"

I nod, warmth still sweeping over my face. But something about Eliza's voice is so soothing. It's no longer the confident voice she used in front of the ETUP kids. And it's not even the rapid-fire, get-it-done tone that was coming out of her mouth just moments ago when we were working on the recycling spreadsheet or watching those videos. It's almost a whisper. Gentle. Like a hug.

"Javi, I'm so sorry, I didn't know. I wouldn't have showed you that stuff if I had." She drops her hand from my shoulder, and it's like I can still feel it there for a moment. Steady. Warm.

"It's okay," I say. "I mean, it sort of sucks. Like, yeah, I can avoid your videos, but it's not like I can avoid the rain or whatever."

She nods, her brow furrowed like she's contemplating a problem she knows there has to be a solution to if only she focuses hard enough.

"Have you, like, *talked* to someone? Like . . . a therapist?"

I shake my head no. Daniela and Rosario would probably tell me I'm wrong, but therapy sounds like something rich white people do. Not guys like me.

"I don't really know a therapist, I guess," I say.

"Neither do I," Eliza says. "But isn't that what they say to do? Teachers and everyone? *Maybe you should talk to someone.*" She sighs, her voice rueful. "I mean, this nebulous *someone* who's supposed to fix all our problems. I'm sorry. I'm not anti-therapy or anything. Not at all. Just . . . Anyway, I'm terrible. I think you *should* talk to someone. Really. I'm just not sure exactly who that should be? I mean, professionally speaking."

A thought occurs to me, but I file it away, not ready to discuss it with Eliza just yet.

"I feel like a jerk," I say. "I mean, my house didn't even flood. Harvey sucked, don't get me wrong. But after the rain left, my life went mostly back to normal. I mean, I had to go over to my brother's girlfriend's parents' house to help them clean out. That was awful and gross."

Eliza nods knowingly, then wrinkles up her nose in disgust. "That smell, right? You can't get it out of your head."

"Nope," I say. "But at least it wasn't my house that was destroyed." I think back to Rosario's mom, sobbing in the backyard, clutching an old burgundy photo album filled with waterlogged Polaroids and handmade birthday cards as Miguel and my dad and me ripped out carpet, cut out Sheetrock, and lugged out bag after bag of stuff that could never be replaced or dried or put back right. Not ever. "I'm sorry," I say, looking over at Eliza, whose eyes are resting on the Morrissey poster across the room. "You did flood. You probably don't want to talk about this."

Eliza exhales. "What happened, happened, you know? I mean . . . I can't make it unhappen. And it could happen again. It probably *will* happen again, and in our lifetimes, if we don't get a handle on what's going on." The earlier warmth in her voice has disappeared a bit, and she sounds a little detached. Like she's answering a teacher's question in chemistry class. Suddenly, she pops up like a jack-in-the-box and slides over to my desk, taking her laptop with her. "We should get back to work. I mean . . . if you're okay to?" She glances at me, genuine concern on her face. But maybe, also, a look that tells me it's time to refocus on the task at hand.

"Yeah, I'm okay now," I say. "And yeah, let's get back to it." Maybe the action of doing something with ETUP will help my nerves. I don't know. I move from the bed to my seat next to her. But before I start doing club stuff again, I summon the courage to say one more thing to Eliza.

"Hey," I say, peering toward her, trying not to make full eye contact. "Thanks. I mean, for listening. For not, like, laughing at me for getting freaked out."

I can sense Eliza gazing at me long enough that I can't help but lift my chin and meet her eyes with mine. If I had to describe her expression, I guess I would say it's one of surprise.

"Laugh at you?" she says, furrowing her brow. "I could never laugh at you about something like that, Javi."

I nod, grateful. "I wouldn't laugh at you, either," I say. "Not that you freak out over the rain."

"Well," says Eliza, firing up her laptop again, her eyes turning away, "why don't I reserve the right to freak out over one thing before the end of the year. Deal?"

I smile. "Deal."

"Okay, so the recycling spreadsheet is looking good," she says, her fingers back to *tap-tap-tapping*. "But we should think about some strategies for promoting Meatless Mondays." She clicks her tongue again, like maybe it triggers a part of her brain that helps her come up with good ideas.

I tip my head back, stare at a hairline crack sprawling out above me that my dad is always muttering he needs to patch. Meatless Mondays. *Meat Is Murder.* Meat Murders the Planet. Go Meatless with ETUP.

"Hey!" I shout, my mouth moving too fast to let my brain catch up. "What if we use some hashtag like 'ETUP your veggies and forget the meat' or something? Like play on the club name a little? And get people to use it on social media showing their meatless meals? Not just on Mondays but any day?"

Eliza whips her face toward mine, her mouth open in a perfect *O* of excitement.

"Javi, that is so genius!" she says. She literally claps her hands. "I mean, total genius. Everyone pronounces it 'eat up' anyway, so I guess go for it."

"Everyone is wrong," I say. "The club is E-T-U-P. At least in my opinion."

"Mine, too, but not everyone is smart like us," Eliza says breezily, opening up another document to type down my idea. She looks me in the eye, shoots me a grin. "I'm really, really glad we're working on this together," she says.

"Me too," I reply, and my stomach does a little flip.

That night, long after Eliza has gone home and after I've made a playlist of my favorite Smiths songs to give her later, I find myself at the dinner table. Mom has made a pot roast, but I only eat the mashed potatoes and veggies on the side. Partly to save the planet but also partly because somewhere in a neighborhood not far from mine, I know Eliza isn't eating any meat, either.

I get to school the next day a little earlier than normal, ignoring Dom's texts that we meet up in the courtyard so he can show me some new skateboarding trick that's sure to blow my mind.

Taking a deep breath, I make my way to the side of the building, near the doors that are closest to where I want to go. I pull one open, the cool blast of Southwest High air-conditioning practically blowing back my hair. Houston weather is strange all the time, but late October is especially bad. It might be warm enough to go swimming or cool enough to need a jacket.

Or the heavens might dump buckets from the skies.

I make my way down to Room 135 and spy the light on, shining through the slim glass window in the middle of the door, with that sign I've seen a million times taped above it.

SOMETHING ON YOUR MIND?
THIS IS A SAFE SPACE TO ASK FOR HELP!

Maybe you should talk to someone, said Eliza. She meant it, too, even though I doubt Eliza has ever talked to anyone in her life. Not like what I'm about to do. The way she behaves, so confident and together so much of the time, I don't know if she even needs to. What was that way she put it? *What happened, happened.* Then she just dove back into ETUP stuff.

What happened, happened. And it might happen again.

And you can't avoid the rain forever.

I glance down either side of the hallway, sort of worried someone I know will see me here. But there are just a few Baldwin girls, probably young enough to be freshmen, sitting in a clump and giggling at their phones. They ignore me.

I knock on the bright blue door three times. The first time soft, the last two times as hard as my heart is hammering.

"Yes, come in," comes a muffled but welcoming voice.

I pull down on the handle and open it, peering in to find Ms. Holiday sitting at her desk in her closet-sized office, the walls, painted a soft blue, surrounded with brightly colored posters that say things like *No one can make you feel inferior without your consent* and *Your voice is valued here.* That last one is written in rainbow letters.

"Hello," says Ms. Holiday, looking up from her laptop, her smile warm and broad. "How can I help you?" She pushes herself away from her desk and folds her hands in her lap, waiting for my answer. Something about that makes me think I'm not interrupting her.

I open my mouth but nothing comes out. The thought of thunder and lightning cuts through my mind, and an image of me crouching in a stairwell flashes through my head.

Ms. Holiday leans over and hauls a folding chair from the corner and opens it, facing it toward her. "Sorry it's so cramped, but I'm glad you're here," she says, patting the seat of the chair. "What's your name?"

"Javier Garza," I say, sliding my backpack to the floor and sitting down on the metal chair.

"Hello, Javier, I'm Ms. Holiday," she says, leaning forward and smiling. "I'm guessing you're here because something is on your mind? Maybe something that's bothering you a bit?"

I nod, stare at my feet.

"Okay," says Ms. Holiday. "Well, the way this works is that whenever you're ready, I'm here to listen. You can take your time."

Something about that, that permission to be silent for as long as I want, has the opposite effect. Maybe that's something they taught Ms. Holiday in social worker school, I don't know. But I do know that before long, I'm looking up, looking at her and her warm smile.

And before I know it, I can't stop talking.

ELIZA

I clap my hands, trying to get the attention of the crowd.

"Hey, listen up, please!"

Javi echoes me, but he sounds a little deeper and more booming.

"Listen up, people!"

He shoots me a smile. This is the fourth meeting of ETUP and he's certainly starting to find his voice up here, even if he still seems a little shaky at the start.

The room full of Southwest and Baldwin kids settles, turning to face us. Ms. Bates slides into a seat at the back of the room like she always does.

"I want to thank Yesenia for bringing in the cookies for our meeting," I say. Yesenia beams from the front row. She and her boyfriend made cookies frosted like the earth, and they've been gobbled up in the first five minutes of this meeting. I try to ignore the fact that they've wrapped each cookie in individual plastic and tied each one with a ribbon, surely also made of some sort of petrochemical.

"I'm wondering," Yesenia says, "if maybe a bake sale wouldn't be a cool idea. Like to raise money for an environmental organization? All the stuff we sell could have, like, an environmental theme?"

My mind floats to dozens and dozens of plastic bags being

sold so we can justify sending a few hundred dollars somewhere. I already envision Ms. Bates's trash can overflowing with single-use bags at the end of the meeting. I know Yesenia means well, but I can barely fix a fake smile on my face when I nod and say, "Yeah, maybe we can consider that for the spring." Hopefully by then she'll forget this idea. Or at least I can convince her to use recyclable packaging materials.

I turn my attention to the whiteboard, going through our achievements for the month of November.

"It's almost Thanksgiving, but we have the recycling program up and running, which is supercool," I say.

"Just remember to let us know if you can't make your shift, so we can schedule someone to help out," Javi adds. He's taken over the spreadsheet, and I've finally stopped double-checking his work, which has always been perfect.

"Can we maybe talk about an education campaign on, like, *how* to recycle?" says Yvonne, my Baldwin acquaintance. "People are putting nasty half-filled chip bags in those bins. I mean, we can't recycle your chewed-on Takis, y'all." She says this last sentence loudly for the benefit of the room, searching the rest of the faces for validation, which she quickly receives in the forms of nods and *yeah*s.

"It's *gross* what some people put in there," echoes a Southwest girl named Carmen. "Like sandwiches with a bite out of it or whatever."

I jot *recycling education campaign* on the board and ask for volunteers to chair that committee. Yvonne and Carmen agree to take the lead.

"It would be cool if we could use the same sort of social media we used for the Meatless Mondays, ETUP your veggies thing," says Javi. "I mean, just a thought."

Yesenia rolls her eyes good-naturedly. "You come up with *one* idea, Javi . . ." Javi blushes a little.

"Hey, it was a *good* idea," I respond, coming to his defense. Javi shoots me a grateful smile, and that tingly, nervous wave of feelings washes over me like it often does when we make eye contact.

Ever since I went to his house after school a few weeks ago, I keep wondering if something else is going to happen between us. And by something else I mean kissing him for hours and hours while we listen to The Smiths. But Javi seems to be all business. And while I'm totally pro–girls making the first move, at least in theory (never having actually made the first move), for some reason I don't know if I should do that with Javi. Not when we're running the club together so smoothly. Not when I'm unsure whether he thinks I'm the most annoying, hyper-organized girl on the planet. I can still hear in my head the way he said *whoa* when he saw my planner the first time. Like he was pretty confident I was a freak of nature more concerned with color-coding my life than making out.

Don't get me wrong. I *do* like color-coding my life. But I think there is also a big part of me that would also really enjoy making out with Javier Garza.

I watch as he jots down a couple of ideas for the recycling education campaign on the board, and the gentle way he laughs as kids in the club recall the funniest posts about Meatless Mondays. It makes me melt a little inside for sure. There's something so, I don't know, *tender* about him, if I had to think of the right word.

"All right, folks," says Ms. Bates, standing up and motioning toward the clock. "This has been a productive meeting. But it's time for us to clear off campus and for me to get home to my life outside of this building. And yes, I do have one." Classic Ms. Bates humor.

Javi and I remind everyone about our next meeting, scheduled for the first week back after Thanksgiving Break. The kids clear out, and I try not to wince too visibly as my worries about the plastic cookie bags are made real; in just a few moments, Ms. Bates's trash can looks like it's overflowing with jellyfish. Javi and I have started gathering our things when Ms. Bates asks us to wait for a moment.

"Yes?" I say, concerned. My mind always goes to concerned when an adult asks me to stay after class. I don't know why, seeing as I've literally never been in trouble for anything. Just something about authority figures, I guess. Especially ones I respect as much as Ms. Bates.

"I just wanted to say," she begins, crossing her arms and smiling broadly, the biggest smile she's offered me so far, "that I'm very impressed with all the hard work being done by this club under your joint leadership. In just a few weeks, you've mobilized students from both Southwest and Baldwin to care about their planet and think about climate in a new way. Splendid job."

I stand a little straighter, reveling in the validation.

"Thank you so much, Ms. Bates," I say. "We certainly couldn't have done it without your guidance and support."

"Yeah," says Javi, "we appreciate it."

Ms. Bates moves behind her desk and picks up her canvas bag, the one that reads *Science Is True Whether You Believe It or Not*. "I'll walk out with you," she says.

As the three of us make our way down the third-floor main hallway, Javi and me on either side of Ms. Bates, I decide to take advantage of this moment to broach an idea.

"I don't mean to keep the club business going," I say, "but . . ."

Ms. Bates glances at me and offers a wry grin.

"Eliza, again, do you ever sleep?"

At this Javi snorts, but I know it's well-meaning. Whatever. I'm used to everyone thinking I'm too much, I guess. I mean, it's not like they're wrong.

"I just wanted to bring up the bus situation," I say. "The idling? I mean, those buses run for almost thirty minutes after school, spewing emissions day after day. If we could get those buses to stop idling, it would do more for the planet than a million bake sales."

Ms. Bates nods, thoughtful. "Public transportation is a good thing for the environment in theory," she says, "but you're right about those buses. They emit diesel fumes, which are so terrible. And the idling seems to go on forever." I nod vigorously in agreement.

"We sent an email to the principals of both schools," says Javi, "but we haven't received a response yet."

"Well," says Ms. Bates, "given this unique school year and everything we are going through, both Southwest and Baldwin, our administrative leadership has been stretched tight. I'm willing to bet Principals Franklin and Lopez receive hundreds of emails every day. I'm not exaggerating, either."

At this point we've made it through a set of side doors. Ms. Bates begins to split off toward the faculty parking lot, but she pauses and turns to face us.

"Perhaps an old-fashioned petition might be the way to get some attention," she says. "It could be a way to show them that students from both campuses care about this issue. For what it's worth, Principal Franklin mentioned to me that she thought the ETUP your veggies Meatless Mondays campaign was quite clever."

Javi puffs with pride next to me.

"Fine, Javi, drink that in," I say, elbowing him gently, trying to ignore the sliver of electricity that slides through me when I touch him, even in this casual way. Then I turn my attention to Ms. Bates. "We can start a petition. Maybe at the next club meeting, I'll designate some members to take that on." It's an okay suggestion, and I know Ms. Bates means well in giving it to us. But it doesn't feel like enough.

"It's not just a problem here," I continue. "Buses idle at every single campus in this district. Have you ever driven by the bus barn that services this part of the city? It's superclose to here, and it's, like, a virtual sea of yellow, carbon-emitting evil."

Ms. Bates smiles at this. "Again, Eliza, I admire your fervor. We'll discuss it soon. But now I really do have to get home to the life that I really do have."

"I'm sorry," I say, a little flustered. "I know I get carried away."

"It's all right," she says, already walking away. "See you tomorrow!"

Javi and I head in the other direction toward the student lot. It's unspoken between us that I'm going to give him a lift home. After we slide into my Nissan, I sink my head into my hands.

"Gah!" I say. "I'm embarrassed."

"What?" says Javi. "What for?"

I sit up, lean my head back, stare at the ceiling.

"Sometimes . . . I'm just too much, you know? I'm overbearing. Prattling on and on about these buses when Ms. Bates wants to go home to . . . I don't know. Her cat. Her husband. Her kids."

Javi considers this. "It's weird when you think about teachers having families. When you run into them in real life, it's so strange. Like imagining them naked or whatever." He holds up his hands, flustered. "I'm not saying I'm imagining Ms. Bates naked!"

I laugh, partly glad that Javi is now as embarrassed as I am.

"I know," I say. "When I was a kid my mom and I ran into my kindergarten teacher at Walgreens and I started crying for some reason. My little-girl brain couldn't comprehend that she existed outside of the classroom." I sigh and turn to face Javi. "Anyway, whatever. I know I can get stuff done. But sometimes I go into overdrive, and I think it scares people." As soon as I say this out loud, it strikes me that it's not a thought I've really ever shared out loud. Not with my mom. Not with Isabella. Maybe only just a little bit to myself. But something about Javier makes it easy to relax, to spill my guts out sometimes.

"I don't think it's overdrive, necessarily," says Javier. "I mean . . . I think you're just . . . you're a driven person."

My cheeks flush with pleasure at this. That warm feeling of possibility that always seems to be enveloping us is dialed up just a notch. "If I were a boy, probably I wouldn't even worry about it," I add.

"Yeah," says Javi, like he's never considered this before. "I don't know. I dig when a girl speaks her mind." He breaks our eye contact, his fingers tapping against the automatic lock. "That first meeting when you were up there, just getting everyone on board to do stuff for the club . . . my first thought was that I could never be like that. It's . . ." He pauses. "I guess what I'm saying is you're . . . dynamic."

Now it's not just warmth between us. The air feels charged with something, the electricity in the air spreading to a pins-and-needles feeling all over me. *Dynamic.* It's better than being called pretty or cute or even appealing. *Dynamic.*

"Thanks," I say at last, breaking the silence that feels both awkward and full of potential. "But . . . I mean . . . you've really come into your own in just a few meetings. Like today. You seemed totally at ease up there in front of everyone."

Javi nods, unsure. "You really think so?"

"Yes, totally!" I reply, finally starting the car. Pulling out of the parking lot and driving toward Javi's house gives me something to do, provides an action that cuts through the tension I know *I'm* feeling. But does Javi feel it, too?

And are we ever going to do anything about it?

We're quiet during the superbrief drive to his house, and

when I pull over, I half-expect the tension to build again. Just then my phone buzzes.

Can you swing by the house and get our mail? Been meaning to and haven't been able to get away this week. Dad is working late and can't.

I type out a quick no problem.

"My mom," I explain. "Just an errand."

Javier nods. "Okay," he says. "I was going to invite you in, but . . ."

"Oh," I say, wondering if I can delay my mom's request. Wondering if we don't make a move today, maybe we never will. "Well . . ."

"No, it's cool," he says, opening the door. "I mean, I don't want to keep you from helping out your mom."

We could make out here in the car right now for a minute, I think. But Javi just gets out of the Nissan. I feel embarrassed and hope I'm not showing it. I'm probably imagining that anything could happen between us. He probably only likes me as a friend. But why does he want to invite me in? Just to work on club stuff? Or what? If only I could read his mind.

"Well, see you," Javi says, shutting the door, offering a wave before jogging up to the front door of his house.

I pull out onto the street and drive toward my old house on Ferris, my mind daydreaming about Javi. There's something so appealing about his gentleness, his quiet demeanor. The way he doesn't mind hanging out with a girl who is louder and bossier than him.

Don't say bossy, I remind myself. *It's just that you have leadership potential.*

Ten minutes later I pull into the house on Ferris, and I check my phone, which I had heard buzz twice while I was driving.

Thanks for the ride. And I meant what I said about you being dynamic. I honestly just double-checked that I used that word right and I did, so . . . anyway, just wanted to say that.

I spend about three minutes considering which GIF, emoji, or just-right mix of cool/cute statement I could send back.

"Screw it," I finally mutter to myself.

I'm always happy to give you a ride. And I'm just really really glad that I asked you to be copresident with me. I really like working with you. Like a lot.

Send.

Ahh!

How many times can I use the word "really" in one text? And that last phrase, *like a lot*. I sound like a silly schoolgirl. I mean, I am a schoolgirl, obviously. But still.

I peer up at my old house, now vacant, the windows stickered with bright-colored city construction permits. The sight of it sends me spinning. I glance down at my phone and see that Javier has read my text. Then I see the three dots pop up that tell me he's responding. My heart picks up speed as the bubble pops up and goes away, pops up and goes away.

He's going to tell me he likes me.

He's going to tell me he's weirded out.

He's going to ask me out on a date.

He's going to tell me he's uncomfortable with my directness and I actually am overbearing.

Finally, after a minute or two, he simply "likes" my last text. Then radio silence.

My face falls and my shoulders drop. I knew it. It was all in my head. I should have never taken such a chance.

"Please, Eliza, just chill out," I admonish, tossing my phone into my backpack. Tomorrow, Javi will probably tell me he has to step back from his club responsibilities or something because I weirded him out. Feeling frustrated and embarrassed, I grab my backpack and slam the car door behind me and walk up to the house that used to be the center of my life before the fates decided to take it all away.

~

There are several days' worth of mail in the mailbox, and I grab the bundle and cram it into my backpack. I spy a few bills and wonder not for the first time about my family's finances. We've always been well off, I know this. So much better off than most. But not as well off as Isabella. Part of me wants to know what my parents are saying in those hushed conversations behind their door at Heather and Dave's house, conversations peppered with words like "deductible" and "adjustor" and "mutual funds" and "credit card." Sometimes I think being an adult gives you more power, but there are parts of it that confuse me. When are you supposed to learn all that stuff? And what do you do if you *don't* have resources like my parents do? The thought overwhelms me, almost as much as my thoughts about plastic bottles breeding do.

I'm about to turn and head back to my car, but something tugs at me. I haven't been inside my house for weeks, and there's a part of me that's curious to see how much progress the contractor has made. I peer in a dusty window, past one of the permitting stickers from the city, and spy fresh, unpainted Sheetrock and electrical cords splayed out like a den of snakes.

The code to the lockbox is the birthday of my maternal grandmother, the one I never met. My mom set the code, and this sort of breaks my heart along with everything else about this place right now. I spin the combination numbers and fetch the house key, then let myself in.

Shutting the front door behind me, I drop my bag and step into what was once my living room.

"Hey!" I shout. There's no one here right now to respond, but I want to hear what my voice sounds like in this strange, vacant place. It echoes, no carpets or furniture or other bodies to absorb the sound.

The staircase leads up to the second floor, where my bedroom is. That was spared, and for that I'm lucky. But here, on the first floor—the dining room to the left, the formal living room to the right, the kitchen and family room toward the back—this is where so much of my life happened. Here, in this space. It's shapeless now, empty. Anonymous. I reach out and touch one of the smooth slabs of Sheetrock, running my hand over it and remembering the sounds that came with tearing down the old walls, the blows and thumps of sledgehammers. The rip and tear of wet carpet.

One of the cruelest things about having your house flood is that you don't have time to grieve. You have to move fast in those first few hours and days. If you don't rush to rip out Sheetrock, drag out rugs, haul the flesh of your house to the curb for the world to peer at when they drive by, the mold will come and invade the bones of your house as fast as the floodwaters did. But floodwaters subside. Mold is nefarious. Tricky. And it doesn't leave without a fight.

I remember Javi talking about cleaning out the home of his brother's girlfriend's parents. How we commiserated about the smell. That sick, unmistakable smell of water damage baking in the Houston heat. A smell matched only by the clinical hospital odor of bleach hauled in by the gallon to try and mitigate the potential mold disaster.

Swollen books and photo albums, molting in the late summer sun.

Furniture passed down from generation to generation, dragged to the curb, abandoned.

Small heaps of books and tchotchkes and musical instruments and favorite holiday sweaters, never to be loved again.

I wander past the living room, past the corner where our Christmas tree always sat, past the space where that square of sun used to stream in through the bay window, the square of sun where I'd rested tummy-down as a little girl and written poems and played with my dolls. Past the room where Heather told my mom that she was finally pregnant with Ethan and my mother got so excited she'd tripped over an end table, the same end table that held corny pictures of my brother from his senior prom. The same end table that had been tossed, lost, destroyed after the flood.

I move past all that and into the kitchen, where unpainted cabinets sit, counters still missing. My mom has decided on a new layout, and I don't like it. I don't like that she wants to get rid of the island where I used to make my morning coffee, even when my dad told me I was too young for coffee. I don't like that she's moved the pantry to the other side of the kitchen, the pantry where Isabella and I would sneak snacks back during sleepovers when we still went to the same school.

Back when we still knew how to talk to each other. Back when we still seemed to *like* each other.

"I hate it," I say out loud, to no one. I don't shout it or yell it or anything. I just say it, my voice echoing off the walls again, strange and eerie in this strange and eerie house. "I hate this stupid kitchen. This is not my kitchen!"

Turning on my heel, I bolt past the living room that's no longer my living room and the dining room that's no longer my dining room and the front door that's no longer my front door. I slam the key back into the lockbox and I spin the combination and I race back to my car and I pull out without looking back at the house that is not my house.

A big shake comes over me, a heaving sensation. I grip the steering wheel and focus on the street in front of me. My heart is hammering, and my throat aches with tears that are begging to come out.

Just go, Eliza. Drive. Don't dwell, just do. Just drive.

Somehow, I make it back to Heather and Dave's, and by the time I pull into the driveway, I've collected myself. I check my reflection in the rearview mirror, making sure I look normal. Fine. Like the Eliza Brady I know the world sees and expects.

"Hey," I say, letting myself in. "Mom, here's the mail!" I drop it on the dining room table and take out my planner and my homework. I have so much to do.

"Thanks, sweetie," my mother responds, wandering in from the kitchen to start sorting through it. "Everything okay over there?"

"Yeah," I respond. "Seems fine."

If I can focus hard enough on my tasks at hand, I'm confident that soon it will be like I never even went to that place at all.

JAVIER

I watch Ms. Holiday's finger as it traces a box in the air, and I listen to her voice as it commands me to breathe in, out, in, out.

"Very good," she says, mimicking the breathing with me. "How does that feel?"

I consider this. "Weird."

Ms. Holiday smiles. "I'll take that."

This is the third time I've come to see Ms. Holiday since I visited her office a month or so ago. And this is the third breathing technique she's taught me, along with words like "traumatic response" and "self-compassion."

"So the goal, Javier, is to recognize when you're starting to feel the symptoms of anxiety as it relates to the weather," she says. "And see that as a signal to start a breathing technique like we've practiced here."

I nod. It makes sense. But Ms. Holiday makes it sound so easy.

"What if I can't do it?" I ask.

She leans back in her chair, tucks some of her blond hair behind her ears, and smiles gently. I can tell why kids at Southwest like her so much. There's something about her vibe, her calm voice, the way every move she makes is slow and relaxed, that makes her office feel like some sort of chill cocoon. The last time I walked out of here into the bustling first-floor hallway, it was almost like I'd forgotten the rest of the school existed.

"Developing this sort of thing takes time," Ms. Holiday answers me, "but with practice it gets easier."

"Yeah, I get it," I say.

But what I really want to say is that there's something corny about these exercises. Of course I'd never say something like that out loud because I would never want to hurt Ms. Holiday's feelings. But there's almost something *girly* about them.

As fast as the thought comes to me, I know it's wrong. Unfair. I can hear Rosario or Daniela or Eliza calling me out. Telling me that way of thinking is stupid. And on one level, I know they're right.

But then I picture Miguel finding me breathing in my room, tracing a box into the air. Wasn't the yoga bad enough?

Ms. Holiday must sense my doubt because she rubs at her chin, a habit I've noticed she has when she's thinking. "I have an idea," she tells me. "We've still got a few minutes before first period. Do you want to come outside with me for a moment?"

I shrug, briefly wondering if anyone I know will spot me with Ms. Holiday and what they might think. No one knows I've been coming here. Not my family, not Eliza. Certainly not Dom and the other guys. But how can I say no to Ms. Holiday? She feels like a teacher, almost. Plus, she's cool.

We head out a side door, and Ms. Holiday guides me to a patch of rocks and weeds near the side of the school. Southwest High doesn't exactly have fancy landscaping, or any landscaping at all. There are a few trees where kids vape and gossip before class, and bushes that tend to grow too high and raggedy before the district cuts them down, and then patches like the one Ms. Holiday is standing in front of.

"I want you to pick out a stone," she says. "It doesn't matter which one. Just whatever rock sort of calls to you."

Calls to me? Ms. Holiday *is* cool, but this feels like some sort of weird New Age stuff. Still, I don't want to hurt her feelings. I squat down, peering briefly over my shoulders to see if I spy anyone I know. But there's no one. My fingers trace the rocks and stones. They're nothing special or gorgeous. Gray and white, small and relatively large. Some are smooth and others rough under my fingertips. I finally pick a medium-sized gray oval, flipping it over in my right hand.

"This one," I say, standing up.

Ms. Holiday leads me back into her office, and we sit down again.

"This stone," she says, "could be sort of a grounding device for you. A way to remember that you have the tools inside of you to handle the weather."

"Okay," I say, uncertain. "But how? Like, what do I do with it?"

"Well," begins Ms. Holiday. "First you just hold it. Take it with you everywhere, in a pocket or a bag. And you know that it's there. And when you feel your anxiety build, you can breathe and touch it, work it over and over in your hands."

I look down at this nothing-special stone that until moments ago was destined to live out its sad existence in a patch of weeds outside my high school. I'm not quite sure it has the power necessary to talk me down when I'm flipping out in the middle of a rainstorm.

"I guess I can . . . try?" I say, uncertain. Mostly because I don't want to disappoint Ms. Holiday. I'm pretty sure this stone is going to live somewhere on my nightstand along with a bunch of other junk.

But Ms. Holiday just seems glad to be making any sort of progress with me.

"Good," she says, nodding. "And the other thing I was thinking . . . That object is from nature. Just like rain is, right? I think another way to deal with this anxiety that you're experiencing, anxiety that's totally understandable, is to spend more time in nature. More time outside. When you do that, you're reminding yourself that this planet has a lot of wonderful gifts that are not scary, not threatening. And it can also motivate you to keep doing the work you're doing with your club."

"Yeah," I say, agreeing. The funny thing is, even though I'm doing all this stuff with ETUP, I've never really considered myself a nature guy. My family is the type to barbecue and hang out at home, not hike or camp. When we were supertiny my parents sometimes drove us to Galveston to play in the ocean, until Daniela read some article that said there was too much poop in the Gulf Coast waters to swim safely. So that put a stop to that.

"How's ETUP going?" Ms. Holiday asks.

"Pretty good," I say. And then a thought occurs to me. "You know, I've been thinking . . . I can't be the only kid at this school who started freaking out about the weather and everything after Harvey."

"You are most certainly not alone, I can assure you," Ms. Holiday answers, offering a soft smile. "I've had several kids from both schools come see me this year to talk about how they're feeling post-Harvey. It was a trauma, just like we've discussed."

"I wonder," I begin, and I rub my thumb against the smooth gray stone. Maybe it's just Ms. Holiday putting ideas in my head, but it sort of does calm me down a little. "Do you think it would be a good idea to do a presentation about this to ETUP? Like how to deal with anxiety about the weather, about climate change? Like I could research and share some techniques?"

What I don't add is that even though I'm not 100 percent sure the techniques will work for me, I figure they might work for other people. And anyway, I don't have to tell people in the presentation that *I'm* trying them.

Ms. Holiday smiles so broadly I can see her gums, and I find myself smiling like a goofball.

"*Is* it a good idea?" I ask, already knowing her answer but wanting to hear it.

"Javier, I think it's a great idea," she says, "and I think it can help you take charge of what you've been feeling and going through. I'm proud of you."

"Cool," I say, nodding. "I'm going to work on it over the Thanksgiving Break."

"Sounds like a plan," says Ms. Holiday as the first bell of the school day rings. "Speaking of, I hope you have a nice one."

"You, too, Ms. Holiday," I say, standing up and grabbing my backpack.

"Come and see me when you get back, all right? And I'm here to help with that presentation, which I know will be awesome."

I thank her again and head out of the door, then slide my hands into my pockets as I walk toward my first class of the day. In my right pocket, my fingertips graze the small stone, and I wonder if it really could hold some of the magic Ms. Holiday promises.

Rosario rubs her belly and pushes back from the dinner table.

"I know I'm eating for two, but that doesn't mean two complete Thanksgiving dinners," she says. "I'm so stuffed."

"First meal with her folks and now this one with us," says Miguel, smiling as he serves himself another helping of tamales. The two Thanksgiving meals don't seem to be slowing him down.

"Ooof, Miguel, how can you," says Rosario, eyeing his generous portion. Then she presses a hand on her chest. "Heartburn. Ouch. Is there any part of pregnancy that's easy?"

"Just wait," says Mom, passing the cranberry sauce to my father. "You're in the last trimester now. That's when things really get wild." But she smiles with sympathy before telling Rosario it will all be worth it when the baby comes.

"I hope so," Rosario says.

Miguel leans over and kisses her on the cheek. "Sorry it's so rough, babe." She glances at him, her face a mix of grateful and exhausted.

"Hey, Javi, you only ate the sides," Daniela says, coming back in from the kitchen with dessert. "No turkey? No tamales?"

Dang. I was hoping no one would notice.

"I'm just . . . trying out not eating meat sometimes," I say.

My entire family eyeballs me like I'm out of my mind.

"This is why you didn't want my fajitas yesterday, isn't it?" my mother asks, peering at me, confused. "And why you asked what was in the soup on Sunday?"

This is the last thing I wanted. Attention. I should have just eaten the meat. It's Thanksgiving, after all, and it's not like I've committed totally to going meat-free like Eliza. I ate the chicken patty they served in the cafeteria last week. And when I was hanging out at Dominic's house Saturday, I had the ham sandwich his mom made me. I guess I'm just trying to eat meat *less*, which Eliza says is a step in the right direction. And the truth is, I'm not a fan of turkey. The tamales were a sacrifice, though, I have to admit.

"I've just been learning, in my club, that there's a connection between not eating meat and helping the planet," I say, cringing at my own words, regretting my choice already. Why did Daniela have to say anything?

Speaking of, my sister cuts herself a huge slice of pie. "As long as there isn't a connection between saving the earth and dessert," she mutters.

I try to explain my reasoning to my family, and nobody reacts much. Dad just grunts a bit.

"Dad, you know Morrissey," I say, desperate. "He's a vegetarian. *Meat Is Murder*?"

"The man is a racist pendejo," my father decrees. "I like his music, but I also like my meat."

"Just forget it," I say under my breath. "Here, pass the tamales." I don't want a fight.

"No, no," my mother says, waving her hands. "Javier, you have the right to eat what you want. It's okay with me. More leftovers for us tomorrow."

Rosario, who is seated next to me, reaches over and pats my arm. "I think it's cool," she says. "Stand up for what you think is right." She takes a sip of her ice water. "What's this club, though?"

Good grief. If only I'd eaten like everybody else, I wouldn't have to be in the spotlight.

"It's about the environment and the planet and stuff we can do to help with climate change," I say. "You know, recycling, learning how to limit our dependence on fossil fuels. That sort of thing."

Rosario tucks her black curls behind her ears and smiles that warm big-sister smile at me. "That sounds important," she says, rubbing her belly again.

But Miguel doesn't smile. Just pushes away his plate and shoots me a look, his brow furrowed.

"Well, those fossil fuels pay my salary, little man," he says. "Unless you want me to go work at Chipotle or something. And they don't pay as good as my friends on the east side of town."

I duck my head, stare at my plate, the remnants of sweet

potatoes and cranberry sauce starting to solidify onto my plate. I can hear Rosario gently try to shush him.

"Yeah, I know," I say. "I didn't mean . . ."

Miguel doesn't say anything, but there's a heaviness in the room all of a sudden. An awkwardness. Something unsaid. Unlike Daniela, Miguel never made school his thing. With Daniela, we all knew she was going to hustle herself into something professional, and picturing my big sister as a nurse is easy to do. But for my big brother? Well, I remember the nights my parents would get into it with him, badgering him to get his grades up to 70, the bare minimum to pass. It didn't matter if he thought a GED would serve him just as well, they pushed back. They wanted him to earn his diploma.

And finally, he did, and I know my folks breathed a huge sigh of relief when he came home one afternoon talking about the fat paycheck he was going to earn working at a refinery near Pasadena. Never mind Daniela's warnings about increased risks for cancers and breathing troubles as he got older. This was good money right now, plus benefits. He could figure out the future later. Then he and Rosario moved in together and a few years after that, Rosario got pregnant. He'd been working for "Big Oil," as Eliza would put it, for almost six years, and he doesn't seem to have a plan to stop.

"Anyway, forget it," says Miguel, reaching for the pie. "No big deal." I can tell he's a little irritated, but he's also not the type to push it. Still, between that and the meat debacle, I'm pretty worried about my ability to digest what I *did* eat.

Just then my phone buzzes in my pocket, and I excuse

myself to the bathroom. Dad has a big thing about no phones at the table. Once I shut the door, I slide out my phone and read a text.

From Eliza.

Why why why do I try to explain things to my family?

She's included a GIF of a woman tugging on her hair and screaming.

What happened? I text back.

A few moments later, she replies.

Huge blowup. My parents said I was being obnoxious talking about meat, the planet, fossil fuels, having a future I can actually picture . . . the usual but on steroids since this was supposed to be A Nice Family Meal and Your Brother Is Home and Enough Eliza!!!!!!!

I grin, not at Eliza's plight, but because it feels like we've had parallel holiday meals. Yeah, maybe hers is a little more intense, but still.

Sounds familiar, I type back. I think my brother hates me now because I told him working for big oil is killing the planet.

Okay, so maybe that's a stretch. Am I trying to impress Eliza? Or just make her feel less alone?

While I'm struggling to answer my own questions, she messages me back.

Totally get it. I'm so sorry. I have to get some air. You want to take an after dinner walk or whatever? Maybe Willow WH? I could pick you up in 15. My family will be glad I'm leaving.

Something pulses through me, makes me catch my breath. As I'm staring at the corny framed cartoon of a dog in a bathtub that my mother has hung in this bathroom for some absurd reason, trying to figure out how to respond, Eliza texts me again.

I mean no pressure or whatever if you can't.

Fumbling with my phone, I text back.

No, it's cool. Let's go. I could use the air too.

Great. See you soon. Do you want me to honk or come in or . . .

Just pull up. I'll be waiting by the window.

I turn and face my reflection in the mirror.

"Be cool, Javier," I command myself, knowing it's like I'm telling myself to slay dragons or walk on water. I'm not cool and I'll never *be* cool.

But the coolest girl I know is coming over here to pick me up in her electric car.

~

"I don't see why Javi gets out of doing the dishes just because some girl is coming over to pick him up," whines Daniela. I can practically feel her shooting a pointed look into my back from the adjoining kitchen as I peer out our living room's bay window.

"Leave Javi alone," says my mother. "He set the table."

"Big deal," my sister protests.

At least my dad and brother are going on a beer and soda run and aren't here to see me get picked up for . . . whatever this is that I'm about to go on with Eliza.

"Your ride on her way?"

I turn and find Rosario standing next to me, holding a plate of half-eaten pecan pie. "Don't judge," she says. "I know I said I was full ten minutes ago, but pregnancy is weird like that." She forks another big bite into her mouth.

"I won't judge," I say, smiling. Rosario is even shorter than me, but everything else about her is big. Big eyes, big smile, big heart.

"So you can tell me," she says, dropping her voice to a dramatic whisper even though Daniela and Mom are blabbing away and ignoring us as they load the dishwasher behind us. "Is this girl someone special?" She winks at me, then pauses. Her face falls.

"Oh wow, I'm so sorry," she says. "Did I just ask you that? I'm not even an official mom yet, and I sound like such a *mom*. Just ignore me."

I laugh as Rosario shoves another forkful of pie into her mouth.

"It's okay," I say. "Eliza is . . . she's really a cool girl. I really like her. She's smart. Intense. Curious."

"Those are all good things, right?" she says, raising an eyebrow at me, the tiny little mole just above her right eyebrow popping up simultaneously.

"Yeah," I say, blushing just a little. "All good things."

"And you met her through this club, right?"

I nod.

Rosario shifts her fork and almost-empty plate to one hand and rubs her belly with the other. She looks at me carefully, like maybe she's seeing something in me for the first time. "Listen,

Javi, I know Miguel was giving you a hard time, but don't let that bug you. I'm glad you're getting involved with all this." She breaks eye contact and peers down at her belly. "I want this little one to grow up on a nice planet, you know?"

I nod, feeling dumb for not making the connection earlier between everything ETUP is doing and my new baby niece on the way. But Rosario is right. The work we're doing is going to have an effect on that little girl's life. A really good effect, I hope.

"I want that, too," I say.

Rosario smiles at me, then gets a look on her face like she's plotting something.

"Hey," she says, lowering her voice again. "We finally picked out a name. Wanna be the first person to know?"

"For sure," I say, feeling honored. "But Daniela is going to be jealous."

Rosario smiles even bigger. "She'll find out soon enough. Anyway, it's Valentina! You better say you love it."

Now it's my turn to smile.

"I really do," I say. It's a great name.

Just then there's a *beep beep* and I spy Eliza's car roll up in front of our house.

"Have fun," Rosario says meaningfully, gently sliding her elbow into my side.

"I'll try," I say, my heart picking up speed as I head out the door and cross our front lawn. I slide into Eliza's Nissan, thinking it's kind of weird to be in this car and in her presence in the evening as the sun has started to make its descent.

Something about it is exciting, too.

"Hey," I say.

"Hey," she says, exhaling. "I'm so glad you were willing to get out. I just . . . cannot anymore with my family."

"I hear you," I say, nodding, feeling slightly guilty that I'm trying to equate her family drama to mine. Especially after my talk with Rosario. Something tells me Eliza's Thanksgiving was worse.

"How'd you manage to leave?" she asks.

I shrug. "Well, we were done eating, and all anyone was going to do was watch football, so it was fine. I just told my parents that you and I were going to Willow Waterhole to work on club stuff. Discuss a cleanup event, maybe?" That *had* been my excuse to go out with Eliza, but the truth is, my parents never really question me. Unlike Miguel, I've never been a problem kid. Never came home too late, never gotten in trouble at school. Never made waves.

Is it something to be proud of or embarrassed by? I'm not really sure.

"Like I said in my texts, I don't think my family particularly cared that I was leaving," Eliza mutters, turning onto a side street near the waterhole. She pulls off to the curb. I spy a couple walking their dog, a mom guiding her little girl on a two-wheeler. Folks burning off Thanksgiving meals, I guess. The sun is setting, painting the sky all orange and pink.

"We could walk down to the detention ponds on the other side of the street," I suggest.

"Sure."

We take off down one of the paths. Kids from Southwest

High sometimes sneak over here to cut class, and I'm not sure I'd be comfortable coming here alone in the dark. Once Daniela and her girlfriends came here for an outdoor study date and came back to our house complaining of finding what looked to be a used condom abandoned in the tall grass. Still, if you can look past the garbage some people leave behind, it can be really pretty and peaceful.

"Look, a heron," says Eliza, pointing out one of the delicate snow-white birds with the elegant poses that make the waterhole their home. At the sound of her voice, the heron flaps its big, broad wings and takes flight, soaring off to parts unknown.

"Even the animals want nothing to do with me," Eliza says, and I can't tell if she's joking or not.

"I want to hang out," I say. My cheeks flush, and I turn away, pretending to be totally engrossed in a sign some government entity has posted that has information about the local watershed and preservation.

Eliza doesn't say anything for a moment. We keep walking for a bit and then she says, "We're hanging out right now, aren't we?" The words hang there, like they're inviting me to respond in a certain way, explain myself further. But I can't seem to do it.

We take a winding path with hardly any other people on it; we pass one or two nature lovers taking photographs and another man walking a small mutt that yaps when we walk past.

"I told you the animals want nothing to do with me," Eliza says, shoving me a little. The feeling of her arm bumping against mine, even though we're both wearing long sleeves, sends my heart racing. Even after she moves back, toward her side of the path, it's like I can still sense her arm touching mine.

"It's wild how this whole thing"—at this Eliza sweeps her arms wide, motioning to the water in front of us—"was built to keep flooding from being superbad around here." She stops, considers this truth. "And still the flooding is *terrible* in this city. You just watch. The next big rain . . . it'll just happen again." She scowls, shoves her hands in the pockets of her gray hoodie. Then, as we turn a corner, pass some benches scrawled with graffiti, Eliza says, "I'm sorry. I . . . shouldn't have brought that up. The rain. I know . . . I mean, I'm sorry. I suck." She sounds defeated.

"No, you don't," I say. "Hey, you want to take a break? On one of those benches?"

Eliza glances over at me. Smiles softly.

"Okay."

"I didn't tell you," I say as we sit down, a few inches apart. "After you suggested, you know, *talking* to someone, I did. Talk to someone, I mean. I went to see Ms. Holiday, the Southwest High social worker."

"Oh wow," says Eliza, turning toward me, a lock of her long hair blowing across her face in the breeze and getting stuck in her mouth. It's sort of adorable. She pulls her hair back into a knot. "Do you think she's helping?"

I consider this for a moment.

"She's definitely trying to help," I say. "She's giving me, like, breathing exercises. Like breathing in a square to calm down." I show her a brief tutorial, and she watches, curious. Even though the exercises felt sort of goofy when Ms. Holiday showed them to me, I don't mind doing them in front of Eliza.

"Plus, she gave me this," I say. I pull the stone I picked out last week from my pocket. Even though I haven't really used it the way Ms. Holiday suggested, I figure it's at least something to carry it around with me. "I'm supposed to touch this to help me relax when I get anxious about the rain. It's . . . uh . . . I forget the word."

"Grounding?" says Eliza, wrinkling her brow.

"Yeah, grounding!" I grin. "You're so smart."

"Ha!" Eliza looks out at the wide expanse of water in front of us, her bright blue eyes tracking another heron that flies down, considers something in the water, and then departs. "I just read a lot. Not as smart as my know-everything, golden-child big brother. But whatever. I don't want to talk about him."

"I don't want to talk about mine, either," I agree, feeling a tug of guilt. Miguel isn't so bad. He really isn't. He can't help it if the best job he can find with his high school diploma is with Big Oil.

"Then let's not talk about them," says Eliza. She exhales, leans back against the bench. "Anyway, I'm glad you're going to talk to Ms. Holiday."

"Yeah," I say. "And . . . I wanted to talk to you about, like, having a club meeting about anxiety around weather. And the climate. Like, I'm pretty sure I'm not the only kid from Southwest or Baldwin who is dealing with this stuff after Harvey. I could work on some slides and give some tips. Like about the techniques Ms. Holiday has shared with me."

Eliz mulls this over, furrows her brow.

"That sounds . . . cool. At the next meeting you can gauge interest and then we can keep talking about the recycling education program and coming down here to clean up the waterhole." She motions with her foot toward a crushed can of Dr Pepper a few yards from the bench and scowls. "Like that could be recycled."

"Yeah," I say. "We can grab it on our way out of here."

The sun is starting to set for real now, and there's a coolness in the air. I peek down at the few inches between Eliza and me. Her thigh is right there, wrapped in denim. Her knees. Her beat-up Converse. Her hands buried inside her gray hoodie.

Her open face and her blue eyes. The way you look into them and just see her mind working.

If I were Miguel, I would know what to do next.

But I'm not Miguel. And I never will be. And I wonder not for the first time if the rest of my life will be me sitting next to girls, wondering what to do next and never figuring out the answer.

"Javi, can I ask you something?" Eliza says. I notice she's suddenly swinging her feet back and forth, kicking up a bit of gravel as she does.

"Sure," I say, turning toward her. She takes a deep breath and looks at me. Stares me right in the eye.

"Do you . . . do you ever think about kissing me?"

Oh wow.

Wow.

Something is happening.

But I freeze. Of course. I totally freeze. And she won't stop staring at me. Not in a creepy or scary way. Just in a superdirect Eliza way.

"I mean, I . . . ?" My voice comes out wobbly. Nervous.

Javi, get it together.

"Like . . . when I sent you that text that one time . . ." She finally looks away, finally gets a little bit flustered. Staring down at her knees, her feet still kicking, she says, "I sent you that text, that day that I babbled on to Ms. Bates about the buses idling? The day you called me dynamic?" She shakes her head, blushes hard now. My heart picks up speed. "Forget it. I'm recalling, like, these superspecific things that you've almost certainly forgotten."

Could she actually be the one who is embarrassed right now?

"I didn't forget."

At last. My brain remembers how to speak.

At this, she looks up at me again, like she's regained some courage.

"You didn't?" she asks, her voice hopeful. My heart is thrumming so hard it hurts, but in the best possible way.

"No," I say. "I didn't." There's a pause as I try to think of something more, but Eliza plows ahead.

"I basically told you . . . I mean, when I told you that I liked working with you, 'like a lot.'" At this she slides her hands out of her pockets and punctuates the end of the sentence with air quotes. "I mean, I said I liked you . . . a lot. And then the next time you texted me it was just about club stuff." She squeezes her eyes shut, shakes her head as if she wishes it would make her disappear. "Forget it."

"No, wait," I say. Even though there's no chance of rain, I find myself sliding one hand into my pocket and squeezing Ms. Holiday's stone for good luck. "Eliza, I read that text maybe five hundred times," I admit. "But . . . I mean, I *wanted* to think it meant something? But I wasn't, like, sure. And I didn't want to embarrass myself. I mean, more than I already have."

Finally, I've explained myself.

And when she hears my words, a lightness seems to come over Eliza. She stops kicking her feet.

"What do you mean? More than you already have?"

I shrug, roll my eyes. "I don't know. I'm not . . . I mean . . . I'm not a cool guy. I'm . . . I don't know what I'm doing."

Eliza breaks out into a grin. At the sight of it, blood starts rushing in my ears, and my heart speeds up to some world-record pace, I'm sure.

"Javier," she whispers, and the way she says my full name, the way she can't really pronounce it in perfect Spanish but the way she tries so hard? It's endearing. And so sweet.

"Yeah?" I manage. The space between us seems to be shrinking although I'm not sure how.

"Javier, I think you're such a cool guy," she says. "Like the coolest guy I know."

I raise my eyebrows, try to calm my heaving heart.

"You're pretty great yourself."

"I really want to kiss you," says Eliza.

"Okay," I say. Because it's all I *can* say.

The last thing I see is Eliza flashing me a big grin, and then reflexively I shut my eyes and before I know it her mouth is on mine, warm and soft. She kisses like she's sure of herself. My hands are reaching for her, one gently around her neck, one around her waist, holding her close to me. For the briefest moment I can't believe I'm pulling this off, but after I have that thought, my brain melts into nothing but how good it feels to be here, on this park bench with Eliza Brady, the most dynamic, beautiful girl I've ever met, kissing her with no plans to stop anytime soon.

ELIZA

I have been kissing Javier Garza for exactly two weeks and one day. Well, two weeks technically. Today is Friday, the day after the two-week anniversary of our first kiss at Willow Waterhole, and I fully intend to kiss him today, too.

Good grief, Eliza, I scold myself. *This is the boy you're kissing.* (Your boyfriend? Maybe.) *It's not necessary to track him in your planner, is it?*

Especially since I want to kiss Javi every day all day forever. He's an ongoing agenda item. I don't need to put him down on a list of tasks.

The door to Ms. Holiday's office opens, and out he comes, his face searching for mine. His sweet brown eyes. His tender smile. His gentleness. It all comes radiating out of him sometimes.

"Hey!" I call, and his gaze finds mine. He grins.

That grin.

"Hey," he says, dodging people traffic as he makes his way toward me. He brushes his lips lightly against mine, just for a moment.

Two weeks and one day.

"How was your talk with Ms. Holiday?" I ask as we head to my car. It's a half day, some staff development stuff. My aunt and uncle and baby Ethan are out of town visiting Dave's parents, and my folks are at work, so Javi is finally going to get to see my place for once.

Well, not my place, but the closest thing I have to one, anyway.

"It was good," says Javier. His hand reaches for mine, his fingers grazing mine until our hands are entwined. He holds hands just right. Sure of himself but not too sure. Don't get me wrong, I love kissing Javi, but I could be totally cool with just holding hands for a couple of hours, too.

As we slide into my Nissan, my phone buzzes. I peer down. It's Isabella.

It's been soooooo long and I'm booooored wanna come over this weekend?

I toss the phone into my backpack and the backpack into the back seat. I'll deal with Isabella's text later. The thought of responding, of hanging out, of telling her about Javi. It would all feel like some sort of weird obligation. Like hanging out with some distant cousin because you have to. This realization pinches just a bit, makes me feel just slightly guilty.

But the truth is, it's hard to think about Isabella when Javi is sitting next to me, picking out what music to listen to.

"So I'm gonna see your place," he says, his eyes scoping out my aunt and uncle's neighborhood. It's not as fancy as where I used to live; most of the houses are original 1950s ranch homes, but in considerably better shape than the ones in Javi's neighborhood.

I wonder what Javi would say if he saw my family's place on Ferris.

"It's sort of my place," I say, turning onto my aunt and uncle's street. "Remember I'm sharing a bedroom with an infant."

Javi laughs. He's familiar with Ethan's weird ability to know when I'm extra tired because he always seems to use those nights to wake up three or four times, wailing his poor little baby head off.

We head in the front door and past the dining room, the table there stacked as usual with mail and odds and ends.

"Most of the time, we all hang out in here," I say, motioning toward the kitchen and the den. It's about the same size as Javi's house, actually, but Heather and Dave have slightly newer appliances and more modern furniture. "And then this is me," I say, doubling back a little and heading down the long hall to the bedrooms.

I crack open the door to Ethan's nursery. Heather and Dave left everything neat and orderly before they went out. All of Ethan's blankets and burp cloths and bottles of baby powder and lotion are lined up on the shelves under the changing table. His stars-and-moon mobile hangs silently over the crib. The puffy, grinning clouds and smiling sun and green trees peer down from the walls, and on the border, animals march around the perimeter of the room in permanent formation.

"It's nature-themed," I say. "Obviously."

Javi looks it over. "I don't know if my brother and his girlfriend have a theme picked out," he says. "I didn't even know people had themes for a baby's room."

"Kind of ironic to me that you can create a perfect fake planet for your kid while the real planet he's living on is melting," I say. Javi nods, but he doesn't say anything.

"That's where you sleep?" he asks, motioning to the twin bed pressed into the corner, the flowered bedspread I've had since middle school pulled tight and neat over the sheets.

"Yes." I can feel my cheeks start to pink up. Maybe because I'm thinking of all the things that can happen on beds that don't involve sleeping. "Let's go get something to eat," I say, shutting the door behind us and silently wishing my cheeks will return to their normal hue by the time we get back to the kitchen.

I'm making my way to the refrigerator to ask Javi what he wants to drink when I feel him behind me, wrapping his arms around my waist.

"Is this okay?" he asks.

Instantly relaxing, I murmur yes, then turn around and put my arms around his neck, sinking into a kiss that leads to another kiss and then another. When we finally take a breath, I whisper, "That makes me feel . . . melty. Warm."

"You're making kissing sound like a grilled cheese sandwich," laughs Javi.

"So?" I ask, smiling and pulling away at last to get back to the fridge. "I really like grilled cheese sandwiches."

We end up on the couch with apples and potato chips and cold cans of ginger ale, Heather's biggest addiction, so there's always a huge supply. After we finish eating, we start fooling around again.

"When are we going to start working on ETUP stuff again?" I whisper as Javi kisses my neck, something I've learned only recently that I really, really like.

"Should we set a timer?" he mumbles into my ear, then laughs. His warm breath feels ticklish and good against my skin.

I pull away a little. "That's a good idea, actually," I say. "For every thirty minutes of work, we can make out for thirty minutes."

Javier laughs so loud I think he's going to fall off the couch. "What about fifteen minutes of work and forty-five minutes of making out?" he offers.

"Negotiations are final," I say, sliding farther away down the couch so I'm not tempted.

"Fine, fine," he agrees, pulling out a notebook and his school-issued laptop from the backpack he's dumped by the couch. I reach for my own laptop and planner. I want to update our recycling schedule, pick a date for a Willow Waterhole trash pickup and put the information on our Instagram, plus check on the petition to get the school buses to stop idling.

"You know, making out is going to have to be put on hold over the break," I say, opening up my calendar. "My grandparents are taking us to this resort outside of Austin. It's called Lost Pines or something." I don't mention that I overheard my father telling my mother that his parents were being very generous with this gift and that Lost Pines costs thousands for a week's stay. My dad's family has some money. My grandparents live in a very nice condominium in Austin, and they belong to a club where you can sign for meals instead of paying for them while you're there.

"That sucks for us," Javier says, opening up some slides he's been working on. I see the words "anxiety" and "weather" complete with a radar image of Hurricane Harvey, the reds and yellows and greens and blues blotting out Houston, devouring it like a monster. "I mean, I hope you'll have a good time. But how long will you be gone?"

"We leave the Saturday after we get out of school and then come back the afternoon of New Year's Eve. We'll be gone almost the entire break."

Javi messes around with font size on the slide, increasing and then decreasing it. "We're not really going anywhere like that," he says. "But I will have, like, five hundred family gatherings and events. Driving to San Antonio to visit my grandparents, driving to Rosario and Miguel's house, driving to Rosario's parents' place. Like, so many gatherings." He rolls his eyes, then tips the laptop toward me. "How does this look?" he asks.

I peer over. "Nice. Flip through it."

Javi previews his slide deck, and I can see that in addition to having information about anxiety and the weather, he's added some new slides, too. The first is some stock clip art illustration of a bunch of teenagers of varying racial backgrounds all with their fists in the air next to a picture of the earth. Hovering above are the words The Planet and Racial Justice.

"I decided this was superimportant, too," he says, moving to the next slide, which shows a picture of a little boy who looks like a young Javi holding an inhaler to his mouth. The body of text next to the picture reads: Did you know a disproportionate percentage of people of color live in places that are polluted with toxic waste? Higher incidents of asthma and cancer in communities of color is just one example of why we need to talk about race and ethnicity when we talk about climate and the environment.

The next slide shows a picture of Black residents trying to evacuate their home during Hurricane Katrina. Next to that image, Javi has typed: In places where climate change has had a negative impact, people of color often don't have the means to flee or rebuild.

And then on a third slide, where Javi has a picture of a map of part of the African coast, are the words Poor countries with large populations of people of color that actually contribute the least to carbon emissions are on track to be some of the most affected by rising sea waters.

"Wow," I say, taking in all this information. Not all of it is totally new to me, but I cringe at the realization that I didn't know more. After Hurricane Harvey, everyone kept talking about how climate change was an equal-opportunity offender, and in some ways, yes, that's true. But obviously, it's really *not* true at all. Suddenly, the image of rich white people terraforming Mars and abandoning everyone else on the planet flies through my mind. Then, just as quickly, I picture the school buses idling, burning fossil fuels while executives at CITGO and Exxon and Schlumberger rack up the big bucks.

Suddenly, my heart starts to pick up speed. A fidgety feeling comes over me.

It's too late, Eliza. We're running out of time.

I squeeze my eyes shut for a moment and tell the mocking voice in my head to be quiet. My heart still racing, I open up the Google form that's been collecting signatures and comments about the buses. I think maybe getting back to work will help me brush off this unsettled feeling.

"Hey," says Javi, and his voice sounds a little hurt. "I wasn't totally done going through the slides."

"Oh, I'm . . . I'm sorry." My voice sounds strange to me, quieter and thin. But I stop what I'm doing and set my laptop on the coffee table. "Didn't mean to interrupt," I say. "Honestly."

Javier says it's okay, and he doesn't seem that upset. But as he quietly walks me through slide after slide of even more depressing statistics, I suddenly find myself wanting to climb out of my own skin. My heart is still moving at superspeed, and now my breathing is faster and my cheeks are warm. Then I notice a picture of a water bottle on one of the slides, and my brain does that thing it's always doing. Mentally calculates the life of that *one* bottle, quickly envisions all the plastic bottles just *one* person throws away in a lifetime filling up this room, this house, this entire neighborhood.

It's too much. It's too late.

The voice is back.

There's not enough time, Eliza. You have to do something now. You have to take action now. There's not enough time. There's no more time! Why don't you just give up?

I feel hot, restless. But I don't want to hurt Javi's feelings again, so I just nod as he speaks. Only now my ears are buzzing. The apples I ate earlier are churning in my stomach, my palms feel clammy. I guess I must look strange enough that Javier notices and puts his laptop down next to mine on the coffee table.

"Hey, are you okay?"

I nod, but I pull my legs up under my chin. Wrap my arms around them. Suddenly, I remember the first time I hung out at Javi's house and *I* was the one who kept talking and *he* was the one who got uncomfortable.

"I just . . . I'm fine," I say, answering his question, trying to catch my breath, still fighting the urge to get up and run, move. Anything to burn off these uncomfortable feelings.

I wonder if getting back to what I was doing before Javi started sharing would help me. "I read depressing statistics all the time, too," I say. "It isn't that they aren't important. But I just . . . sometimes I like to focus on . . . action. It helps me feel better about everything, you know?" I take a breath, try to get control of myself.

Javi nods like he gets it but not totally. Still, he doesn't push.

"I'm sorry, I shouldn't have gone on and on," he says. "But . . . you seem a little shaken up. Do you want to . . . talk about this?" I think about the hours he's spent with Ms. Holiday, discussing his feelings. I wonder if he's trying the same techniques on me. Something about that is really sweet, honestly, but right now, I don't want to talk about anything. I keep thinking working on club stuff will help, but the truth is I can't quite focus on that, either.

"Hey," Javi says, his brow furrowed, his eyes full of concern for me. "Eliza?"

I just sit there, my knees still under my chin. Suddenly, I can't speak.

Javi scoots over, the warmth of his body soon pressed up against me. Finally, something feels good. I curl up in a ball, snuggle up as close as I can to his chest. I'm taller than Javi, but right now I feel smaller. Vulnerable. I want to vanish into his Southwest High T-shirt, disappear into its sea of blue. I finally take a deep, slow breath. My heart begins to slow just a little bit.

Suddenly, just as I'm starting to calm down, there's a sound in the dining room. Keys dropping, steps coming toward us. Javi and I turn, surprised looks on our faces, our limbs still basically entwined.

"Eliza?" asks my father. Then his eyes take in everything on the couch in one moment. "Oh."

Javi and I pull apart—not that we were doing much, but it sure doesn't look that way—and Javi stands up, flustered. I stand up, too, because I figure if we're all standing, that makes it one millionth of a percent less awkward.

"Dad, this is Javier Garza," I say. Poor Javi. He looks like he's about to pass out.

"Hello," my father says, reaching out his hand. "I'm Matt Brady."

"Hello, Mr. Brady, sir," Javi says, almost stuttering.

"You can call me Matt," my father says. Suddenly, I realize my dad appears as uncomfortable as Javi and me.

"We were working on our club," I say. "The environmental one. You know we're copresidents."

My dad nods like he doesn't really believe me. I'm grateful that at least our open laptops have club stuff on the screens.

"Well, Javier, nice to meet you," my dad says, walking to the kitchen sink to pour himself a glass of water. I'm pretty sure he's just giving himself something to do. "I'm sure my daughter has let you know of my allegiance to evil Big Oil." He says this last sentence like it's a joke, only I know it's not entirely one.

Poor Javi doesn't know what to say to that. He does this awkward chuckle and remains silent.

"Listen, I'm going to take Javier home," I say. "I didn't think you'd be getting here so early." Javier starts to pack his stuff, rushing, it seems, to get out of here.

"I took the afternoon off," he says. "Dentist appointment and I wanted to stop by the house to check on stuff." He drinks the water and keeps his eyes trained out the window over the kitchen sink.

"It was nice to meet you, Mr. Brady," says Javier. "I mean, Matt."

"Nice to meet you, too, Javier," my father says, turning around and giving a half wave. I can't tell if he's upset or just weirded out.

In the car on the way back to Javi's house, Javi keeps pretending to bang his head on the dashboard in mock self-destruction.

"I can't believe that's how I met your dad," he says. "Dang. That was so awkward. It was terrible."

"I know," I say, sighing. "But . . . I mean, I don't think he hated you or anything."

"You were basically in my lap when he met me," Javi says.

I shrug. "Yeah, true. But my dad . . . I have to give him credit. He's never been one of those dudes that's, like, I'm going to get my shotgun if you come near my daughter. That's not his style."

"I guess no shotgun is a start," Javi mutters, his voice thick with sarcasm.

"It's more that I've never really had a boyfriend," I say. "So I think I just surprised him."

Javi groans, buries his face in his hands. "I'm never going over there again."

"Don't say that," I tell him, gently shoving him with my elbow.

"We do have more privacy at my house," he answers as I pull up in front of his house. "For ETUP and . . . other things."

I grin, but with my dad fresh on my mind and how unsettled I'd been feeling right before he walked in, I'm not exactly down for a car make-out session. After a quick kiss and another reassurance that my dad won't beat him up, Javi heads for his front door and I make my way back home, where I find my dad watching television. *SportsCenter* as usual, or as I like to call it, Dudes Yell at Each Other.

"Hey," I say.

My dad presses mute on the remote.

I take a chance and sit down, but I'm not sure what to say. My dad scratches at his forearm, clearly uncomfortable.

"I'm sorry I surprised you," he says. After a beat, he says, "So is Javier your . . . I don't know if people say *boyfriend* and *girlfriend* anymore, but . . ." He's staring at a now-silent commentator on *SportsCenter*, clearly preferring to make eye contact with him rather than me.

"Yeah," I say. "I mean, only recently."

My dad nods slowly. "Your mom probably would like to meet him at some point." He doesn't say anything about wanting to get to know him more.

"Okay," I say.

"I saw what you were working on. For your club? About the buses idling?"

I get up off the couch and shut my laptop, then draw it back to my chest. I don't sit back down.

"What, is it something top secret?" my father asks. I get that he's trying to make a joke, but it falls flat with me. He could have asked me more about Javier at least.

"Do you not want me dating someone who's Mexican?" I ask.

My father falls back into the couch like I just shoved him, and hard, too.

"What?" he asks, looking at me at last. "Eliza, what makes you say that? That's absurd. I didn't raise you to think like that, and you know it." He's right. I know he's right. But something in me has been set off.

"You hardly asked about him!" I say. "And then all you want to do is pick on my club stuff." This isn't really true, I know. It *feels* true, somehow. But logically I know it's not. Still, I'm irritated. I'm irritated that my father works for the oil industry and doesn't seem to care. I'm irritated that he clearly likes my older brother more than me, no matter what I do. I'm irritated that he came home early on the *one* day that Javier and I were going to have my house—wait, not *my* house, not *really*—all to ourselves.

And I'm irritated—no, I'm freaked out—by whatever it is that happened to me when Javi started showing me his slides.

My father throws up his hands. "I didn't think you'd want me to ask about the guy you were . . . *making out with* . . . on the couch! I thought that would embarrass you!"

"We weren't making out!" I shout.

My father grabs the remote, signaling to me that this conversation, or rather, this attempt at conversation, is over.

"Eliza, I cannot win with you. Ever." At this he unmutes the television. The guy on *SportsCenter* is shouting about some football player with a torn Achilles tendon as if that were the most important thing on the planet. I almost want to shout over him, yell at him *and* at my dad that there are so many things more important than sports or holidays or dental appointments or home repairs, and that I wish someone in my family other than just me would pay attention to them. But all I can think to do is turn on my heel and storm off, making sure I slam the door to the nursery extra loud behind me.

They call us Clutch City.

As in we come through in a clutch.

And what bigger clutch situation is there than when your world is underwater, drowning in rain that doesn't ever seem to stop?

In the immediate aftermath, we showed what makes this place valuable. Beautiful. We proved we were the same city that had welcomed our friends from New Orleans with open arms after they endured their own weather trauma, their own ferocious storm. We made headlines again for our compassion, this time the compassion we gave to each other.

We showed up at the houses of strangers and mucked out old carpet, thick with bayou water. We opened up free day cares at our houses of worship to welcome children whose parents had to figure out how to rebuild their lives. We donated money and canned goods and new underwear and bottles of bleach. We found ways, big and small, to prove to ourselves and each other that our humanity was still here, that it hadn't been swept away like everything else in the flood.

We have so many stories of those days after the storm. The English as a Second Language teacher with her band of students working to clean out flooded homes. The neighbors who'd lost everything gathering in a local synagogue to make breakfast for each other. The explosion of posts on community Facebook pages offering help of all kinds, including ice-cold Dr Peppers upon request. The goodness was enough to make us cry, a release after so much horror.

On one of the talk shows, the columnist from the New York Times *made a point that made us proud. That we, Houstonians, make up the most ethnically diverse city in the country, and if we can come together—so can this nation. We nodded in agreement. Even with our flaws, in many ways we'd lived this truth for a long time.*

The sun came back out. The planet kept spinning. And the trauma lived on in our bodies and hearts and minds. We were proud of who we were and what we'd done for each other, but every time thunder cracked the sky, we peered up with fear and wondered if and when we would have to do it all over again.

JAVIER

Eliza pulls her Nissan to the curb.

"Whose car?" she says, pointing to the Honda Civic in the driveway.

"Oh, that's my brother's girlfriend's car," I say. "Rosario. I don't know why she's here."

"When's the baby due?"

"Next month," I answer. "She's huge."

Eliza elbows me. "Be nice. It can't be easy." Still staring at Rosario's car, she murmurs, "I wonder if I'll ever have a kid. Sometimes I don't think it would be ethical."

I frown, eye her carefully.

"Why?" I ask, confused.

Eliza sighs. "Ugh, I don't want to get into something super-depressing now, when Winter Break is finally upon us. I just meant . . . you know, because of climate change. Like, I look at sweet baby Ethan and imagine how bad things might be for *him*, and I can't even imagine having a kid of my own, you know?"

I don't know what to say. I've never denied the severity of the situation we find ourselves in. Like I'd shared with Ms. Holiday in our session yesterday afternoon, working on my presentation about climate anxiety and racial justice has only opened my eyes even more about what we as humans have to do to reverse what's happening right now. But the idea of not having kids? It kind of breaks my heart that's how Eliza feels. And it makes me remember what Rosario said to me on Thanksgiving, about wanting a nice planet for her baby.

"Anyway, forget it," Eliza continues. "Let's not think about that. I'm leaving tomorrow morning and won't see you for almost two weeks. I hate it." She frowns, then slowly transforms that frown into a smile, complete with a knowing look that ends with the two of us kissing in the front seat of her car for a good five minutes.

"I hate that you're leaving, too," I manage when we finally pull apart for a moment. "It would have been cool to have extra time to just hang out. No school. Take a break from club stuff."

Eliza shakes her head like she's scolding me. "No breaks for me. I have to finish a dialectical journal assignment for AP Lang and work on some college essays. And think about ETUP's spring semester agenda."

"Eliza," I say, and now I'm the one who acts like *she's* in trouble, "you gotta take a break sometime."

She rolls her eyes, then says, "Okay, let's take a break right now, then."

More kissing. Dang, it feels so good to kiss her. It's difficult not to let my mind wander to what could happen between us after we move on from kissing, but I don't think Eliza is ready for that just yet, and to be honest, I'm not 100 percent sure I am, either.

But I can't help but fantasize a little about Eliza and Javier's spring semester agenda.

Finally, she has to go, and after we promise each other that we'll text and FaceTime every day, I watch her drive off, trying not to think too much about the fact that we won't see each other for what feels like forever.

As I head inside, I try not to notice something else. Or at least, I try not to obsess on it, because Ms. Holiday says noticing is okay, but panicking is a sign I need self-care. I kind of dislike that term, "self-care." It's corny. It makes me think of moms taking bubble baths after a long day or something, not a thing for a teenage boy. But anyway, that's what Ms. Holiday says.

A dark, gloomy cluster of rain clouds is building in the sky, thick as carpet. I remember Ms. Holiday's stone, which I've carried around mostly out of obligation. Not necessarily because I think it will work. I let my hands briefly run over the outside of my right pocket, to make sure it's there. And then I take my keys out to let myself in.

"Rosario?" I shout. "Miguel?"

"It's just me, and I'm in your parents' bedroom!" Rosario's voice calls out. I make my way down to the end of the hallway and find Rosario standing over several stacks of baby clothes on my mom and dad's bed.

"Hey," I say. "What's up?" I know Eliza said it was rude, but she really does look like she could have this baby any day. A tiny sliver of olive skin peeks out from underneath her lime-green shirt, the one that says *Yes, I'm Still Pregnant* on it.

"I'm off today," she says, "and your mom wanted me to drop by and sort through some of these clothes the women at the church gave me. See what I want and what I don't want." She holds up a tiny T-shirt that looks to be about the size of my palm. Printed on the front are the words *Party at My Crib at 2 O'Clock!* What is it with corny sayings on maternity and baby clothes? But Rosario grins at me like it's the most hilarious thing she's ever seen in her life.

"The trouble is, I want *everything*," she says, folding the small piece of clothing and placing it carefully in a paper sack from Kroger. "Miguel is going to freak out when I come home with more clothes. But I want Valentina to be the best-dressed baby on the block. Or at least in the day care." She digs through more stuff.

"That's nice she got all that stuff for you," I say.

"Yeah, your mom is the best," she says before holding up some frilly yellow thing. I'm not even sure if it's a dress or a shirt or a pair of pajamas. "*Wow*, look at this, Javi!" She laughs. I just nod and smile like it's awesome.

Just then my phone buzzes. I pull it out of my back pocket.

I already miss you and also you are such a good kisser.

Oh man. Geez. Wow.

"Javi?" Rosario's voice calls me out of my stupor. She's wearing an amused expression. "You are standing there with the stupidest grin on your face, you know."

I blush and tuck my phone away, like Rosario can read the words from where she's standing. Then again, from the way she's looking at me, I have a feeling she can guess who they're from.

"Your ride from Thanksgiving?" she asks, reading my mind.

"Maybe," I say, but we both know I'm not fooling her.

"Well, you'd better go respond immediately," she says, turning her attention back to the stack of baby clothes. "But from the look on your face, that must have been some text."

Feeling like the coolest guy in the world (me, feeling cool!), I head back to the kitchen, where I grab a Jumex and a bag of potato chips and make my way to my bedroom.

I throw on *The Queen Is Dead*, situate myself comfortably on my bed, and consider how to reply to Eliza.

Takes one to know one, I tap back at last. And I miss you so much already too.

Just then Dominic texts, asking if I want to hang out tomorrow at Monroe Park.

Sure that's cool, I respond. He mentions JoJo and Felipe might be there, too. I think the guys have a sense something might be up with Eliza and me even though I haven't mentioned it yet. But maybe tomorrow might be the day I officially tell them I have the *greatest* girlfriend in the world. They might be surprised it's a Baldwin girl, but I know they'll be cool about it.

I stretch out even more on my bed, starting to feel pretty good about this break. Even though Eliza won't be around, I'm looking forward to nearly two weeks without homework. Two weeks of sleeping in, hanging out with my friends, flirting via text with Eliza, and letting my mind wander about what happens next between us.

I'm feeling so good, in fact, that the slow rumble of thunder outside doesn't set me off right away. My ears perk up. My breath grows just a bit more shallow.

When you feel your body start to get anxious, that's a sign that you have to start to take care of yourself. Ms. Holiday's words run through my head as another slow roll of thunder builds, followed by the gradual slapping of fat raindrops against the window over my desk.

Just then, another text from Eliza pops over my phone.

You okay? Wanna talk? It's followed by an umbrella and a red heart.

I soften at the sight of it. And part of me *does* want to talk to her, but I also want to see how I can handle this right now, alone in my room.

I'm cool thanks. You should focus on packing. I know you have to go soon.

She sends me back an exploding heart GIF and the demand that I text or call her if I need to.

I sit up on the side of my bed and peer out my bedroom window. The sky is definitely darkening.

There can't be any harm in at least trying one of the breathing techniques that Ms. Holiday taught me, here alone in my room where no one can see me. Here where it doesn't matter if it's corny or not, as long as it works. I figure I'll start with the one where you breathe in and out as your finger traces a box. I do this four or five times, focusing on my breathing so I can't pay as much attention to what's happening outside. Then I slide my hand into my pocket and pull out the stone I picked out. I stare at it, at the small, glinting slivers of iridescent something bleeding through it. At the small ridges and smooth spots and the heaviness of it in my fingers. I take another deep breath.

I'm doing it. I can do it. I can get through this storm. I know I can.

I'm already imagining telling Ms. Holiday all about this personal victory when I hear Rosario's voice, only this time coming from the den off the kitchen.

"Javi, can you come here for a second?" she asks.

I slide my stone back into my pocket and head into the den. There, I find Rosario lying on our couch on her left side, her hand resting on her belly. There's a slight frown on her face, and she's biting her bottom lip.

"Can you bring me a glass of orange juice?" she asks.

"Yeah, of course," I say, not sure what's going on. "A big glass or . . . ?"

"Any size, it's fine." Her voice is tight. Anxious. I glance outside the big bay window at the front of the house. Even though it's not even five o'clock yet, it seems much later because the sky has grown so dark.

I pour Rosario some juice in an orange plastic cup that says *Houston Astros* on it. For some reason she seems too nervous to handle glass.

"Are you okay?" I ask, handing her the drink. She sits up and gulps it down. "Want more?"

"No, that's good for now," she says, lying back down on her side. She puts her hand on her belly, starts moving it all over. Her face looks like mine when I'm stuck on a problem in math class.

A sense of unease starts to build inside of me, along with the storm brewing outside. Something is wrong, but I don't know if I should say anything. If I should call Miguel, or my parents.

"Rosario, what's going on?"

She sits up, her face starting to crumple into panic.

"I haven't felt the baby move. It just hit me while I was going through the clothes. Normally I feel her kicking at least a few times every so often." She presses her palms against her belly, like she's trying to communicate with Valentina through telepathy. I feel totally out of my depth, confused about what to do and say next.

"They say if this happens you're supposed to drink something sugary and then keep track of their kicks, but there's been nothing!" At this her voice breaks and her eyes start to spill tears, just as a loud crack of thunder splits the sky outside.

When you start to panic, practice self-care.

Ms. Holiday's reminder was easier to take when it was just me in my bedroom, chilling to The Smiths and thinking about how I could relax over break.

"Let me call Miguel," I say, pulling my phone from my pocket.

"Wait," she says, "let me call the doctor first. It might be easier for him to meet us there . . . or at the hospital." This last phrase comes out laced with so much anxiety she can barely get the words out.

"What can I do?" I ask. "Do you want more orange juice?"

Rosario shakes her head no. "Thanks, Javi. Let me just make the call." She walks back toward my parents' bedroom, I guess for some privacy.

I stand in the middle of our den, my ears tuned equally to the sound of Rosario's voice and the drumming of rain on our roof. A sinking feeling courses through me.

No, Javier. Stay cool. Rosario needs you.

I take the stone out of my pocket and worry my thumb over it, more times than I can count. Then I start pacing up and down our den, my eyes taking in the framed school pictures of Miguel, Daniela, and me when we were small, our chubby faces smiling and showing off missing baby teeth. Part of me wants to call or text Eliza, but I'm too tense to get my thoughts in order. Too stressed about what happens next.

At last Rosario walks out of my parents' bedroom, moving with purpose even if her face is still pale and covered in panic.

"They want me to come into the doctor's office," she says, grabbing her purse and keys off the kitchen table. I can see her hands are shaking. She drops the keys to her Honda on the hardwood floor, where they land with a loud clatter.

"Wait," I say, reaching for them. "You're in no position to drive, Rosario. You have to wait until Miguel gets here."

"From the east side of town? At this time? It's almost rush hour, Javier, and it's starting to storm outside. I'm going to call him and tell him to meet me at the doctor's office." At this she pulls her phone out, then collapses into sobs.

"I can't do it! I can't call him!" She places her phone down on the kitchen table and presses both palms against her belly. "Move, Valentina. Please!"

I know what I have to do. Even though the idea is almost too scary to say out loud, I have to. There's no doubt in my mind.

"Rosario, I'm going to drive you," I say. The keys are already in my hand, and before I can think about it too much, I race into my bedroom and grab my wallet from my backpack.

"Javi, you only just got your license," says Rosario, taking a shaky breath. "And it's the Med Center." The Med Center is a twisting maze of massive hospitals and parking garages, apparently always under construction, with difficult-to-read signs and lots of honking horns and sirens. My mom once told me she chooses doctors *because* their offices aren't located there.

"I turn seventeen next month," I remind her. "I've been driving for almost a year!" True, most of that driving has been in our neighborhood, running errands to Kroger and Walgreens for my parents.

And never in the middle of a torrential Houston thunderstorm.

"Javier, are you sure?"

"Yes," I lie. "Rosario, let's stop talking about it. Come on!"

Afraid to slow down even to grab my raincoat or an umbrella, I usher Rosario into the Honda. The cold December rain hits the nape of my neck and my forearms, and even in the few seconds it takes to make it to the car, my hair is half soaked. There's a moment when I sit in the front seat and feel a hot surge of anxiety so powerful I honestly think I might hurl right here in Rosario's car, but I force myself to take a deep breath in, then out. Rosario is too busy buckling her seatbelt to notice, fortunately. I adjust the seat and the mirrors just like they taught us in driver's ed, flip on the headlights and windshield wipers, and put the car in reverse, my heart beating as hard and as fast as the wipers swishing in front of my face.

Rosario is giving me directions, one hand on her belly the entire time. I want to ask her if she's felt Valentina move yet, but I figure if that happened, she would tell me. I also need to use every bit of mental energy to focus on driving.

We have to get onto the freeway briefly, and I find myself leaning forward, so close to the steering wheel it probably isn't safe. But it's so hard to drive in this downpour. I'm crawling along in the right lane, worried I'm not going fast enough but also too terrified to go any faster. The drumbeat of the rain on the roof of the car sounds like machine-gun fire, and there's a constant squeak in one of the windshield wipers that keeps my heart racing and my breathing shallow. At one point, I dig my thumbnails into the steering wheel so hard I'm sure I've left moon-shaped marks.

"Wow, this rain is awful," Rosario says. She's calmed down as much as possible after spending the first few moments in the car in a frantic phone call with Miguel. ("I don't know. Javi's driving me. I'm not sure. I'm freaking out, too. Get to Dr. Ortiz's office, but drive safe, please. Yes. Yes. No. I'll text you as soon as I know something.")

I swallow, keep my eyes trained on the pickup truck in front of me, convinced that any moment I'll lose control and send

Rosario and me slamming into the back bumper. I shudder briefly at the thought.

"Okay, exit Fannin," Rosario directs, her hands still pressed hopefully against her belly. As I maneuver the car down the exit ramp, I finally allow myself the thought that something might be seriously wrong with Valentina. I don't know anything about babies or being pregnant, but from the way Rosario is acting and the way her doctor wanted her to come in right away, it must be serious. I know this baby was a surprise, but from the way Miguel and Rosario have been acting, I also know they can't wait to meet their daughter.

I really want to meet her, too. The idea of being a fun tío started to sink in recently. Playing music for Valentina, making her little origami swans. Taking her to the playground near Monroe Elementary and pushing her on the swings.

"Turn here, this parking garage," says Rosario, motioning to a garage attached to a massive multistory building. "You can drop me off and park. We're almost there and I just want to get inside." She sniffs, tries to hold back tears. Like a magical off switch has been hit somewhere, the rain goes from torrential to nothing as I pull into the safety of the garage. I turn the wipers off and exhale.

Rosario lets herself out and motions where to pull in to park.

"I've got it, but tell me where to find you," I say.

"Houston Women's Specialists," she says. "Third floor."

Before I can respond that I've heard her, she's slammed the car door and rushed off. I have to go up several floors in the garage before I find a spot. At last, I turn off the ignition and slide the keys out, taking a moment to stare at them in my right hand.

I did it. I actually made it here in the rain with Rosario.

I give myself only a second to be proud. I'm too worried about Rosario and the baby. Navigating the signs out of the parking garage and to Rosario's doctor takes my last bit of energy, and by the time I open the door into the doctor's office waiting room, I realize my entire body feels on fire from exhaustion, like my legs might cut right out from under me.

"Can I help you?" comes a voice from the front desk; it belongs to a short blond woman in pink scrubs. I guess this is definitely a waiting room where a teenage boy all by himself stands out, seeing as it's full of pregnant women checking their phones and flipping through magazines.

"Uh, yeah, I drove my brother's girlfriend here?" I start, making my way to the front desk. "Rosario Rayo?"

"Have a seat and hang on," she says, motioning toward the sea of chairs.

The windows facing out onto the rest of the Med Center reveal a brightening sky, small patches of blue emerging from gray. Hurricane Harvey came for four days and pounded my city, but this storm is more classic H-Town. All bluster and drama and force, gone as quickly as it came.

I take a seat and pull my phone out and set to crafting a text to Eliza. I'm not sure if I should text my parents. I don't want to freak them out without being able to give any sort of news. Maybe I should just call them? No, that would be too scary without more information.

I start a new text to Eliza to tell her what's going on and ask her what I should do when Miguel tears into the waiting room, practically slamming the door off its hinges in the process. He must have broken every speed limit and rule of the road to get here so fast. I jump up.

"Javi!" he shouts. At this point he's caught the attention of half the waiting room, and there are several concerned gazes trained on him. "Have they told you anything?"

I'm about to tell him no when a different woman behind the front desk, an older Black woman in purple scrubs, comes around and offers to guide him to where they're checking out Rosario. I don't even have a chance to answer Miguel's questions before he disappears behind a door with the woman.

I finally do manage to text Eliza, my eyes darting up to the door every second in the hopes that I'll get some sort of news soon.

OMG that's so scary . . . definitely wait to tell your parents. Do you know anything yet?

No just in the waiting room. I drove her here in the rain.

Seriously?

Yes. I'm not sure how but I did it.

I don't get to read Eliza's response because just then, Miguel and Rosario come out from behind the door Miguel had disappeared through a few minutes earlier. The first thing I notice is Rosario's broad smile, and suddenly I feel a million pounds lighter.

"Everything okay?" I say, getting up from the chair.

"Oh, Javier, you're the actual best," Rosario says, pulling me in for a tight hug. Miguel reaches over and rubs my head like I'm ten.

"What happened?" I ask. The few people in the waiting room who can overhear us are peering over and smiling, vicariously enjoying our good news.

"They put a fetal heart monitor on and she's just fine," Rosario says, patting her belly. "The doctor explained that sometimes toward the end it's harder to feel the baby move because they get so big. I'm used to her being active around this time of day, but it's possible she was sleeping. And just as they were taking the monitor off, she kicked me!"

"She's big on afternoon naps like me," says Miguel. Relief is etched all over his face, and he can't take his eyes off Rosario.

The three of us head out of the office, Rosario practically skipping out. As we wait for the elevator, she touches her belly again and starts laughing. "What a stinker. *Now* she's kicking up a storm. Feel, Javi." Rosario grabs my hand without asking permission, presses it against her stomach. There's a *tap, tap, tapping* under my hand, like Valentina is trying to knock hello. It's admittedly a little freaky, but of course I don't say that.

"Wow," I manage.

"She wants to thank you for getting us here safely," says Rosario.

I shrug like it was nothing.

As we head down the elevator in the direction of the parking garage, Rosario demands the keys to the Honda. "You take your brother home in your truck," she commands Miguel. "Poor Javi deserves a break after what it took to get us here."

"Are you sure you're okay to drive home?" Miguel asks, frowning.

"I could fly home I'm so happy," says Rosario. It's amazing how much better she looks. Her face is pink and glowing, and she can't stop smiling. "Please. I'll go home and start cooking. Oh! She just kicked again!"

Finally, Miguel is convinced, and we part ways in the garage. Miguel doesn't say much as we wind down the levels of the garage to Fannin Street, but as we pull out into full-blown Med Center rush hour traffic, he exhales hard.

"Javi," he starts, gently punching my left shoulder, "thanks a lot, man. You're the hero today."

Me. The hero. My big brother, essentially the coolest dude I know, thinks *I'm* the hero. On the same day my girlfriend tells me I'm a great kisser.

Seriously, is this my life?

"I'm not a hero," I say, even though I'm pretty sure I'll be replaying Miguel's words in my head on the regular for the rest of my life. "It was nothing." But then, mulling it over, I recalculate. I want to be honest because honestly? I'm really proud of what I did. "Actually, I was scared out of my mind," I admit. "I . . . ever since Harvey . . ." I search for the words.

"The rain?" asks Miguel. "I know it makes you nervous."

"Yeah," I say, nodding, not embarrassed. "But doing this . . . It helped me know I can be okay. I can handle it."

Miguel nods. "That's cool. You really can handle it, Javi."

I nod back in response, and as Miguel comes to a red light, I finally sneak a peek at my phone to read Eliza's response to my last message. She's texted a bunch of excited GIFs and messages that say how excited she is for me. I smile in spite of myself.

We pause at a stoplight and Miguel notices me peering into the screen like a goofball.

"What's making you grin like that?" he says, amused.

I flush. "This girl," I say. "Actually, my girlfriend."

The light turns green and Miguel pulls forward. "Your girlfriend?" His eyebrows dart up, just a little. But I can tell he's happy for me. I pull up Eliza's picture, the one of the two of us on the ETUP Instagram.

"This is her," I say, flashing the screen in his direction. Miguel waits until it's safe to glance over. His eyebrows go up again.

"Let me guess. She goes to Baldwin?" I know he's saying this because she's white.

"Yeah," I say. "But she's cool. I promise. Her name is Eliza."

"Huh," Miguel says, contemplating this development. "How'd you meet?"

I remind him about the ETUP club and how she asked me to be copresident. This time, I don't focus too much on the Big Oil thing. I mostly just talk about the recycling program and our plans to do cleanups at Willow Waterhole.

"You should," says Miguel. "People can be nasty throwing their stuff around there."

"Yeah," I say. My mind floats back to my first kiss with Eliza on that bench overlooking the water, but I don't tell Miguel about that. That's just for Eliza and me.

"Actually, she sort of helped me with the rain thing," I say, as Miguel finally manages to crawl onto the freeway heading home. Traffic is practically at a standstill. I stare out the front window, the sea of idling cars in between us and home, and imagine what Eliza would say about fossil fuels.

"How'd she help?" my brother asks.

I wonder how Miguel will react to news that I'm talking to Ms. Holiday. Will he think it's weird? It's not anything I can picture him doing. He barely ever talks about how he's feeling beyond just the basics. But something about this conversation makes me think I can tell him.

"She told me to talk to someone," I say, answering his question. "Do you remember that social worker at Southwest? This white lady named Ms. Holiday?"

Miguel thinks for a moment, then quietly curses at some driver in front of him in a Toyota that doesn't know what he's doing.

"Holiday? Like tiny? Blond hair?"

"Yeah," I say.

"I think I remember her," he says. "I remember kids saying she was cool."

I nod, agreeing with this assessment.

"She is pretty cool," I say. "Anyway, Eliza said maybe talking to someone would help me feel better about everything, so I started seeing her, talking to her. She gave me breathing exercises to calm me down when I get nervous, and even though she was really nice, at first I thought they were sort of stupid. But I tried them for the first time today, right before I ended up having to take Rosario to the doctor." I think about the stone in my pocket, but I don't say anything about that.

Maybe Miguel would understand it, but right now it feels too personal.

"Breathing exercises?" says Miguel. "Like . . . what?" He seems genuinely curious if not still a little confused.

"Uh, well . . ." I start, sifting through all the exercises Ms. Holiday has shared with me. I end up settling on the box breathing because it's easy to show Miguel while he navigates the traffic.

"You breathe in like this," I say, drawing a line on the invisible box in front of me, "then hold it, then exhale," I say, drawing another line. Then I do it once more, finishing out the box. It's kind of awkward doing this in front of my brother. I'm a little embarrassed. But really only a little bit.

"So that helps, like, chill you out?" Miguel asks, looking at me, surprised.

"I know it sounds kind of weird, but yeah, I guess it does."

Miguel nods, processing all this. Then he puts on some music, maybe to signal we're done talking, and we head home.

When we finally pull into the driveway, I ask Miguel if he wants to come in.

"Nah," he says, "I want to get home to Rosario. You'll fill in the folks and Daniela, yeah?"

"Yeah, for sure," I say.

"Milk it for all it's worth," says Miguel. "Get Mom to order from that Italian place you like, to celebrate."

I laugh. "All I did was drive your girlfriend to the doctor," I say, even though I know it's bigger than that. "And she ended up being okay anyway."

“Yeah, but Javi,” Miguel argues, “if Rosario had tried to drive herself as panicked as I know she was . . . and in this weather.” All of a sudden his voice breaks, just barely, and he squeezes his eyes shut. Takes a moment to gain control again.

I honestly can’t remember the last time I saw my big brother cry, and I just sit there in his truck, not making a sound.

I can only hope that sometimes, when Miguel really does need to cry, he lets it out.

“Anyway,” he says, punching me in the shoulder again, “thanks, little brother. Or maybe I should just say brother.”

In a movie, Miguel and I would probably hug right here in the cab of his truck, but I know that’s not going to happen. And that’s okay, honestly.

Miguel’s words are enough for me.

ELIZA

Ethan's cry breaks through the fuzzy borders of my dreams for the third time.

"Oh please, kid, give me a break," I mutter into my pillow. I really want to say something worse than that, but it feels wrong to curse in front of a baby.

Even a very cute baby who's preventing you from getting any sleep the night before you have to go back to school after Winter Break.

I sit up, groggy and irritated, as Heather rushes into the room. I'm sure she would have heard Ethan's wails even without the baby monitor.

"Eliza, I'm so sorry," she whispers, reaching for a frantic Ethan, whose fat little baby arms are outstretched so pitifully in desperation for his mom that I can't be angry at him. Still, what is the point of whispering?

"It's his ears," she says. "I think they're infected. I'm taking him in tomorrow. Shh, sweetie, shh, I'm so sorry it hurts." She holds him close and bounces him gently, which I can't think would make infected ears feel any better. Suddenly, Dave enters the room in boxers and his Baylor T-shirt with the holes in it, hovering around his wife and baby, asking what he can do to help.

"I think I'm going to the couch," I announce, bleary-eyed,

dragging my bedspread and pillow with me. The bright light from the hallway streams in, and I wince.

"Again, Eliza, I'm so sorry," Heather repeats.

"It's okay," I say. "It's not your fault." And really, it isn't. Shouldn't *I* be the one apologizing to *Ethan*? It is his room, after all, and it's probably the best version of the natural world he's ever going to get to enjoy, even if it's totally fake.

I stumble into the den and collapse onto the couch that's long enough for my 5'10" frame but that sinks in the middle like an uncomfortable hammock. I finally do curse, under my breath, and toss and turn until around four in the morning, when I manage to pass out into something resembling sleep. I wake up to my mother shaking me gently on the shoulder.

"Eliza, school. Sweetie, are you okay?"

I startle, for a moment not sure if I'm in my bed in the house on Ferris, in my bed in Ethan's room, or back in the hotel at the Lost Pines resort, where I spent most of my time texting Javi and ignoring my dad and brother bonding.

"Huh? Where?"

"You're in the den, Eliza," my mother says, her voice soft. I'm sure she can't remember the last time she had to wake me up for school. I certainly can't. "Was it Ethan?"

"Yeah," I manage, remembering at last what happened the night before. I yawn. "Oh, Mom, I'm so exhausted."

"Eliza, I'm sorry," she says.

"It's okay," I mutter, stumbling off the couch and making my way to the shower in the hall bathroom, only to find my dad is using it.

"Sorry, Eliza," he shouts through the closed door.

Sorry, sorry, sorry. It's all anyone can say to me lately, it seems.

Sorry about the baby waking you.

Sorry you have to sleep on the couch.

Sorry I got to the shower first.

Sorry the house won't be ready by next week like we thought.

Sorry I made fun of your club.

Those last two had been courtesy of my father and brother, respectively, while we were on "vacation" over the break. It would have been preferable to stay home in Heather and Dave's place, invading their first Christmas with Ethan, instead of stuck making awkward small talk with my family while finding out that the move to the Ferris house was on hold for just a little bit longer *and* discovering my brother Mark found ETUP to more of a joke than anything serious. (*"I'm sorry, eat up? Like, food?"*)

When I finally manage to shower and head to school, I'm running late, and I barely have time to answer Javi's text about meeting up in the courtyard for lunch. I tell him yes, please, that I'm having a terrible day.

Naturally, it only gets worse.

In AP Lang class, Ms. Carter passes back the papers we were supposed to write on social class in America, synthesizing a bunch of our in-class reading and outside sources.

"I'm not going to lie to you," she says. "I spent the better part of my break grading these so I could hand them back to you today." She pauses, like she expects us to applaud, but most of us just sit anxiously as she wanders around the room, tossing our fat, stapled papers on our desks.

I flip to the last page. I'd stayed up until two in the morning the night before this was due, trying to make it just right. I don't normally like to wait until the last minute to work on major assignments, but that week had been especially packed with club meetings and two major tests on the same day.

I stare at my grade:

85.

My stomach tenses. An 85? I haven't made a B on a major assignment since, well, since I'm not sure when. My eyes work to process it. Underneath the score is a brief note from Ms. Carter, scrawled in her loopy, difficult-to-read cursive.

Strong thesis, Eliza, and excellent command of the language as always. Unfortunately, I felt your commentary was lacking in spots, particularly in your analysis of Jay Gatsby as a member of the upper class. Still, I appreciate your efforts.

"I appreciate your efforts"? It sounds like she's patting me on the head because I'm a toddler who just finished all her vegetables.

"How'd you do?" asks OC, eyeing me. She loves to compare scores. Always.

"Fine," I say, sliding my paper into the folder I keep for graded work.

"I got a 90," she says, clearly irritated. "Like, let me give you the lowest possible version of an A."

"The worst," I say as the bell rings. I hang back because I want to talk to Ms. Carter, but I don't want OC to see. She'll figure out that my grade is lower than I wanted, and I don't want anyone to know that. I act like I'm going to pack up my stuff to go and accidentally-on-purpose spill my set of flair pens off the side of my desk. They clatter and spin out in all directions as they land on the tiled floor.

"Here, let me help you," says OC.

"No, it's okay," I say, waving her off. We're practically the only kids left in the room now.

"Well, here," she says, handing me the peach pen that's traveled all the way to under her desk.

I thank her and then slowly collect the rest of the pens, standing up when I sense that the only people still here are Ms. Carter and me.

"You okay, Eliza?" she asks from behind her desk, where she's opening up a brown paper bag and pulling out an apple and a Diet Coke.

"Yes, sorry, I just spilled something," I say, pausing to slide my paper out of the folder. "Actually, if you have a second, I just had a quick question about . . ."

Ms. Carter sighs and stops fiddling with her lunch. I can tell she doesn't want to be having this conversation right now. "Eliza, my dear," she says. "It's an 85. It's a B. A good, solid B. The paper was good and solid and slightly above the class average. And with all your other high marks in the class, you still have an A average if that's what you're worried about."

I step back a little, flustered. The words "slightly above the class average" are ringing around in my head. Only slightly above?

"I know, I recognize that," I say, "but I was just wondering if . . ."

Ms. Carter looks up at me, holds her hand up to stop me from continuing.

"Eliza," she says, her voice quiet but firm. "I am not going to raise your grade. I'm happy to talk about this essay at a later time if you'd sincerely like to understand how you could improve an already good piece of writing. But today, on this first day back from break, I just want to eat my lunch in peace, okay?"

I'm not used to teachers snapping at me like this. And yes, Ms. Carter doesn't really *snap* so much as make it very clear that she wants me to leave her classroom immediately. My cheeks are red now, and I'm so discombobulated I think I might drop my pens all over again, this time for real.

"Okay, thank you," I say. "Sorry."

"There's nothing to be sorry about, Eliza," she says, but I don't hear the rest because I'm barreling out of the classroom, embarrassed, hot tears teasing my eyes as I look for the closest girls' restroom. Once inside, I hide in a stall and take a few deep breaths, fighting the urge to totally lose it.

You're being absurd, Eliza. You can try to talk to Ms. Carter later. She just needed to eat lunch. Get it together. I dig my fingernails into my palms hard until I gain control, then walk back out and splash some cold water on my face. It's time for lunch and for meeting up with Javi. I can't believe I haven't seen him all break.

I venture down to the courtyard with my lunch and spot him alone on the perimeter, sitting on a bench, engrossed in his phone. It strikes me again how cute and kind and gentle he is, and how lucky I am that I get to be the one to kiss him. Even though we've texted all break long, nothing could make up for seeing him in person.

"Hey," I say, approaching him. He looks up, his deep brown eyes lighting up when he sees me. My mood instantly lifts.

"Hey!" he says, standing up. Even though there are people around us, he pulls me close and kisses me. We don't go full-on PDA or anything; that's not our style. But I hear a few voices in the background shouting and making fun. Somebody tells us to get a room, but I don't care.

Finally, we sit down, and I lean into him, setting my head against his shoulder. He feels steady. Calm. There's something about being around Javi that relaxes me. Slows me down. I don't think I realized it until this very minute.

"I missed you," I say. "A lot."

"Same," he says, taking my hand in his. "I wish we could have seen each other yesterday."

"I know," I say, sitting up and gazing in his direction. "We got home later than we thought we would on Sunday, and my parents insisted I spend yesterday unpacking and getting everything organized for going back to school." This isn't a lie. They did want me to get everything straightened up, but there was a part of me—no matter how much I wanted to see Javi—that relished the process of doing laundry, hanging up my clothes, and organizing my school stuff for the spring semester.

"It's cool," he says. "Break was boring without you."

"Same," I say. "I mean, Lost Pines was nice. Pretty. But . . ." I feel awkward. Lost Pines was fancy. Expensive. I know I'm lucky that I even got to go there at all. But the truth is I didn't have the greatest time. Not just because I wasn't near Javi, but because my family was getting on my nerves so much.

"You made it sound like things were sort of rough with your dad," Javi says, reading my mind.

"Yeah," I say, "and my brother. And then finding out we aren't moving back to our house next week. Just . . . I don't know." Irritation starts to course through me. "Honestly, I don't want to talk about it." Javier stiffens a little, and I squeeze his hand in response. "I'm sorry, that came out sort of harsh."

"No, it's cool," he says. "I get it." But I'm not sure he really can. From what I've figured out, he gets along great with his family.

"How's Rosario?" I ask, changing the subject.

"Good," he replies. "No more false alarms. She's due early next month, so she's really ready."

Squeezing his hand first, I detach from him slowly and open up my reusable lunch sack and take out a peach and an egg salad sandwich. "Still the hero?" I ask. "I mean for taking her to the doctor?"

Javi laughs. "I guess, maybe." But I can tell he's still pretty pumped about what he was able to do.

"I'm proud of you," I say, in between bites of my sandwich. "I mean it. Did you tell Ms. Holiday?"

Javi starts eating his own lunch, a few slices of cheese pizza he bought from the outside vendors that are allowed to sell in the courtyard sometimes. "I haven't told her yet," he says. "But I want to." He takes a big bite of pizza, then wipes a trickle of grease off his chin with his thumb. I wonder for a moment if it's weird that I find the act sexy.

We eat and catch up. He tells me about trying to skateboard with Dominic and Felipe over break and falling and scraping his leg. I tell him about this mystery novel I read at Lost Pines, the first book I'd allowed myself to read for pleasure in ages. As we finish eating, I mention my 85 in Ms. Carter's class.

Javi grins, and I can't help but feel prickly when he does.

"What?" I say, trying to make my voice light and failing.

"Nothing," he says. "It's just . . . an 85. Eliza, that's not a bad grade."

"To me, it is," I say, annoyed. Why is it bad I have these high standards for myself? Why do some teachers act like I'm silly for wanting to earn the highest grades possible? I mean, if they thought grades were meaningless, why would they give them at all? I say as much to Javi, who shakes his head, frustrated.

"Look, I'm sorry," he says. "I didn't mean . . . like . . . forget it. Maybe you should try talking to her again when she's not busy."

I slide my reusable water bottle into my lunch sack and zip it closed. "I think I will," I say, more determined than ever.

"So, club meeting this week?" Javi asks, and I get the sense he wants to change the topic.

"Yeah," I say, pulling out my notebook. "I was thinking about what we could cover. We could staff another Willow Waterhole cleanup, and figure out other action items for the spring."

Javi doesn't respond, but I sense him eyeing my planner, neatly cluttered with to-do lists in varying colors, the various bullet points I've made dotting the pages like freckles on a face.

"Well," Javi starts, his eyes still on the planner, "what about my presentation on managing weather anxiety and racial justice and climate change? I could use this meeting to share it. Over the break I tightened up the slides and found some cool videos that we could show, too."

I nod, my eyes scanning the calendar portion of the planner sitting in my lap. If ETUP keeps meeting every two weeks, and we're already in January, that really doesn't leave a ton of meetings before May arrives. The end of the school year is always way too busy for club meetings, with final exams and prom. And there are so many things we could still try to get done before the end of the year.

"Where are we on that petition for the idling school buses?" I ask, gliding over Javier's comments. I don't feel very good doing this. In fact, I feel lousy. It's not that I don't think Javi's presentation is full of good, accurate information. I know it is. But if we spend a whole meeting just talking, isn't that one less meeting where we're *not* doing or planning? I want our first meeting back to be about what we can accomplish, not just our sad feelings about awful stuff.

"I emailed it in over break," says Javi, his voice sharpening. "Did you hear what I said about the presentation?"

"Yeah," I say. Across the courtyard I spy two Baldwin boys I don't know attempting to toss their half-empty water bottles into a trash can. They're yelping and insulting each other for missing.

"Pick it up and try again, idiot!" one shouts to the other.

A burning, restless feeling starts to build inside of me. I can sense my heart starting to pick up speed, too. One of the boys tosses the bottle again and misses one more time. I mentally start to multiply all the plastic water bottles that boy has used and tossed in this one school year alone.

"Forget it, leave it," he says, and he and his friend start to walk away.

Before I realize what I'm doing, I find myself marching across the courtyard, filled with fury.

"Hey," I say to their backs. A few kids nearby turn to look at me. "Hey!" I shout again. One of the boys turns around, eyes me like I'm an insect.

"What?" he asks.

I grab the water bottle and unscrew the plastic cap. One cap. One of literally billions of plastic caps all over this planet that will be used for five seconds and never disappear. Ever. They'll be here, littering our planet, when Rosario's baby is born, and when Rosario's baby's baby is born.

If we even last long enough for that to happen.

"You can recycle this, you know," I spit, dumping the bottle over and letting the remaining water splash out onto the courtyard. I feel a few drops spray against my bare calves.

"Uh, thanks for the information," the boy replies, his voice cut with sarcasm. He turns around again. His friend is laughing, already moving on.

"Thanks for not caring!" I shout to their backs. The few kids watching the exchange start giggling. One of the boys flashes me his middle finger without turning around to face me.

I head back toward Javi, my fingers crushing the plastic bottle in my hand.

"Sorry," I say, slamming back down on the bench.

Javi takes a deep breath.

"What?" I say as I shove the bottle into my backpack so I can recycle it later. "They were just going to leave it there on the ground."

"Okay," Javi responds, like he's a grown-up and I'm some annoying kid. I don't like the way he's acting.

"What?" I say again, this time my voice a degree louder. My heart is still racing and I know my cheeks are flushed.

"I just . . ." Javi starts, then pauses. "Look, am I going to deliver this presentation in a club meeting or not?" His voice quavers, just the slightest bit.

"I know it's a really good presentation," I say. "What if we linked to it on the ETUP Instagram? And directed people to go there? We could come up with a hashtag for it like you did for Meatless Mondays."

Javi frowns, then looks away. He's silent.

"It's just that . . . I mean . . ." I start, already feeling like the biggest jerk but somehow unable to stop myself. I'm starting to feel prickly, restless, like I did the day my dad caught Javi and me on the couch.

"I know this is important information," I say, "but I want our club meetings to focus on action, right? *Doing* stuff, not just talking about it."

"You know, educating ourselves *is* doing stuff," Javier says, his tone curt, his eyes still avoiding me. "And so is learning to deal with our emotions about all of this. Like I've been doing with Ms. Holiday, you know?"

I nod, my mouth set in a firm line. I find myself biting my bottom lip. My heart still hasn't slowed.

"Eliza," Javi says, and I can sense his face and tone softening, "are you . . . okay?"

Of course I'm okay. I have to be okay. I have to be more than okay if I'm going to get anything done. I'm okay, okay, okay.

"I'm fine," I say, and it comes out more like a snap than a statement. Javi recoils a little, hurt.

"I was just asking," he says.

"Look," I say, feeling the urge to run, only I don't know where, "can you just put the presentation on Instagram and we'll deal with this later?"

Javi doesn't respond, and I know that I've screwed up royally.

He leans down and picks up his backpack, then stands up. "Okay, Eliza," he says, his voice almost monotone. "I get it. I'll share it on Instagram."

I'm digging myself a hole, and I can't seem to stop.

"Wait, are we in a fight?" I ask, jumping up. "Are you mad at me?"

Javi scowls, refuses to look at me.

"Eliza, it's not about being mad or in a fight," he says, sliding his backpack over his shoulders. "I worked hard on that presentation, and I deserve to present it. It's important, even if it's not, like, an *action item* as you put it. I wanted to share it, and you don't want me to. Whatever. It's fine. This is your club anyway, and we all know it."

"Wait, what?" I start, grateful to have a point of order that I actually feel I can genuinely argue against. "That's not true. I asked you to be copresident."

"Yes," he says quietly. "You did." I notice the more excited I get, the calmer Javi seems to be. It's disconcerting.

"Then how can you say it's my club?" I fire back. My throat starts to ache, like I'm going to cry. I won't let myself. "That's just not true!"

Javi holds up both hands. "Eliza, I need to take a break, okay?" He starts walking away, out of the courtyard. Naturally, I follow him. I need to fix this. Now.

"What's wrong?" I ask as we reach a set of doors leading into the school building. "You're this upset because I don't want to waste time on a presentation?" As soon as the words come out of my mouth, I'm filled with regret. Javier winces, then shakes his head. True anger passes over his face for the first time. His mouth is set in a firm line, his eyes cloud over.

"Eliza," he says, still not raising his voice, "you have to leave me alone right now."

At this I finally give up, standing back as Javier walks into the building, swallowed up by a sea of Baldwin and Southwest kids heading to class.

"Move," says a voice behind me just before someone runs into me, causing me to stumble.

"Sorry," I mutter, moving off to the side, out of everyone's way. "I'm sorry," I whisper again. But I've said it to the wrong person, and I've said it much too late.

~

I have a theory. When you're having a bad day, your brain starts to automatically look for more bad things just to confirm for you that this really is a crummy day in your life. Like confirmation bias. You'd think being aware of this theory, which seems pretty plausible, would prevent me from falling prey to it, but today, this terrible Tuesday full of little sleep and bad grades and an awful moment with Javi, I just lean into it for the second half of the day.

We get yet another major history assignment with an unreasonable deadline.

The printing company our literary magazine uses sends our club sponsor an email saying that they're going out of business and we need to find another printer on short notice.

While using the bathroom, I notice a pimple beginning to erupt on my chin.

And when I walk out of the building at last, my ears are immediately drawn to the sound of school buses idling by the side of the building, spewing their toxicity into the air for no reason whatsoever. The petitions, the emails, none of it is working. Nobody is listening. If you think about it, this whole miserable day started because of stuff like this. After all, if it wasn't for climate change and Harvey, wouldn't I have gotten a decent night's sleep?

Nobody cares. Nothing matters.

My heart starts to race, its rapid beats like the ticking of a stopwatch.

You're running out of time, Eliza. We're all running out of time.

I stomp to my car and drive home, furious at this day, at myself, at a world that's on fire without enough people who care.

Why didn't I just let Javi do his presentation even if it's not connected to an action? Why do I have to insist on my way all the time? Why am I so unreasonable? Why am I like this? Why?

By the time I pull into Heather and Dave's driveway, I'm exhausted and restless at the same time, a horrible combination. I pull my phone out, hopeful, but there's no response from Javi to my last three desperate texts.

I'm sorry.

Can we talk after school?

I'm an idiot.

He's not going to give me a chance. I slump in my seat, press my forehead against the steering wheel. A lump builds in my throat, begging me to let it out.

Just cry, Eliza. Just cry.

A few warm tears start to slip down my cheeks until I taste salt on the edges of my lips. I hate feeling this way, weak and out of control. And I hate crying. I always feel *worse* on the rare occasion I let myself cry. Wrung out. Pathetic.

And feelings get nothing *done*.

"Stop it," I say out loud. "Just stop."

I take a big, shaky breath and blink back the remaining tears threatening to escape, then scold myself a little for getting so out of control. Finally, when I think I'm ready to face my family, I head inside, where I find my mom in the den chatting on her phone.

"Sounds good. Love you, too."

When she's finished with her call, she looks up.

"Your dad has some good news to share," she says. "He's coming home early. We ordered Fadi's for dinner. Hope that's okay." That's one win, I guess. A lot of Middle Eastern food is vegetarian, at least.

"That's good," I say, opening up the refrigerator to get a ginger ale. "What's the news?"

"He wants to share in person," she says. "But I have an idea." She smiles like an excited schoolgirl.

"Is it the house?" I ask, my heart lifting. "Are we getting in next week after all?" I lean back against the counter and open my soda.

My mom's face falls. "No, Eliza. I'm sorry. It's not that. But it shouldn't be much longer, I promise." She tips her head, examines me with pity. Something else I can't stand. "You know, Eliza, you've been very patient through all of this. I know it hasn't been easy."

I want to be grateful, and I am, but I'm so fried from this miserable day it's like I can't really let myself show it.

"I'll just be glad when we can get back there," I say. *Even though I'm afraid it won't really feel like my house again.* I don't say that, though.

Heather and Ethan are out for a walk, but they get home shortly before my father with the takeout from Fadi's. Dave has to work late, Heather says, so we should dive right in.

"So what's the surprise?" I ask my father, setting out plates.

"Let's wait until we're seated," my dad insists, smiling at my mom, who's opening a bottle of white wine.

"Well, Ethan's excited, right, Ethan?" my aunt says to my baby cousin as she straps him into his high chair. Ethan bangs on the tray in front of him in response, and everyone laughs, even me.

I scoop a heap of tabbouleh and then some hummus on my plate before reaching for some of the coriander potatoes that I love. I ignore the butter chicken that my parents and Heather can't seem to get enough of. Heather plops some green baby food from a jar into Ethan's mouth in between bites.

"Mmmm, this chicken!" she announces. "So good."

I force myself not to roll my eyes.

"So," I say, "*now* will you tell us the good news?" I really have no idea what it could be if it doesn't involve us moving back home sooner.

"The promotion came through today," he announces, peering around at all of us. My mom's knowing smile breaks into an enormous grin.

"I knew it!" she says. "Did Bob let you know today?"

"This morning," my father says. "Shortly after I got there. He called me into his office and Tony was in there, too, and I knew it was happening."

Bob. Tony. *I knew it*, says my mom. The two of them are talking about my dad's work life like we should all know who these people are and what any of this means. I stare at my untouched potatoes, growing colder by the moment.

"Honey, I'm so glad," my mother says.

"Let's make a toast!" says Heather. "Ethan can use his sippy cup."

His sippy cup made of plastic that will get tossed out somewhere, to fester in a landfill for all time. Plastic made from oil that my father helps pump out of the ground. A job he's apparently so good at that they can't help but give him more money and bigger job titles for it.

"Eliza?" my mother asks. "Aren't you going to say anything?"

I want to explode. Jump up and scream at my father. Yell at him until he understands that he's complicit in the death of our planet. How can he forgive himself?

But I can't. I don't have the energy for it. This day has exhausted me too much.

No one will ever get it. Not my parents. Not my brother.

Maybe not even Javi.

No one will ever get that we're running out of time. That we're sitting here, laughing and talking and eating takeout, and it's all pointless. The earth is being destroyed and humanity is dying. We are literally running out of time and no one around me seems to grasp the urgency.

"Eliza?" my mother presses, her tone having moved from questioning to outright frustrated.

"Congratulations," I say, my voice flat. My eyes still on the dinner I no longer feel like eating. Then, to try and achieve some level of authenticity so I'll be left alone, I add, "That's great news." Still, I don't look him in the eye.

There's an uncomfortable silence. I haven't rocked the boat

in an obvious way, but still, we all know it's the wrong reaction. But I guess my parents would rather take this than some lecture about fossil fuels for the ten millionth time.

"Thank you, Eliza," my dad says, his voice as flat as mine.

Another pause. I shovel some of the potatoes into my mouth, then a spoonful of tabbouleh. It all tastes like cardboard sliding down my throat. Finally, Ethan giggles and babbles and provides enough of a distraction for the adults at the table to forget about me, the weird, intense Eliza who takes everything too seriously and doesn't know how to relax.

"May I be excused?" I ask after I eat a reasonable amount of food.

My mother peers at my father, then says, "Fine." She seems relieved to be rid of me.

I head into my—no, *Ethan's*—bedroom and collapse onto my bed with my phone. My only messages are homework questions from OC and OP. Isabella has given up talking to me, and even though I know in my heart our friendship was ready to end, the reality stings on today of all days.

Nothing from Javi.

I slide in my headphones and punish myself by watching YouTube video after YouTube video about climate change, natural disasters, starving polar bears. Mudslides, floods, droughts, all of it coming and no one will stop it. I hate how it makes me feel, how much it fills me with despair. But it's like I can't stop watching and scrolling and consuming all this terrible news.

Then something occurs to me, and once it does, it's like I can't give up on the idea. There's got to be a way to make people pay attention. People like my dad, who don't give a damn about my future. Or Ethan's future. Or Valentina's future.

Being a nerd who loves research and does well in school comes in handy. I search up a few YouTube videos. It looks surprisingly easy. All I really need is a pair of needle-nose pliers. I bet Heather and Dave have some in their neatly organized garage.

~

I pretend to fall asleep, but really, I don't. I wait with my eyes closed, counting my breaths, until I know everyone in the house, even Ethan, is asleep.

The pliers are in my backpack. I went into the garage earlier in the evening under the pretense of finishing some laundry. A half-full can of black spray paint from some home project is in there, too, and I grab that when no one is looking.

Other than a simple "good night," I didn't talk to anyone all evening, and no one spoke to me. Just a good night and the pliers and the spray paint in the backpack and pretending to be asleep until I could sneak out.

You always hear about teenagers sneaking out to party or go meet a crush or run away and the truth is, it's surprisingly easy to do. At least it is for me. Heather and Dave don't have a dog that will bark and wake everyone. Everyone in the house is a deep sleeper besides Ethan, and even he's coming through for me this evening. I peek into the crib as I creep out, and he's curled up in a little ball, his pacifier firmly in place, his sweet little baby brain off in dreamland.

I glance at the time as I pull down the street toward my destination. It's 12:45 A.M. I have plenty of time, but I want to get this done as quickly as possible.

I know where the bus barn is, practically next door to Southwest High, protected by a sad little chain-link fence. I park on a side street in the residential neighborhood bordering the barn. The January air, even in Houston, is brisk. If I listen carefully, I can hear the rush of traffic on Highway 90 not far from here and the occasional dog bark, but that's it.

My heart is thumping, but I feel weirdly calm. Focused. I realize it's the same tunnel vision I get when I'm working on a major assignment, or soothing myself by organizing my planner and writing out lists of tasks to accomplish.

Don't dwell, Eliza. Just do.

I reach the gate, which is locked, of course. Undeterred, I toss my backpack over the fence, hear it land against the pavement with a smack, then scale the chain link with the determination and agility of someone more athletic than I actually am in real life.

But this almost doesn't feel like real life. Not at all.

I check my phone. Just after one o'clock in the morning. I'm making great time.

My mind runs through the YouTube videos I've committed to memory. I hope it's as easy as they made it look.

I head to the closest bus, squat down, and dig in my backpack for the pliers. There, underneath the gigantic tire, is a crushed plastic water bottle. I want to laugh it's so perfect.

Unscrewing the valve cap and setting it aside, I worm the pliers through until I reach what I think I'm looking for and screw and tug. As soon as the snake-hissing sound of escaping air hits the cool winter air, I know I've done it.

Don't dwell, Eliza. Just do.

One tire per bus should maximize my efforts, and that's just what I do, jumping from bus to bus and emptying exactly one tire on each vehicle, rendering each bus useless.

With each tug and pull of the pliers, I feel something breaking inside of me. Something cracking. I realize I'm crying as I race from vehicle to vehicle, and I don't try to stop it this time. I just brush the tears aside with one hand so they don't get in the way of my work.

Pull, tug.

Mark, the water's coming in through the bathroom.

Run, race.

Oh no, it's happening.

Pull, tug.

Eliza, take all you can carry upstairs! Hurry!

Move, squat.

My mother's photo albums, no!

Hiss, deflate.

Mom, Dad, why is this happening?

Choking back sobs, I keep going, unable to stop. Waiting to feel better, but the better doesn't come. All I know to do is to keep yanking out the valve cores until I'm surrounded by a chorus of hissing sounds. I get faster at it, but reaching every bus would be impossible, and I know I have to stop eventually. Once I've disabled about fifty buses, I race back to the front of the barn, where I've left my backpack. Taking out the can of spray paint, I shake it up. Then, on the two buses closest to the entrance, I spray out my fury.

FOSSIL FUELS KILL. STOP IDLING BUSES.

Adrenaline still coursing through me, I gather my supplies and head back to my car, then drive home with my hands tight around the steering wheel, my mind a blank, unable to picture what might happen next.

JAVIER

I wake up with a headache. I guess that's only natural after crying yourself to sleep, but it still sucks. Rubbing my eyes, I force myself to sit up. It's a Wednesday in early January, my girlfriend and I are in a fight, and everything sucks.

In the shower, I recount yesterday's events in the courtyard for the millionth time. How insistent Eliza was in everything she was doing and how, for the first time, this bothered me more than it attracted me. It was like I was seeing the inverse of her, the confident part of her in some sort of over-the-top overdrive.

She'd acted like she didn't care at all about the presentation I'd worked so hard on, and I'd been weirded out by the way she'd gone over and yelled at that kid in the courtyard for tossing the water bottle. It was like nothing could stop her or calm her down, definitely not me.

My phone taunts me with her unanswered texts. I want to talk to her, sort of, but I'm also still upset, and I don't know what I'm supposed to say. Getting dressed, I think about our first kiss at Willow Waterhole. How she took charge and leaned in and how good she tasted. And then I feel like I'm going to start crying again.

"Okay, Javier," I mutter to myself as I cram my school stuff into my backpack and head into the kitchen. "Chill out for now."

In the kitchen, I find my mom on her phone, pacing up and down. "Okay, yes. Yes, I'm sure it'll be on the news. I can't imagine. Okay, I'll get there when I can."

I open the fridge and peer around for the orange juice. "Is everything okay? It's not Rosario, is it?"

"No," my mother answers as I pull out the orange juice and close the fridge door. "That was one of the teachers from work. There's been something with the school buses at the bus barn," she tells me as she texts someone. "Some sort of vandalism. A few of our kids from the apartments on Franklin Street can't make it to school, so the principal is thinking about doing some carpools with the teachers and staff." As she sends the last text, she scowls. "What sort of person wrecks buses for kids?"

A strange, sick sensation starts washing over me.

"Did they find out who did it?" I ask.

"No, not yet," she says, grabbing her keys and purse off the kitchen counter and heading for the front door. "But they will, I'm sure. That place has cameras all over. Bye, mijo. I'm going to head in early and try to help out."

"Okay," I say, my voice sounding flat and empty. "Good luck."

I check my phone again. Some dumb texts about dumb stuff from Dom. Nothing from Eliza. I shower, dress, and head out the door, waving to Mrs. Green but faking my morning cheer. My stomach is churning.

I flip through my phone and check the school district's Twitter account. There's an alert about some bus routes being canceled because of the vandalism, and a few angry parents and kids responding that the school district should have tighter security at the bus barn.

As I approach Southwest High, my phone buzzes.

Can you meet me in the courtyard? Please Javi. I'm scared. I messed up. I'm sorry.

Eliza.

This is different from her pleading texts from the night before. More urgent. I'm still angry with her, and I know I have a right to be. But something tells me this is serious. Really serious.

My heart pounding hard, I make my way to the courtyard as fast as I can, trying to imagine if my worst fears could possibly be true.

She couldn't.

She wouldn't.

Not Eliza, so focused on her résumé and her planner and her perfect grades. Why would she do something so risky?

I find her hovering by some oak trees at the edge of the courtyard, walking in a circle. She's wearing blue jeans and a dark gray hoodie, her hair pulled back in a messy ponytail. As I approach, I see her face is pale, two dark half-moons settled under her eyes, which for the first time that I can remember aren't sparkling with confidence and energy.

"Javi," she says, her voice almost a whisper. "Oh no, Javi."

"Eliza, did you do that to the buses?" I ask, finding the courage in me to cut right to the matter at hand.

She draws her hands up to her face, covers her mouth, bursts into quiet tears.

Nods yes.

"Eliza!" I cry, unable to stop myself. "What were you thinking?"

She shakes her head no, in protest to my angry reprimand. Tears pour down her face. My heart is torn between wanting to help her, comfort her, and shake her for being so reckless.

"I . . . I . . . thought it could . . . get us some . . ." she starts.

"What exactly did you do?" I ask, trying to calm myself. Needing the facts.

In between shaky breaths, Eliza explains how she used YouTube to figure out how to take the air out of the tires, then spray painted anti–fossil fuels slogans on two of the buses.

"Oh no," I say, my voice tight and low. "Eliza, they know our club submitted that petition about the idling. And *I* was the one who submitted it through *my* email account. They'll see that slogan and know it was ETUP."

Eliza shakes her head again, rapidly. "No, no, I won't let them do anything to you. I'll tell them it was all my fault. I'll take all the blame."

"What if they don't believe that?" I say, my anger building as I imagine myself getting hauled into Mr. Lopez's office and arrested for Eliza's thoughtless stunt. "Look at you. Look at me. The white Baldwin girl from the nice neighborhood, or me, the Mexican kid who goes to Southwest?" My voice is bitter, sharp. I hate that she hasn't considered any of this. "And another thing," I go on, unable to stop myself, "did you ever stop to think about how a lot of kids get to school? Kids whose parents aren't *rich* enough to buy them their own electric cars?" Maybe it's a low blow, but I'm so mad I keep going. "Eliza, you know my mom works at Monroe Elementary, but what you don't know is that she's going to have to drive all over the place picking up kids today who can't get to school because *you* made it so they can't! You didn't think about them, did you?"

At this, Eliza shuts her eyes tight. She still hasn't taken her hands down from her face. And then, suddenly, she turns and runs, out of the courtyard and into the building.

"Eliza, wait!" I shout, but she doesn't come back and I don't go after her. I'm angry, but I'm also worried for her. She seems so fragile, and even though I know I have a right to feel the way I do, in my anger I worry I've just kicked the last chair out from under her. At the same time, I also have no idea what is going to happen next, and I'm scared, too.

The bell for first period rings, and I head toward Ms. Gomez's class, my mind a blur. I think about stopping to try and find Ms. Holiday, but what would I say? Am I supposed to turn Eliza in? Defend myself in advance? These problems are all way too huge for me to figure out how to solve or even begin to solve.

As I take my seat in English class, I check my phone. The buses are on a few local news sites, and it's the lead story on KPRC. My ears are ringing and my hands are practically shaking as Ms. Gomez cheerfully delivers instructions on the day's lesson. As I numbly try to follow, I notice a school police officer arrive at the classroom door. I've seen her around campus. She's a tall white woman with a tight red ponytail and a face that never seems to smile.

"I need Javier Garza," she barks into the room, startling Ms. Gomez, who hasn't noticed her yet even if I have.

Ms. Gomez frowns, confused, and glances in my direction.

"Is everything okay?" she asks, but whether she's directing the question at me or the officer is hard to say. Anyway, I'm too nervous to answer.

"Just need to see him, please," the officer says again.

There's a ripple of whispers as I get my stuff and head toward the hall. I'm not on most people's radars at Southwest High, and I am definitely not the sort of kid who gets called out by the cops.

"What's this about?" I ask the officer as she escorts me toward the main office.

"We'll talk about it when we get there," she says. There's a burst of static and yammering from the radio on her belt. She pulls it close to her mouth and says something so loud and fast I don't understand it. The whole exchange sets my already frayed nerves on edge.

At last we make it to the main office, and I follow the officer down several hallways I've never seen, past desks with people behind them who I've never met. This is the administrative wing, and it's weird—and terrifying—to be in it.

"Here he is," the officer says, motioning me into an office where I see Principal Lopez and Ms. Franklin, the Baldwin High principal, along with Ms. Bates.

"Javier, have a seat for us, won't you?" Mr. Lopez states, pointing at the only empty seat left in the room. "I think you know Ms.

Franklin, the principal of Baldwin, and I know you know Ms. Bates."

Ms. Bates gazes at me, her eyes full of sympathy, and something in me relaxes just a tiny bit.

"Hello, Javier," she says. Her voice is steady and soothing.

The police officer leans against the open door, her arms crossed. I turn away and try to act like she's not there.

"Javier, I'm going to get right to the point," Mr. Lopez says. "We have reason to believe that the club for which you serve as copresident, ETUP, might have been behind some vandalism that took place last night with the district school buses. And we want to know what you might know about that."

He's being vague, probably on purpose. Mom said the bus barn had cameras, so surely by now they've seen Eliza on video. But what if the cameras weren't working? What if all they have to go on is the anti–fossil fuels message and the damaged tires? And they think it must be my fault? They can link the petition to my email, after all.

I take a breath and exhale. It sounds shaky, even to me. I wipe my sweaty palms on the knees of my worn jeans. They must think I'm guilty from how I'm acting.

"Javier," says Ms. Bates. I look up, make eye contact. She has big, warm brown eyes. Ms. Bates has always intimidated me a little bit, but for sure right now she's the least scary person in this room. "For what it's worth, I don't think you were involved. And I've made that very clear to Mr. Lopez and Ms. Franklin." At this she turns her gaze on the two principals and blinks once, twice.

She stays calm and collected but her stare is fixed on them, and it's not the nicest stare I've ever seen. But it's like she's trying to send them a message telepathically or something. A message that says *Lay off Javier.*

But what am I supposed to do? Rat out Eliza? If they have camera footage, can they tell that it's her and not me?

"I wasn't involved in what happened with the buses," I say. That much I can say with confidence. "I can tell you that I helped to collect signatures for a petition to stop the buses from idling, and I turned the petition in. That was something ETUP did, yes. And it was something I believed in. That the buses shouldn't idle." I glance at Ms. Bates, then screw up the courage to face the two principals. "But I did not touch those buses. I had nothing to do with that."

Ms. Franklin nods and Mr. Lopez just stares at me. No one says anything.

"Can I go?" I ask, desperate to get out of there. As soon as I say the words, I'm sure I sound guilty. Only a guilty person would want to leave that office. But I'm not guilty. I just don't want to be cornered into ratting out Eliza. Even if I am upset, confused, and just about ready to explode over her stupid stunt, I still care about her. I still admire her.

And I'm still worried for her.

"Javier, do you know who did vandalize the buses?" Mr. Lopez asks, laying the question out as straightforwardly as possible. It's impossible to deflect. I either answer it or I don't.

"Javier," Ms. Bates says. But I can only hear her because by this point I have my eyes trained on the nubby, thin gray carpet that covers Mr. Lopez's office floor. "Javier, I know it's scary, but we need you to tell the truth. I think maybe we can find out a way to help this person, not just get them in trouble."

The blood is rushing through my ears, and I'm starting to feel swimmy, unsteady, even if I'm still sitting down. How can I snitch on Eliza? How can I turn in this girl who has come to mean so much to me?

"Javier . . ." Mr. Lopez begins again, only he never gets to finish. There is a loud, sudden disruption in the hall outside Mr. Lopez's office. All of us turn in that direction, and the police officer makes a motion like she's going to leave and see what's going on.

"No!" someone screams. A girl's voice.

Eliza's voice.

And suddenly, there in the doorframe, is Eliza, her face a blotchy mess. Tears and snot pouring down her cheeks and running into her mouth. Her breathing rapid and loud. As soon as I process that it's her, another district police officer runs up, an older Hispanic guy who has patrolled Southwest High since I was a freshman.

"Hey!" he shouts, grabbing her right arm. "I told you to wait."

The red-haired officer takes Eliza's other arm, even though she's not fighting or resisting or anything.

No, she's just screaming, I realize. Screaming at the top of her lungs and sobbing. Mr. Lopez and Ms. Franklin jump up. Ms. Bates, too.

"Eliza," I say, standing up because what else can I do. "Eliza, it's okay. It's okay."

Even though I know it's not. What's happening to Eliza in this office is the furthest thing from okay.

It's one of the scariest things I've ever witnessed.

I've never seen another person so upset. So clearly falling apart. I've never seen anyone cry like this. Make sounds like this.

"It wasn't him!" she screams through her tears, so upset we can barely understand her. "It wasn't Javi! He had nothing to do with it. Nothing! It was me and I did it! I did it! I'm sorry, but I did it! Javi, I'm sorry!"

And at this, Eliza heaves, like maybe she's going to puke right there on the floor of Mr. Lopez's office. If she had, it wouldn't have surprised me. But she only collapses on the ground, ripping her arms from the grasp of the officers, her blond hair spilling out of its ponytail. She pounds the floor with one fist and screams, howls. The police officers stand there, staring.

I can't process what I'm seeing. It's like she's not Eliza anymore. She's transformed into some sort of wounded animal or desperate creature. I want to help her, but I also want to look away because it hurts to see her like this. It's all too much. Honestly, it's terrifying.

"Eliza," says Ms. Bates, coming toward her, her voice steady but loud. It has to be loud to have a chance of being heard over Eliza's noises. Ms. Bates kneels down and puts her hand on Eliza's back, rests it as gently as she can on Eliza's gray hoodie. But Eliza just sobs and smacks the ground and screams over and over that she did it and I didn't. That she did it and she's sorry.

I open my mouth, but I can't think of what to say. I don't think Eliza would even hear me given the way she's acting.

Just then, as Eliza pauses to catch her breath, I overhear Ms. Franklin murmur something to Mr. Lopez about calling for the school nurse, or maybe even an ambulance, and suddenly something hits me hard, and I know what I have to do. Stepping around Eliza as carefully as I can, darting past the cops, ignoring the shouts of my name insisting that I return, I race out of the maze of administrative office past the curious gazes of clerks and run run run down the first-floor hallway all the way to Ms. Holiday's office, my heart drumming in my chest so hard that I think it might burst.

ELIZA

The email from Ms. Bates arrived in my inbox on Thursday, but I haven't had the guts to read it until now, Saturday morning. And now that I have, I just keep reading it over and over again. My impulse is to respond right away with some bright, cheerful acknowledgment, but something in me—something new—says to wait. Hold on.

Maybe it's okay not to respond right away.

Maybe it's okay not to have the perfect words.

Eliza,

I wanted you to know I've been thinking about you quite a lot these past few days. I've been worried about you, but I also have every faith that you will be okay with a little time and lots of care.

I know you understand that what you did was wrong, and you are prepared to face the consequences. And when you come back to school, we can talk about it if you'd like. I'm excited to continue to serve as ETUP's sponsor.

And I also want you to know that I still believe you have a lot to offer your community and this world of ours, and I know that you will go on to do great things with that big brain and heart of yours.

Please reach out if there is anything I can do. Something tells me schoolwork might be on your mind; let's not worry about schoolwork right now. There will be time to catch up on that later.

Sincerely,
Ms. Bates

I read Ms. Bates's words one final time, then slide my phone onto the floor and dig under the covers, burying my head under my bedspread. I catch a whiff of my armpits. I think I'm starting to stink a little.

There's a soft rapping at the door.

"Yes?" I call.

My mom comes in with a plate of toast and a glass of orange juice. I think she's figured it's easier to handle all of this if she acts like I've come down with something, and maybe I have. I'm not sure. Anyway, she's been very gentle and quiet with me since Wednesday, and I've mostly appreciated it.

"Hungry?" she asks hopefully.

"A little," I say. I can't really tell if I'm hungry or not. Or sleepy or not. Or anything or not. I've spent most of the week in bed, and even Ethan crying in the middle of the night hasn't done much to disturb that.

She places the plate on my bed and hands me the juice. I

dutifully take a few bites and sips and then tell her I'm full. She takes the plate and glass back from me.

"Your dad was wondering if . . ." She pauses as if she's afraid what she's about to say might set me off. And who can blame her? "Your dad was wondering if maybe you'd like to go on a little drive. He really wants to talk to you, Eliza."

I nod. I can't think of any reason why not, I guess. My options seem pretty limited right now in terms of saying no to my parents.

"I'll tell him you'll get dressed and be out soon," she says, her voice a little lighter, her shoulders dropping a little in what I guess is relief.

"Okay," I say, and then, just as she opens the door, I mutter, "Mom, I'm really sorry."

"I know you are," she says, a sigh escaping her lips. My heart aches hearing it.

I throw on some clothes and roll on some deodorant, then brush my teeth and splash water on my face. Heather, Dave, and Ethan are out doing something. They've been trying to stay out of the house and out of our hair as much as possible these past few days, which only makes me feel worse considering it's *their* house.

I wander into the den, where my father is on his phone and my mother is sorting through some papers on the coffee table.

"Dad?" I ask. "Mom said you wanted to see me?"

My parents glance at each other, then my dad nods and slides his phone into his pocket.

"Thought we'd go check out the house," he says. "Lots

of progress made this week. It looks like we'll be back in by Valentine's Day."

It's good news, I know, and I am happy about it in an abstract sort of way. But like everything this week, it's like I'm feeling it through a fog or a filmy piece of fabric. Like I'm sensing it but not as much as I should or could be.

Plus Valentine's Day makes me think of Javi. Of his dark brown eyes. His gentle steadiness. I think about the last time I saw him, crouched down next to me on the floor of Mr. Lopez's office, his hand on my shoulder, his voice telling me to look at him, focus on him. His words shouting about Ms. Holiday and how she was here to help me.

I haven't seen him since. No texts or calls, either.

Wordlessly, my dad and I get into his Volvo and head to the house on Ferris. My mind stays fixed on Javier, then drifts against my will back to Mr. Lopez's office on Wednesday afternoon, on the absolute worst day of my life. Worse even than the day our house flooded.

It's difficult to piece everything together. I remember Ms. Holiday walking me out into the hallway, somehow, and trying to help me breathe. I remember my parents showing up, although how long it took for them to get there I can't say. I remember the school nurse coming in to take my blood pressure, check my eyes and my reflexes. She asked if I'd used drugs, and I'd said something about being too perfect for drugs.

I remember Ms. Holiday explaining to me that my parents were at the school and meeting with Mr. Lopez and Ms. Franklin. She'd dismissed the nurse by this point and the two of us were in her tiny office, and I remember asking her if this was where she met with Javier, and she'd said yes.

"Eliza, I want you to follow my finger as I make this box," she'd said. "Follow my finger as we breathe." And I remembered Javi telling me that Ms. Holiday had taught this to him, and it had helped him feel better when it rained, and I fixated on that finger and on the air in Ms. Holiday's tiny office traveling in and out of my tired, anxious lungs, and I began to feel a little bit better. But only just.

My parents had taken me right from the school to my pediatrician, Dr. Carlisle, the same tiny, pale woman with black hair in a tight bun who'd seen me in the hospital and always complimented me and commented on how well I seemed to be doing and how perfectly I was growing along the growth curve and how perfectly I was meeting every milestone and how perfectly I was becoming a young adult. That same Dr. Carlisle had to meet with my parents while I cried alone in the waiting room, and then she prescribed something to help me sleep that night and gave my parents the names of some therapists on a printed-out piece of paper that my mother clutched in her hand like money she was afraid she'd drop and lose.

"Eliza, would you say that recently you've had little pleasure or interest in doing things?

"Eliza, would say that recently you've felt depressed, irritable, or hopeless?

"Eliza, in the past few months have you felt sad most days, even if some days you felt okay?

"Eliza, have you thought about hurting yourself?"

My answers were robotic, hollow. But they're the truth.

Maybe.

Yes.

I'm not sure.

I don't think so.

When Dr. Carlisle finished her questions, she had paused and looked at me, her head tilted to the side, her eyes sad.

"Eliza, you're going to get better. We're going to get you some help."

"Okay," I'd said, and I'd started to cry again. And then, my voice cracking, I'd managed to whisper one more thing.

"I want to feel better than this."

The rerun of that awful afternoon comes to a halt as my dad pulls up into our driveway of the house on Ferris. My eyes take in the front stoop, the front door. It's a new front door, unrecognizable to me, but I remember pictures taken in the front yard on Halloween, on my middle school graduation, on my first day at Baldwin High.

"Want to check it out?" my dad says, sliding his keys from the ignition.

"Sure," I say, and I follow him up the steps and inside, where everything smells new, like wood chips and fresh paint. It's a lot further along since the last time I was here, and I silently trace my fingers along the wall as I walk with my dad toward the kitchen. The layout is different, as I've come to expect.

"This doesn't look like the old kitchen," I say.

My dad puts his hands in his pockets and looks around, observing.

"You're right," he says. "Your mom made some changes. I guess they'll take some getting used to."

"I guess," I say. I still don't think I like it much, but maybe I could come around to it if I gave it a chance. I don't know.

"Let's go outside for a little bit," he says, and we head out through the French doors in the breakfast nook and into the backyard. My mom must have purchased some new patio furniture—the old set with the red-and-white stripes that always reminded me of candy canes was destroyed in the flood. This set is a little fancier, a little more solid.

"Maybe these won't float away in the next hurricane," I say, sitting down on one of the chairs.

"I can't tell if you're making a joke or if you're serious," my father answers as he joins me, but he smiles as he says it.

"Me neither," I admit.

We sit in silence for a while, my eyes gazing out over the site of former birthday parties and backyard barbecues. I remember how Isabella and I used to spend summers in middle school out here in the backyard, trying to dye our hair with Kool-Aid and the backyard hose because my mother said it was too messy inside the house.

And I remember how this same space transformed into a murky lake when Harvey struck, swallowing up everything until my house—and my life—became practically unrecognizable to me.

I glance over at my dad, and I'm stunned to find him staring out at the backyard with me, only he has tears in his eyes. I can't really recall the last time I saw my father cry. He got choked up the day we put Mark on the plane for MIT, but he didn't actually cry.

And right now, my dad is crying. Not huge heaving sobs or anything. Just red-rimmed eyes and a tear running down his cheek. He wipes it away and sniffs.

"Dad," I say. "Dad, I'm so sorry. I'm really sorry for what I've done."

He deserves that apology. I know he does.

He turns to look at me, his face soft.

"Eliza, I'm not . . . I mean, I'm not happy about what you've done. And you know you're going to have to face consequences."

I nod. Two-week suspension. Appearing before a juvenile court judge. Community service hours. This was all listed out in front of me yesterday afternoon, after my parents and I met with school district officials. Lawyer Uncle Dave came along with us. A few weeks ago, such a list of punishments would have been unthinkable to me. And now I feel fortunate that they're all that I'm facing. Javi's words in the courtyard after I trashed the buses haven't left me; I know kids who don't have my skin color or my parents wouldn't be so lucky.

"But, Eliza," my father continues, blinking back the tears in his eyes, trying to gain some control, "what I'm the most upset about is . . . us. You and me. I'm worried about you. Really worried. And I . . . I miss you. I miss talking to you. I miss just . . . being your dad."

The lump in my throat is immediate, and I try to take this in. I mean, my dad and I have barely exchanged more than the basics of communication with each other for what feels like forever. At these words from him, it feels like something has cracked open, and it makes me feel scared and hopeful all at once. I think back to those afternoons watching *SpongeBob* when I was little. Making "science experiments" with shaving cream and food coloring. Chasing after him in the park and tackling him when he let me tag him. What happened to that? How did it all disappear?

I tuck a lock of hair behind my ear and reach out to touch my dad on the arm. It feels awkward, but he seems to appreciate it. He rubs the top of my head like I'm four, and that's awkward, too, but it's sort of nice.

"I guess," I say, looking back out at the yard, taking a shaky breath and taking a chance, too. Because at this point, I don't feel I have anything to lose. "I guess I thought maybe you didn't want much to do with me anymore. That . . . that you didn't like me that much anymore. That you just wished I'd be more like Mark or something, going into engineering."

Out of the corner of my eye, I can see my dad shake his head, confused.

"No, Eliza. Of course I love Mark. He's my son. But you're my daughter. My only daughter. My little girl. We were close, once. And then . . . all of a sudden . . . you're in high school. You're so passionate about things. You have a boyfriend out of nowhere. And . . ." He pauses, and I can sense him choosing his words like he's walking over a field full of land mines. "You seem to think I'm the cause of all the evil on the planet." At this he stares at his feet.

That hurts. It does. And a part of me recoils, gets ready to pounce and shout and scream. It would be the easiest response, really.

But I also know, deep down inside, that it wouldn't be the right one.

"I don't think you're the cause of all the evil on the planet, Dad," I say, searching for the right thing to say. I think about how I can get up in front of a room full of kids for an ETUP meeting and speak without notes or even thinking ahead. How confident I feel in moments like that, so sure of myself. And it all feels like a lie because the truth is, most of the time I'm really scared. Not of the speaking in front of others part, I guess. But of losing control. Of not being perfect. Of not being able to *fix* things.

"I just feel . . ." I'm trying to find the right words and unable to. I decide to just speak from the heart as best as I can. "I mean, Dad, I . . . I am sincerely, genuinely worried about the earth. I don't want to get into a fight with you. I really don't. But the science is real, Dad. We don't have a future with fossil fuels. And I don't know how you can't see it." There's a moment of tension then, like this headway we're making—if that's what you can call it—could all fall apart. But my dad just sits there, like he's holding my words in his hands, examining them. Considering them.

"Eliza, I'm worried, too," he says at last. "I went to A&M. I believe in science. I believe climate change is real, I believe humans caused it, and I believe it contributed to Harvey."

This catches me off guard. I guess I never really thought my father felt this way.

"Look what I was watching the other day," he says, and at this he slides out his phone and fools around with it until he pulls up a TED Talk I recognize, delivered by this English professor who is pretty urgent about the need to act on climate change. I've seen it before myself.

"You were watching this?" I ask, incredulous.

My dad offers me a rueful smile.

"Yeah," he says. "I like to stay informed. This guy is interesting."

I nod, feeling sort of guilty I'd never noticed my dad listening to this sort of video before. But this discovery also prompts another question.

"But, Dad, if you think this way, if you watch these videos, how can you keep your job?" I ask, my voice tightening, my eyes gazing at him. "How can you work for this Big Oil company when you *know* fossil fuels are killing this planet?" At the word "know" I pound the armrest of the new fancy patio furniture.

My dad closes his eyes, shakes his head.

"Eliza, it's not so easy," he says. He opens his eyes and looks at me, then continues. "Your mother works hard, but it's my salary that pays for Mark to go to MIT. It's my salary that paid for your car, for this house."

I sit with this. Wrestle with it. Despite my best efforts, so much of what I have, own, what I'm able to do . . . it's all tied up in my dad's oil job. And so much of Houston is entrenched in this industry. How to untangle this knot? The question is almost enough to raise my anxiety again, so I take a slow deep breath, visualizing Ms. Holiday's finger moving in the shape of a box as I do.

"You okay, Eliza?"

I nod. I am. But I can't help but push my father a little more.

"Dad, don't you *ever* think about getting another job? Maybe not tomorrow, but someday?"

My father exhales, scratches at the back of his neck. Considers this.

"Sometimes," he says. "Honestly, yes. Sometimes. And your words are always rattling around in my head when I think about it." This makes me feel pretty proud, I can't help it.

And while in my heart I know I can't blame my dad alone for the fact that my childhood home filled up with water and everything else that's happening on the earth—I also can't ignore everything I've learned over these past few years.

"Dad, I'm really sorry if I've made you feel that I blame you for our house. I don't. And I know my actions with the buses were reckless and I didn't take into account that I'd be hurting people, people with fewer resources than me. But I also know that moving away from dependency on oil and gas is the right thing. I'm never not going to think that."

My dad nods. Takes a deep breath. Thinks. It feels good to say all this to my father. To give him a chance to listen to me. To not fight but really talk.

"Lots of people have jobs in the oil industry," my father says. "And trust me when I tell you that the vast majority of those people are good, hardworking people like me who want to feed their families and keep a roof over their heads, and this is the industry in this city that makes that possible."

My mind flashes to Javi telling me about his older brother, the one with a baby on the way. About how he makes more money at a dangerous refinery job with a high school diploma than he could most places, and how wrong that seems to me.

"For *now* it's the industry," I say. "But, Dad, I really want to work to change that. That's, like, my life's goal." And as I say it, I realize that *is* what I want to do. Like, for a job. I want to make a life out of working to protect the planet and the people on it.

"You're talking about undoing literally decades of systems put in place long before you or even I was born," continues my dad. "And I'm not saying it's not possible, or that it shouldn't happen . . ." At this he stops himself. Pauses. Looks at me. Really looks.

"Then again," he says, his voice cracking, "I admire you for that goal. I think it's a good one, actually." His eyes fill up with tears.

Just like my father's voice, something in me cracks clean through. Suddenly, hot tears are pouring out of my eyes, and my throat aches. Shaking, I lean forward, my face in my hands. My whole body crying. Hard.

I can sense my dad scooting his patio chair closer, then I feel his warm, big dad hand on my back, rubbing gently.

Whenever I was sick to my stomach as a little girl, my father was always the one who could calm me down the fastest. It was always my dad who crouched down next to me by the toilet, his hand on my back like he's doing now. His warm, steady voice promising that it would be okay very soon.

It feels good to let out these tears.

"Eliza," my father says after he's let me cry for a moment—and maybe he's shed some tears, too—"you remind me so much of me. You really do."

Sitting up and wiping at my face with the sleeves of my sweatshirt, I peer at him, curious.

"Mom always says that," I say. "That we have the same work ethic."

Dad grins. Maybe the most genuinely happy smile I've seen on his face in the past week.

"Mom's right," he says. "The way you write everything down in that planner. The way you color-code your life."

My eyebrows pop up, surprised.

"You've noticed that?" I ask.

"Of course," my father says. "And I've noticed that you stay up too late, and that you take too much on, and that you're worried about not being perfect. And, Eliza, you need to know that you don't need to be perfect."

"Dad, please don't say I just need to be me," I say. "Please don't say that."

My father laughs out loud. "Okay," he says. "I won't say that. But . . ." His tone turns serious. "The truth is, I worry about you, Eliza. I worry about you because I know how I was at your age, and how I still am now, sometimes. And the truth is, though I really admire your goals—and I hope you believe me now when I say that—you need to remember that you can't bend everything to your will, and you can't personally ensure nothing bad happens. We can do our best and hope for the best, but sometimes, we also have to let go a little. That's life."

Tears start to well up in me again, and I let them fall. It feels good, like I've had so many tears bottled up inside of me for months and months and they just have to come out now, all at once. I lean toward my dad and bury myself in his chest, press my tearstained face against his Houston Astros sweatshirt. He holds me close, rubs the top of my head, and lets me stay there for as long as I need, which turns out to be a long time. When I'm finally able to talk again, I pull back, take a deep, shaky breath.

"Dad, I think I really need help," I say. "Like someone to talk to. Not just you or Mom but, like, a professional."

My father nods. "You've been through so much," he says. "We all have." He peers over his shoulder at our new old house. "And moving back in here isn't going to make all of that disappear. I know that."

"Yeah," I say, exhausted all of a sudden. Like I just ran around the block at top speed or did a million push-ups.

"I know your mom is making some appointments with the therapists that Dr. Carlisle recommended," he says. "That's a start, okay?"

I nod, afraid if I speak I'll start to cry again.

We sit there for a little while longer until my father suggests it's time to head back. We ride in silence until I finally say, "Thanks for asking me to do this, Dad. I'm glad we did."

“So am I,” says my father as we turn onto Heather and Dave’s street. I’m thinking it might be the right time to get into a fresh pair of pajamas and slide back into bed when Dad says, “Hey, who is that parked in front of the house?”

It’s a dark blue early-model pickup truck I don’t recognize, but as we pull into the driveway, I spy someone opening the driver’s-side door. After my father parks, I climb out of his car and turn to see Javier standing there waiting for me.

JAVIER

"Hey," I say, lifting my hand uncertainly.

Eliza smiles. She looks pale and tired, and she's wearing what could pass as pajamas, but she is smiling at least.

"Hi," she replies.

Her dad is standing there, too, and I'm reminded of that awkward afternoon when he found us on the couch together.

"Hello, sir," I say. "I'm Javier Garza. We met before?"

Mr. Brady offers me a smile, and it seems like a real smile, too. "It's good to see you, Javier."

"Good to see you, too, sir."

"You don't have to call him sir," says Eliza, glancing in her father's direction.

"Yeah, you don't, but I do appreciate it," agrees Eliza's dad.

"No problem," I say.

There's an awkward silence.

"Javier, would you like to come in for a bit?" Mr. Brady asks. His voice is kind.

"Okay," I say, getting anxious. This actually wasn't the plan I had in my head when I drove over here in Miguel's truck, but I can't exactly decline.

"Wait," says Eliza, turning to her father, "would it be okay if we went for a drive instead? Like maybe to Willow Waterhole?" She looks at me. "I mean, if that's okay with you, Javi?"

"Yeah," I say. "Totally okay." This had been my plan all along. It's like Eliza read my mind or something.

Mr. Brady nods. "That would be nice, I'm sure."

"Can you hang on just a second?" she says to me. "I'll be right back."

She darts inside, and her father offers me a wave and follows after her. A few moments later she comes back out, her hair pulled back into a neat ponytail, her hoodie replaced by a dark blue long-sleeved shirt. She still has her pajama pants and sandals on.

"Okay, I'm ready," she says.

We get into the truck and I realize every time I've been in a vehicle with Eliza it's been her Nissan and she's been the one driving.

"This is Miguel's truck," I say, just to say something. Eliza's smile when she spotted me lifted me up for a moment, but now that we're together and alone, there's a tentativeness to everything. Like we're both unsure if she's going to speak or if I should fill up the air with some of my ramblings. I choose the latter.

"Oh," says Eliza. "How come you have it?"

"He saved up to buy a new one," I tell her. "Well, a new used one. Just before the baby came."

I wait for her to say something about this truck guzzling fossil fuels, but she doesn't. She *does* pick up on my news, though.

"Wait, Rosario had the baby?" she says. "I didn't see you post anything." Her voice drops. "Not that I've been looking at my phone much beyond just, like, texts and stuff."

"She just came yesterday." When we reach a red light, I show her a picture of baby Valentina at the hospital, all wrapped up like a burrito.

"Oh, wow," says Eliza. "She's got so much hair. And she's so much tinier than Ethan even though I think about him as a baby still, and he is." She hands me my phone. "They start out so tiny. Wait, is everything okay? Isn't she early?"

I slide the phone back into my jeans pocket. "Only by a few weeks. And she's good. Totally healthy. Rosario, too." I go on to tell Eliza how we all went to the hospital this morning, and I peered into the little crib next to Rosario's bed and stared trying to drink in the fact that this little stranger is my niece, and now I'm an uncle. Tío Javi. Wild. That's what Miguel kept calling me in between slapping me on the back. *Tío Javi.* I thought he was going to explode with happiness.

"Wow, congrats, Javi," Eliza says.

By this time we're at Willow Waterhole, and after I park the truck, we head out on the same path we walked that Thanksgiving night, the night we kissed for the first time. It's so nice out. January in Houston is usually when we get our best weather. Clear skies. No humidity. Warm enough you can get away with shorts but not so hot you can't wear long sleeves if you want to.

Perfect.

We make our way along wordlessly, passing by other people walking their dogs or bird-watching or just enjoying the day. I think about reaching out and taking Eliza's hand. Part of me wants to. But part of me can tell she isn't ready; she still seems sort of unsteady and upset, and anyway, she crosses her arms tight across her chest after a little bit.

And honestly, maybe I'm not ready for that just yet either. Maybe Eliza and I just need to go on a walk and talk first.

But I hope I get to hold her hand again one day.

"Are you cold?" I ask, when she pulls her arms across herself even tighter.

"No, I'm okay," she says. "Maybe just a little."

As we approach a bench—*our* bench—I suggest we sit down.

"Sure," she says. "Yeah."

And then, as soon we as sit down, Eliza turns and looks at me with her bright blue eyes. Right at me in that way she does sometimes. Direct. And she clasps her hands in her lap and takes a deep breath.

"Javier," she begins, "listen. I'm so sorry. I am really, really sorry. And I feel like I should be crying, but I just had this long, superemotional conversation with my dad, and I didn't even think that was, like, *possible*, and I think I'm all cried out. But I wanted you to know that I'm so *sorry*."

"For the buses?" I ask. Because I'm pretty sure that's what she's getting at.

"Yes, of course for the buses, and the fact that I didn't even think about the implications of that. But also because of the presentation. The one I didn't want to let you use club time for. That was a mistake. Just a mistake of enormous proportions. I wanted to focus on action, on doing because . . . I think because focusing on anything other than that scared me too much, maybe? Like if somehow I could just work and work I wouldn't have to . . . feel stuff? I don't know if I'm making sense."

As Eliza is speaking, something dawns on me.

"I wonder," I say, "if you just going and going with ETUP and never stopping was, like, your version of hiding in the stairwell when it rains."

Eliza considers this and nods.

"Yeah, honestly," she answers. "That's . . . so smart. It makes a lot of sense." She takes a deep breath, turns and looks ahead at the enormous expanse of water. "Oh, Javi, I thought maybe after what happened I'd never see you again."

I match her gaze and notice a white heron standing serenely in front of us until it senses something and lifts off, and in a moment it's yards away. I turn back to Eliza, and her chin wobbles just a bit.

"Hey," I say, hoping my voice is as soft and reassuring as I want it to be, "I'm glad I'm seeing you again. I mean, I wanted an apology, but I also wanted to see you again."

Eliza nods, her eyes glossing over with tears.

"Hey, I thought you said you didn't want to cry."

"I *don't*," says Eliza, blinking hard and then giving in. "Maybe this is what happens when you hold it in for too long." She sniffs and wipes at her eyes with the cuffs of her sleeves. "No wonder I need to see a therapist." She rolls her eyes a little, like she's trying to make a joke, only I can tell she isn't really trying to be funny.

"Listen," I say, "thanks for apologizing."

"I could apologize a million times and it wouldn't be enough," she mutters, sinking back against the bench, tipping her eyes up toward the clear blue sky. "Anyway, let me try one more time while we're here. Javier, I am so so so sorry."

"I know you are, Eliza," I say. "You don't have to say it again."

"Well, I will, so get ready."

"I'll try to prepare myself."

She grins at last, and something about this, this talking about the future—it feels good. Reassuring.

Honestly, after that horrible Wednesday afternoon, after Eliza broke down on the floor, after I ran and got Ms. Holiday, after I was escorted back to class by the red-haired lady cop—who kept looking at me like I'd done something wrong even though I *hadn't*—after all of that, I wasn't even sure I'd get to see Eliza again.

I screw up my courage and tell her that.

"It was that scary, huh?" she asks me. "I mean, for you to think maybe you'd never see me again?"

I nod, and now I also feel like I might cry. I don't even have to close my eyes to imagine Eliza on the floor, her blond hair spilling out, her fist pounding on Mr. Lopez's carpet over and over again.

"It was scary," I answer.

"I'm sorry," Eliza says softly, her tone matching mine. "See? I told you I'd keep on apologizing."

And at this, she leans and rests her head on my shoulder.

"Is this okay?"

"Yeah." And then I do reach over and take her hand in mine, warm and still. "Is *this* okay?" I ask.

"Yes," says Eliza. "But that's all I want to do right now. I'm not ready to kiss again yet. I feel too . . . I don't know. I guess just not in a kissing mood."

“That’s fine,” I say. “This is nice, too. Just this.”

We sit there in silence for a little bit until Eliza lifts her head up, but she keeps her hand in mine.

“If you want to know,” she says, “the truth is, I scared myself, too. I just . . . I don’t know the words for it and for what happened to me. But I’m so glad you went to get Ms. Holiday, Javi. I think she was the only one who really knew what to do in the moment.”

“I’m glad I thought about it, too,” I say, recalling the sound of my shoes slapping the tiled floor as I ran down the empty hallway. The way I could barely catch my breath when I pulled Ms. Holiday’s office door open without knocking. The way she jumped a bit when I did. “I’m glad she helped you, even if it was only a little bit.”

Eliza nods. “She really did. She did that box breathing thing. It worked.” She squeezes my hand. “But, Javi, I need more help. My parents want me to start meeting with someone two days a week. And they promised the school district I’d be doing that, too.” Eliza goes on to explain what else she has to do in the wake of the buses. Community service. Suspension. Appearing before a juvenile court judge.

“Honestly, I’m lucky,” she says. “It could be worse.”

I consider what I want to say next. About whether or not I should say it. But here in this beautiful space with Eliza, I want to say everything that’s in my heart.

“Eliza, I was . . . I am so . . . I care about you so much, and I want you to be okay,” I tell her. “And the way you were acting, even before the buses. I was so worried about you. You’re . . .” She looks up at me, her face open, waiting. So pretty. So smart.

"You're such a great person," I say, "and the fact that we met, the fact that it took a natural disaster to put us in each other's lives . . . I don't know. I mean, Hurricane Harvey sucked, and I hate that it happened, and if it hadn't happened, I wouldn't be sitting here with you."

"Oh, Javi," Eliza responds, and she squeezes my hand again. "That's, like, the best thing anyone has ever said to me. Honestly. And I am so glad we met. And I'm so glad I kissed you right here on this bench because I knew you were never going to do it first, and that's fine, but . . . Javi." She pauses. My heart locks up like maybe she's going to say she never wants to kiss me again *ever*. "Javi, I really am scared about what happens next."

She must sense my wariness because she smiles gently even though her eyes are sad.

"Not with us, to be clear," she says. Then she motions out in front of her with her free hand, at the wide expanse of water. At the green spaces that will bloom and overflow with Texas bluebonnets in the springtime. At the snow-white heron that disappeared moments earlier and has now returned to stand regally in front of us. "I'm really scared about this. All of *this*. What if we don't act in time? What if we lose this? Okay, so maybe we won't lose it tomorrow, but . . ." She closes her eyes, takes a deep breath. I can feel her grief and her worry coursing through her, and I recognize it because it's mine, too.

But we're not alone. We are not alone in our grief and our worry.

Out of my pocket I take the stone that Ms. Holiday helped me pick out. The one I carry with me always. This stone that came from the earth and belongs to the earth. This stone that will be here long after Eliza and me.

"I want to give you something that helped me," I say, showing her the stone before I slide it into her hand, the hand that's clutched in mine. It rests there, nestled warm and solid in our grip.

"You told me about this," says Eliza. "The stone that made you feel better? The one that Ms. Holiday gave you?"

"Yeah," I say. "That one."

I can sense her palm press against it, and as she does so, she presses the stone into my palm, too.

"But how does it work?" she asks.

I squeeze her hand and the stone, gently, so it doesn't hurt either of us.

"Well, first you just hold it," I say. "First you're just glad that it's there."

Eliza nods, considering this.

"Okay," she says, her expression focused and her voice determined. "Let's try it."

And so the two of us sit there, the stone between our palms. And we are glad it is there. We are glad it is there and we are glad we are there to cradle it gently between us.

There is something about living your life near the ocean's edge, where the waters rise higher than they have records for, where we know now, with certainty, that we can be swallowed up by the rain at a moment's notice.

To live our lives this way is to catch a glimpse of a possible future.

To be gifted with the ability to prophesize. And, on bad days, to live life this way is to feel like Cassandra from the Greek myths, cursed with the ability to see and warn, yet be ignored.

To live life this way is to know with certainty that we must change our way of living.

In the aftermath, we became anxious. We could not sleep when it rained. We cried when it thundered.

But in the aftermath, we came together in ways that were admirable. We proved that people can unite as one, that we can accomplish big things. Not just in one city but all over this planet.

The future is not inevitable. We can do difficult things when we try. We can put our hands in each other's hands and face the future and make a brighter horizon. We can get there, you and I.

Acknowledgments

First of all, thank you to Jill Kubit, one of my oldest and dearest friends, for encouraging me to write this novel for years and years until I finally did it. Your work for our planet and our children's futures through DearTomorrow is inspiring, and I am so grateful for you. Do you remember during the summer of 1995 after our freshman year in college, I told you I would dedicate a book to you? I do. My friend, it happened.

A million thanks to Kate Meltzer and Emilia Sowersby for shepherding this novel to publication with such care and kindness, and many thanks to everyone at Macmillan for getting my books out into the world. I am grateful for all of you.

I wouldn't be here without Kerry Sparks, agent extraordinaire, and the entire team at Levine Greenberg Rostan. All of you always make me feel so cared for.

Several people informed the writing of this novel to ensure it would be an accurate and sensitive portrayal of teenagers dealing with eco-anxiety. Thank you to Lara Hulin, LCSW, a real-life Ms. Holiday, and Larissa Dooley, PhD, of the See Change Institute, for all your insight. The lovely Domino Perez, PhD, also deserves so much gratitude for her thoughtful notes, particularly in regard to the character of Javier and his family.

Thank you to friend and fellow author Jessica Brody, whose

online writing courses helped me break through a particularly bad case of writer's block.

A big hurrah for all the wonderful people at Houston's Blue Willow Bookshop who have cheered on my career since day one, and hugs to all my fellow writers out there and the community we have built. You know who you are.

Thank you to my second family at Bellaire High School, especially my students. Your passion for making the world a better place keeps me going on hard days. In so many ways, this book is for you.

And last but certainly not least, a million thanks to my husband, Kevin, for everything. Texas-sized love to you and Elliott forever.

Resources Guide

by Jill Kubit of DearTomorrow

Reading Eliza and Javier's story may prompt all sorts of reactions. You may relate to their anxieties and feel inspired to act on the issue of climate change. You might wonder how to get started. Below are some resources we hope will guide you.

ACKNOWLEDGE YOUR FEELINGS ABOUT CLIMATE CHANGE

"She closes her eyes, takes a deep breath. I can feel her grief and her worry coursing through her, and I recognize it because it's mine, too. But we're not alone. We are not alone in our grief and our worry."

In *Down Came the Rain*, Javi and Eliza deal with the very real psychological and emotional impacts of living through Hurricane Harvey. They are not alone.

Children around the world are living through more severe wildfires, storms, and floods due to climate change, and kids are increasingly feeling worried. A survey of 10,000 young people from ten countries found that 59 percent are very or extremely worried about climate change and 75 percent say the "future is frightening."

One of the world's leading climate psychologists, Caroline Hickman, PhD, says that these fears are a normal reaction to the changing climate.

If you are worried, you are not alone. Concerns about the climate crisis are common; however, it is also important to share your concerns and feelings with adults and friends you trust.

Here are some steps you can take:

1. **Talk to a parent, grandparent, or teacher about your concerns and feelings.** One of the most important things you can do is to share with someone that you trust. See tips below for how to talk about climate change.
2. **Write and reflect on your feelings.** *All the Feelings Under the Sun: How to Deal with Climate Change* by Leslie Davenport is an excellent resource for tweens and teens to explore and process feelings about the climate crisis and eco-justice.
3. **If you are very concerned and this worry is getting in the way of your daily activities, ask for help.** A trusted adult can help you get the resources you need at your school or from a mental health professional.

Want to learn more? All We Can Save and *Gen Dread* have pulled together some of the best resources in the US for climate psychology and eco-anxiety:

Resources for Working with Climate Emotions: allwecansave.earth/emotions

TALK ABOUT CLIMATE

"I decide to just speak from the heart as best I can. 'I mean, Dad, I . . . I am sincerely, genuinely worried about the earth. I don't want to get into a fight with you. I really don't. But the science is real, Dad. We don't have a future with fossil fuels.'"

One of the most important actions you can take on climate is to talk about it. Talking from your own perspective and speaking from the heart shows that you care deeply about the issue and helps create the change we need. Here are a few tips for having good conversations on climate:

1. **Talk with people you know.** People trust their friends, family members, and the people they know. Choose someone in your life who is important to you and engage them in a conversation about climate change.
2. **Listen.** Start by asking questions about what is important to them. Listen closely to their answers. Then connect climate change to what they care about most.
3. **Share your thoughts and feelings.** Share your thoughts and feelings about the climate crisis and what changes you would like to see. Speak from the heart and don't be afraid to share your fears, as well as your hopes, for your community and your future.

Here are a few excellent resources:

The Secret to Talking About Climate Change: ourclimateourfuture.org/video/secret-talking-climate-change

Talking Climate Handbook: How to Have a Climate Conversation, by Climate Outreach: climateoutreach.org/reports/how-to-have-a-climate-change-conversation-talking-climate

Trying to Talk to Family Member about Climate Change? Here's How: climateoutreach.org/media/katharine-hayhoe-talk-climate-change-podcast

IMAGINE THE FUTURE YOU WANT

"Javi, I really am scared about what happens next."

At the end of the novel, Eliza turns to Javier and expresses her concerns about what happens next, about an unknown future.

Many people feel doom and gloom about our climate future. Living with the immediacy of social media and instantaneous information, we don't spend a lot of time imagining what a positive future looks like. To build a better, more just, and sustainable world, we must first dream it.

Here are three recommended projects that can help us reflect on what the climate means in our lives and how we can imagine a more positive future. These projects can be done with friends or in your school:

DearTomorrow: deartomorrow.org

Climate Ribbon: theclimateribbon.org

Imagine 2200: grist.org/fix/series/imagine-2200-climate-fiction

ADVOCATE FOR SOLUTIONS IN SCHOOL

"I want this club to be action-oriented. Not just sitting around talking about the problem of climate change . . . but really doing *something about it."*

Start a climate club in your school, and advocate for solutions for your own school and community. Make it fun by recruiting friends to colead the club with you. Find adult allies—teachers, principals, and parents—who support your efforts.

Dream big! There are hundreds of things you could do. Here are a few ideas for meaningful climate actions to get you started:

1. **Influence decision makers.** As a young person, you have the power to influence adults who are key decision makers in government, businesses, and organizations. Develop a plan to advocate for policy and infrastructure changes at the national, state, city, or community level. Start a petition, write to a decision maker, ask for a meeting to express your concerns, or connect your group with a youth-led school strike, divestment, or climate justice campaigns.
2. **Advocate for climate curriculum.** Talk to your teacher, principal, or district leadership about bringing climate education into your school's curriculum. Advocate for more outdoor and nature experiences to help your school community build stronger connections with the natural world and climate solutions.
3. **Reduce your school's emissions.** Advocate for renewable energy (solar panels on the rooftop of your school),

sustainable transportation practices (get electric school buses, create safe, walkable and bikeable communities, advocate for free public transport, create a culture of carpooling), and/or smart food choices (more plant-based meals, composting and gardening, addressing food waste).

For a step-by-step guide on passing a climate resolution in your school board, check out Schools for Climate Action: schoolsforclimateaction.weebly.com

Want more ideas? Check out this very comprehensive K12 Climate Action Plan: k12climateaction.org/img/K12-ClimateActionPlan-Complete-Screen.pdf

Not sure how you and your group can best contribute to climate solutions? Try using the Climate Action Venn Diagram to help align your skills and interests with the work needed in your community: ayanaelizabeth.com/climatevenn

GET INVOLVED IN YOUTH-LED CLIMATE JUSTICE ORGANIZATIONS

"But in the aftermath, we came together in ways that were admirable. We proved that people can unite as one, that we can accomplish big things. Not just in one city but all over this planet."

There are so many amazing youth-led climate justice organizations in the US and around the globe. Get inspired by these ten climate campaigns and organizations:

Fridays for Future: fridaysforfuture.org

Climate Mobilization: theclimatemobilization.org
Earth Uprising: earthuprising.org
EcoTok Collective: ecotokcollective.com
Our Climate: ourclimate.us
Plus 1 Vote: plus1.vote
Power Shift Network: powershift.org
Rise Up Movement: riseupmovementafrica.org
Sunrise Movement: sunrisemovement.org
Zero Hour: thisiszerohour.org

Jill Kubit is the cofounder of the award-winning Dear-Tomorrow storytelling project and Our Kids' Climate global parent network. Her work is focused on inspiring and motivating people and communities to deeply engage in bold climate solutions. For more information about her work, visit deartomorrow.org and ourkidsclimate.org